$ 15 —
1st new
ed #810

COLD
WATER
CORPSE

COLD WATER CORPSE

by
Glynn Marsh Alam

MEMENTO MORI MYSTERIES

Memento Mori Mysteries
Published by
Avocet Press Inc
19 Paul Court, Pearl River, NY 10965
http://www.avocetpress.com
mysteries@avocetpress.com

AVOCET PRESS

Copyright ©2003 by Glynn Marsh Alam

All rights reserved. No part of this book may be reproduced or transmitted in any form or by any means, electronic or mechanical, including photocopying, recording, or by any information storage and retrieval system, without written permission from the author, except for the inclusion of brief quotations in review.

This novel is a work of fiction and each character in it is fictional. No reference to any living person is intended or should be inferred.

Library of Congress Cataloging-in-Publication Data
Alam, Glynn Marsh, 1943-
Cold water corpse : a Luanne Fogarty mystery / by Glynn Marsh Alam.
  p. cm.
  ISBN 0-9725078-0-9 (alk. paper)
  1. Fogarty, Luanne (Fictitious character)—Fiction. 2. Women
detectives—Florida—Tallahassee Region—Fiction. 3. Tallahassee Region
(Fla.)—Fiction. 4. Serial murders—Fiction. 5. Women divers—Fiction.
  6. Carnivals—Fiction. I. Title.
PS3551.L213 C65 2003
813'.54—dc21
2002153992

Printed in the USA
First Edition

To Jennifer Ann Clark

A drought in north Florida is an alien thing. In a land of hot-blanket mist that drapes old boards in mildew and houses herds of frogs, the dryness encroaches like a desert sidewinder, turning puddles into black, cracked earth where mosquito eggs die before they hatch. Green grass sticks up brown shoots that crack underfoot. Water edges back from the shores, and sandbars appear in the middle of a swamp lake. After tadpoles and minnows hatch, hundreds of white birds gather in the shallows to gulp down the next generation. When the water finally goes away, deep holes appear, sinkholes that until now were invisible to any human but a diver. The caves meander into the earth, most leading to dead ends. They form a maze that, if one could manage it, might, at the end, find the Gulf of Mexico. The cavers take hold now, vertically descending into spaces that house warm bacteria and rotting alligator hides. When the months bring no more rain, the foliage runs rampant, covering a lake bottom with oxygen-choking weeds, forming trap doors to the pits below where the bodies of animals, including the human kind, dry in the heat.

CHAPTER 1

Alligators eat just about anything that comes from live flesh—birds, turtles, frogs, puppy dogs, humans. They lie on the banks of the Palmetto River during humid daytime to soak up the sun rays, warming their cold reptilian blood. But when the stomach growls, the gator prowls. Swishing his tail to propel his body along the shore line, just beneath the surface, he stops dead still and raises the nose and eyes just above the water level to catch a glimpse of the baby deer on the bank. Dropping down with the stealth of a silent missile, he rises suddenly and grabs the graceful neck, dragging his dinner to the depths to drown it, then depositing it in his territorial shallows to rot a little before gulping it whole—hooves, hide, and bones. The natural process here is the food chain. The deer won't, in turn, eat the gator, nor will the bird or the fish. But while a gator will devour the cutest of human children, humans will turn on the gator.

"You've been to this farm before?" I asked Pasquin, my ancient neighbor and swamp swami, who guided his motor boat on the third off-shoot watery lane from the main river. I had grown weary of the north Florida heat that pounded right through my straw hat, a cast off from Pasquin's wardrobe. He kept three or four old hats in his boat, stashed alongside the cooler that sat in the middle. It was packed with only ice at the moment.

"More than once. Mama sends me down here every year to get

her supply." He patted the edge of the boat as though encouraging it to keep on trucking through the thick hydrilla, an alien grass that threatened ecological balance in this part of the river system. "Rinks' family has been raising gator meat about forty years now."

"It's my first time seeing it," I said and leaned back in the boat. I placed the hat over my face to block out the sun. My hair felt like the roots were burning away. "Can't you go a little faster to stir up a breeze?"

"Not here. Drought has lowered the banks and the grass is thicker than ticks on your doggie." He revved the motor slightly, but immediately slowed again. "Don't want you to have to go over the side and clear off a matt of the stuff."

I had been on the last leg of teaching linguistics classes at the university when Vernon, my significant swamp diving companion or whatever one would call a lover who swam dangerous caves with you, asked if I'd like to work the sheriff's department booth at the fair this year. The fair, an institution in this part of the state, was half local produce and cattle show, half carnival rides and freak shows. It lasted a week and was popular with people from all the counties in north Florida.

Bizarre food items tended to appear at the fair, and booths often tried to outdo each other. Mama, from Mama's Table down on the river, had fed so many deputies over the years that she had taken over as cook and food organizer for the entire department. Besides the regular burgers with grilled onions, she dished up cheese grits, apple fritters, fried chicken legs—and alligator tail.

"Pasquin," I peeked from under the hat, "do you eat gator?"

"Have," he nodded. "Tastes a little like chicken, little like pork without the fat."

"I tasted it once. Wasn't too bad, but I felt queasy knowing what it was."

Pasquin chuckled. Reaction to gator meat couldn't faze a man who had, for eighty years or more, eaten about anything the river had to offer. His preference for the hot cajun stuff of his ancestors appeared on his table in his swamp house, when he wasn't sampling some delicacy from Mama's Table in Fogarty Spring.

"Grass coming up in the water lane," he said. The boat slowed to nearly a stop.

"It's taken over everywhere!" I said as I sat up. Up until now, the center part of the river, the deepest part, had been clear, the grass approaching from both sides. Here it came together, bobbing up and down in front of us like some river monster just daring us to cross it.

"Not more than a few inches below the surface," said Pasquin. "Be ready to swim." He moved closer to the grass. The wake of the boat bounced the stuff harder, and fronds began to appear above the surface. "Grab the oars," he said.

With the engine cut, Pasquin and I rowed over the grass. The motor rested out of the water, poking from the back of the boat like a useless barnacle. I pressed the oar into the water, pushing against heavy growth.

"Wonder why they don't use the hydrilla puller down here," I said. More than once we had watched the boat with paddle wheels lumber down the main river and yank the stuff from the bottom. It all got piled onto a metal conveyor belt and run up on shore to a dump truck. But plenty more grass refilled the river. It didn't need deep roots and air and sun, not much anyway.

"Too many narrow lanes around here to pull it all up," said Pasquin. "Gator on the far side." He nodded to a bank where a bull gator nearly seven feet long rested. "Near the lily pads. Wonder what he's got there." Pasquin took off his hat and pointed it to an area just below the reptile.

"Could be a deer," I said, stretching my neck and shading my eyes with the hat. "Is he likely to sun next to his marinade?" I wondered about this, something no one ever brought up in all the years I had lived on this river. Would a gator rest near his captured prey? Could he smell the decay? I had no idea, but I was betting if anything got near that prey, the gator would be off the bank in a flash, jaws open and ready to fight.

"Pasquin," I said as I raised slightly out of my seat. "Does a deer wear a bra?"

"You're calling from where?" Detective Tony Amado sounded angry, like how dare I let him know that a human body lay in the shallows of a third off-shoot lane of Palmetto River.

"From Rinks' Alligator Farm," I yelled even though the line was clear. "Forgot to bring the cell phone with me. We'll meet you at the spot, okay?"

I replaced the phone on its cradle and brushed my hands on my pants leg. Something greasy and old had been on the receiver. The phone, an ancient black dial model, sat on the edge of a wide railing that fronted a lean-to. I glanced under the tin roof. Mounds of dirt barely hid pieces of alligator hide. A few flies clustered in spots, but most of the stuff was too old to be of any use to them. I figured Rinks killed the gators and used both the skin and the meat to make a living. But there had to be scraps. That's what he called this place, the scrap hut. "Go up to the scrap hut and use the phone there," he said when Pasquin and I finally pulled onto shore.

Down the hill, on both sides of the landing, wire fences penned in what seemed like mounds of alligators. They rested in shallow pools of water or basked on muddy rims of earth. Most touched another gator in some fashion, a foot resting on a tail, a tail across a neck, an entire body crossing the mid-section of another. These were bred gators, raised from birth in pools, fed chickens until they nearly burst. They had no need to hunt or fix territorial limits.

Rinks and Pasquin had gone inside the main storage building, a refrigerated area where the gator meat was chopped and placed in carrying containers. Rinks would pack nearly fifty pounds in the cooler today. Pasquin would return each day for a fresh supply.

"All chopped into cubes," said Rinks as he closed the cooler. In spite of the strange smell of blood and swamp water, I felt relieved at the cold that surrounded me.

"This stuff will keep, won't it?" I asked as I helped the two men lift the cooler onto a dolly. "We've got to meet Amado on the river. Looks like one of your friends caught him a human dinner."

Rinks laughed. "Stupid tourists. They come out here and try to swim in bull gator territory. Some college boy again?" He hoisted his denim overalls in an attempt to scratch himself. Dark green debris, like the stuff on the phone, dotted the material. He wore no shirt. Flabby arms spotted with tufts of hair flew out from the sides. He wore a baseball cap on his head, the logo long since faded. A chewed toothpick stuck from a corner of his mouth. His bulk and loose-flesh arms belied a man who could still get into a gator pen and hold the animal's mouth shut with one hand, while tying a rope around it with the other.

"Maybe some college girl," I said. I shivered inside. What would a girl be doing in the water alone? But then I thought of myself. Swimming alone was therapy for me. I even put on the scuba tank at times and pulled a professional no-no by going to the cave entrance near my house. Going inside the cave would be really stupid, but I had my moments of insanity.

"Girl?" He pulled the toothpick from his mouth and used it to scratch under the hat brim. He frowned, and I expected the next sentence to be something about how ladies ought to stay home cooking and leave the river to the boys. Instead, he shrugged. "Well, ain't no gator I've known to prefer male to female dinner." He patted Pasquin on the shoulder. "I'll get one of the boys to help you get the cooler into the boat."

Amado and his river patrol were already at the spot when Pasquin and I returned. Vernon, in swim trunks but with no diving gear, stood up in a boat a few feet from the body. The gator was long gone.

"You going to track and shoot that bull?" asked Pasquin. We held his boat steady in the water with the two oars.

"Gator's not guilty," said Amado. He stood in the shallows, his pants legs rolled up to his knees. Anyone else would be mud covered and wet. From his waist up, he appeared freshly dressed, crisp white shirt, dark tie, smooth dark hair. "I'm not even sure the beast knew she was here."

I pushed on the oar to get closer. We touched the yellow tape that had been tied to tree branches in an attempt to cordon off the scene.

"Drowning?" said Pasquin. He shot me a dirty look and held his oar steady.

"Could be," said Tony, "but not an accidental one. Crime techs will be here shortly."

We waited on the quiet river. Loman, Amado's sergeant, stood barefoot in the water beside his boss. One pants leg came unrolled and floated in the cool water. He looked down, his heavy-lidded eyes covering the surprise, and cursed. He leaned over his ample belly and pulled at the pants but finally gave up and watched the other side unroll and fall into the water. "Might as well take them off," he said.

"Got your hearts and flowers jockstrap on?" asked Vernon who now balanced against a cypress tree. He had climbed out of the boat and placed himself precariously on one of the knees that grew out of the water. Every few minutes he would rock on the thin root and have to level himself with the other arm.

"I'll knock your ass off backwards, you keep that up," said Loman. He slapped at sweat and insects that hovered around his neck. He jerked at his tie and unbuttoned the top buttons of the shirt. "Hell, it's hot!" He leaned over, grabbed a handful of water, and splashed it on his face.

"It is today, but not the first of the week," said Tony. He glanced at the body that lay amid lily pads; the only indication that something was there was the pinkish outline. "The water is cold; so was the weather. She could have been in here for a while."

"Maybe the gator doesn't know about her now, but he would if she had been here a while," I said. "How do you know it's not an accident?"

"You have to come closer. Big gap between the chin and the collar bone." Tony pointed downward.

A siren sounded down the river. The rest of Amado's force would be here, dragging the crime scene techs with them. With solid shore nearly fifteen feet back into the forest, they would work from boats and eventually crawl around in grass and lily pads.

"You fellows find these on purpose," said Marshall Long. His enormous bulk sat like a stiff Buddha in the back of a patrol boat. He held on each side like a child on a terrifying carnival ride.

"Blame Luanne and Pasquin," said Loman. "They found her." He nodded towards the body.

The men sat quietly for a moment, all eyes on Marshall. "Her?" He asked. Amado nodded toward the victim. "Okay, you heroes get me out of here." Marshall's jowls shook as he tried to rise. The boat swayed back and forth, and he sat down again, creating a wave on both sides. "I can't do this alone!" His big voice bellowed into the swamp; birds took flight.

"You're not going to get into the water, are you?" Vernon said. He waded towards the boat; muscular arms that often held me in the comfort of a bed now reached toward the man who was known to devour an entire coconut custard pie after three helpings of raw oysters.

"No, but I got to get in a position to see the body!" Marshall struggled to bend forward over his front. It wasn't going to happen alone.

Two uniformed deputies in the front of the boat and the assistant tech in the back finally managed to push and pull until Marshall went onto his knees inside the vessel. Water splashed, and the men let go to grab the evidence kits.

"That's better," said Marshall as he adjusted his elbows on the seat cushion in front of him. "Now get this boat as close as you can."

I nodded to Pasquin, and we paddled behind the patrol boat until the edges touched. We each held a side, while the deputies steadied it with poles. Marshall leaned over the water, his side of the boat slanting downward with his weight. The pilot rolled his eyes and leaned the other way.

"Looks kind of new," said Marshall. He had gloved his hands and pushed one arm into the water. "Neck nearly severed." He brushed aside some lily pads. Small catfish scattered. "That's right, little fishies, no dinner for you tonight." Marshall wiggled his butt backward in an effort to see the bottom part of the body. The boat rocked with him. "No clothes other than the bra." He pulled on the garment. It came out of the water with a lily vine attached. "Not your normal bra, is it?"

I stretched my neck. "Bikini top," I said. "She must have been in a bathing suit."

Marshall leaned over once more, and the pilot's face turned white. "Let us know when you're going to do that!" He shouted.

Marshall used both arms to brush aside more river grass. "No bottoms anywhere that I can see." He moved more grass. "Need to check around the area. You guys on shore or in the mud or wherever you are, look for clothing, maybe a towel."

When there seemed nothing more to be found from looking at the body in the water, Marshall gave the order to call in the next boat that would deliver the body to the morgue in Tallahassee. It would be the divers' turn now. They wouldn't need tanks in these shallows, but they would know how to lift her out, to place her in a plastic bag that would conceal her indignity and hang onto any water-logged evidence.

"Looks like another one," said Marshall as he created a monster wake when he turned upright in the boat.

CHAPTER 2

The main double gate of the fairgrounds stood open for horse trailers and loaded supply trucks. Most of the year, this was a vast field with no trees and a few Quonset-like huts, water fountains, and cement bathrooms. It would metamorph today into rows of tents, sawdust-covered grounds, and colorful rides flashing through the air with humans screaming in terror, all the while safely attached to welded steel.

Workers in lemon yellow vests lined off the mowed grass with white chalk for the hundreds of cars that would pack the makeshift parking lot. Teenagers, those not interested in the latest bulimic fashion or rapster, guided terrified calves and squealing piglets into the huts set aside for farm animals. Fed and groomed for months, they would first stand the judgment of contests. The kid may walk off with a blue ribbon, but the animal would walk to the slaughter house.

Beyond the animal huts and several yards removed from the tiny office tents, the bull riding rodeo fences were erected. Here, cowboys danced when somebody spat chewed tobacco too near their fancy boots. The Brahmas would be brought in huge trucks, roped around their stomachs and their testicles, then ridden for all the fury and prize cash money in north Florida. It was a macho thing. "Ride the bull if you can't ride anything else," I whispered as a tight-jeaned, boot-shod man hiked his silver belt buckle. He tipped his stetson as he passed me.

A tattered man with a beard and dirty toga robe stood outside the fence, shouting warnings of how God would punish any who dared pass the gates of iniquity to gaze at freaks and go for thrill rides. He held up a sign that read *God is on His Way.* "Probably planted by carnival promoters," I said as I motioned for Vernon to pull the car inside the gates and haul the utility trailer to a booth several yards across the grounds. There, deputies out of uniform nailed up the sign: *Sheriff's Department.* A smaller sign ran down he side advertising cheese grits, fried gator tail, and pecan pie from Mama's Table in Fogarty Spring. Mama, herself, scooted about the inside of the booth, setting up the deep pots she would use to brew up the concoctions people dared eat only on outings like the fair. On the other end of the booth, Deputy Harlie hung out his sign— *Grilled Burgers.* He and Mama would get on each other's nerves but good before the week ended.

"Gator meat has arrived," I said when Vernon pulled the car behind the booth. He backed it around so that the trailer could be unhitched and left there throughout the day. The meat, kept in a cooler inside the trailer, would be removed only when needed. All she had to do was add the batter and drop the cubes in the deep fryer.

"When do the freaks arrive?" asked Mama when she jerked her paper towel roll away from Harlie.

The man, nearing retirement, had been the chief burger griller for nearly twenty years, and for most of those years, all they served were grilled onions smothered onto overcooked beef atop a bun. But the past ten years had seen a burst of growth in the county, a youthful crop of emigrants from Miami and points south, from New York, and oddly, from California, itching to try out the folk stuff of Southern tales. Gator meat had never been so popular. And grits were catching on. Mama, who'd eaten anything live that a swamp chef could cook, dished it up for the cops on the swamp beat. She was the logical choice for the novelty cook at the booth.

"Mostly already here," he said and glanced up at Mama. The few hairs he had left swept over his head like dead tree branches over a sand bar. Mama, her wide hips taking up most of the spare space between tables, gave a bump against the one holding his patties. The meat, separated by wax paper sheets, shimmied before he could grab an edge. "You need something over here?" he asked.

"The plug," she said and shoved the end of an extension cord into the air as though giving him the finger. He pointed with his shoe to a surge protector against the wall.

"I ain't bending over, old man." Mama stuck the cord in his face.

He bounced his head in defiance for a moment, then snatched the cord and planted it into the outlet. "Might be funny if somebody tripped on that fat wire," he said and turned back to stacking bundles of hamburger buns.

"Going to be a long week, huh?" I said as I stepped up the wooden stairs from the rear of the booth. "You and Harlie going to make it?"

Mama grunted and shook her peroxided hair. She could stand ground against any male, but this one she provoked like it was good sport. A smile twitched at the corner of her mouth. "You got gator tail?"

"In the cooler," I said and pointed to the trailer. Vernon joined us and handed her the key.

"Like to feed that old man to a gator," she said, "but wouldn't nobody eat the stuff after it ate him." She nodded toward Harlie who put a thumb to his nose and waved his fingers in the air.

Before the bantering evolved into talented swampy insults, Vernon's cell phone rang. He headed to the car to talk, while I helped both Mama and Harlie stack supplies on each side of the booth. I felt like a Red Cross worker between enemy camps. Finally, what could have been a battleground of who owned which shelves, petered down to grunts and huffs.

"We need to go meet the guy bringing in the side shows," said Vernon. "He's supposed to sign in with the department." Vernon pulled out the paper from a folder on the back seat of the car.

"Wonder if it's that sleaze they had last year," said Harlie. "Man had enough grease to slide all the way to jail."

"Did just that, I hear." Vernon grinned up at the jostling for space between the two cooks. "Got a different man this year." He checked the paper. "Cannon, it says here."

Mr. Cannon sure wasn't greasy. He came from curly stock, a salt and pepper mass of tight twists encircled a bearded face. He wore the denims of a sixties protester rather than the cheap slick jacket of a carnival barker. We met him under a partially pitched tent where he argued with a man whose girth threatened to flatten the plastic chair under him.

"You got to put my trailer on the grounds. I can't do this back and forth thing, Cannon!" The man moved his mouth, a hole inside mounds of flesh that draped over his bare shoulders like a sheet. He wore only a pair of Bermuda shorts, the seams threatening to pop their thread domino style at any moment. A canvas poster lay on the ground near the tent. *See the World's Smallest Woman Tame the World's Largest Man* blazed atop a painting of a facsimile of this man before me. On his knee sat a petite portrait of a woman in a circus tutu. It was tacky stuff from the fifties, but it still drew the crowds, if for nothing else but to say, "better you than me."

"All your acts here yet?" asked Vernon as he handed over the paper.

"Coming in now," said Cannon as he ticked off a list on the paper. "Fat Man right here, Sword and Fire over there, Snake Boy backed up to the gate about now," he turned round to watch a trailer ease into the spot. The painting on the side played on primitive fears with giant cobras rising into the air and bearing foot-long fangs. A scantily clad female cringed in horror as a python encircled her legs.

"Bet Snake Boy wouldn't be so brave in my swamp," I half whispered.

"Not so brave here, either," said Cannon. "Kid took over from his daddy. Has nightmares just about every nap he takes."

"Only three acts?" said Vernon.

"Got a clown troupe somewhere down the road. Not much circus business anymore. Formed their own troop and joined the carnival circuit. So-so act. Bunch of drunks...," Cannon stopped and looked up at Vernon, realizing he was talking to a deputy. "I keep them under watch, sir. All the time."

"Good idea," said Vernon. "You going to sign that paper?"

"Can't see the clown trailer yet." He turned his back on us and gazed down the road that led from the main highway. He loosened one button in the middle of his shirt and scratched a hairy chest. "Can I bring this to you?" He turned back to Vernon.

"I got to have it by the time I leave here, and that's in about thirty minutes."

"I'll get it to you." He nodded and moved toward the road.

"Hey!" called the fat man. "You gonna put my trailer in here?"

"Not now!" called Cannon and disappeared into a mass of trailers, tents, and trucks.

Vernon and I stood, awkward and embarrassed. I finally turned to the large man and introduced myself. "And this is Lieutenant Vernon Drake of the Sheriff's Department."

We all shook hands, the fat man staring at us like we were the show freaks.

"Jubile Taylor," he said finally. "Been like this all my life." He patted the three folds of flesh that began at the chin and ended sitting on his thighs. "I got a trailer special made, and I need it here, not in some park two miles away."

"Don't most of the show people live off the grounds?" I asked.

"I ain't most; I'm me, and I got needs." He looked into the distance, then clapped his hands together. "There she comes!"

Two trailers pulled by vans drove into the area, crowding it until the outside road was blocked. As soon as they came to a stop, the door opened on one and a child-like woman emerged. She wore studded denim and a cowboy hat on her head.

"Jubile!" she cried. "We got lost when we got off the interstate." She ran to the big man and hugged one leg like a child who hadn't seen her daddy for a week. He pulled off her hat, sat it atop his own head where it perched like an apple, then reached over and grabbed her by the arms and pulled her to one knee. She winced a little until she was firmly in place.

"You got to pick me up by the waist, Jubile. My sockets can't take that anymore."

It was difficult not to stare. The woman, tinier than a third grader, had the lined face of someone near sixty. Her high-pitched voice had the roughness of a hard woman who had been in too many smoke-filled trailers.

"Hello," she said to me, "I'm Julene." She stuck out a tiny arm, and I had to bend to shake her hand. "Julene and Jubile," she said. "We pretend we're married."

"Not possible," said the fat man who began to laugh.

"Nope, not possible," added Julene, who giggled along with him. Both finally burst into howls. "It's not what you think," said Julene who snorted between shrill cackles.

"Did you see the clown trailer?" asked Vernon. He fidgeted,

then held my hand.

"They're back on the road somewhere," said Julene who had begun to bounce and dart for her hat. Unless she stood on the man's leg, she would never reach it. He teased by holding her still with his palm on her head.

"Let's go meet them, " said Vernon. He jerked on my arm.

"Guess you'd get kind of funny if you lead this life," I said as I followed him toward the gate. "Must get claustrophobic being on display all the time."

"Must be," said Vernon. "Wonder what they do to…," he hesitated, then broke into a grin, "you know."

I shrugged and grinned back at him. Vernon was not only a deputy and a diving partner; he was my cozy companion, too. "Maybe it's just not possible."

"Doubt that," he said. "There's Cannon. Looks like the clowns have arrived."

A large camper pulled onto the grounds. The only sign that it might include circus performers was the clown logo on one corner. Four heads decorated in fright wigs, red noses and painted smiles stared from the side of the camper shell. The man driving the four-seater truck looked like a surly laborer. A woman with long thin hair the same color as the straw on the ground sat beside him. She may have been young underneath the heavy liquid make-up.

"Where the hell you been?" said Cannon. "And who is that?" He nodded toward the woman. He didn't wait for an answer but leaned into the window and took a whiff. "Beer, right?"

"Nothing else," said the driver. His dark brown skin was the same color as his buzz-cut hair. His thin, lined face and hoarse voice told of a lifelong smoker. "This here is Yasmina. She just hitched a ride into the grounds." He winked at Cannon and tilted his head toward the woman who had not said a word. She looked bored with the entire scene. The driver squirmed. "Gotta find the men's room."

Vernon moved beside Cannon. The lawman's presence seemed to rattle him for a second. He said, "This is Billy Zigfield, head clown, named for the Hollywood follies man." He looked toward the trailer. "Others in the back?"

Zigfield grunted and nodded. When he pressed the gas pedal and moved into a parking place, we stepped back. "Idiot!" said Cannon. "You don't move that close to people." Zigfield flipped him a finger. The woman Yasmina took herself out of the passenger side, slammed the door, and disappeared through the maze of tents, huts, and booths.

"Not funny outside the big top, these guys," said Cannon. "Not funny at all."

He placed the paper atop a parked car and signed.

The fairgrounds filled with trailers and animals and carnival rides, and on the outskirts, drug dealers. The sheriff's department, along with the city police and some undercover people set up stakeouts on the rims of the tents, waited for the addicts in need to make their purchases. We expected arrests. The fair really had changed from the days of my youth.

"We got something," said Deputy Loman, Amado's sleepy-eyed sergeant. He had approached us quietly from the back, huffing like he had been running.

"Drugs, already?" I asked.

"Not drugs. Luanne, you got to come with me. Vernon, you got to get to the station.

"The girls?" asked Vernon.

"Yeah," said Drake. "One more, and Marshall found something in the lab."

"That makes three for this area," I said. I followed Loman across wood chips and onto dry grass in the parking lot. "Is there a connection?"

"Maybe four, and yeah, seems like a connection. That's why Marshall Long wants you. Says you might be able to help."

Before Loman could continue, Cannon approached with two men. Like Mutt and Jeff, they introduced themselves as Sword and Fire. "I swallow swords," said the tall, thin one. "Fire swallows, well, you know." He pointed to his short mate.

"Fire," I nodded. "Do you ever get mixed up?"

"Nope," the short one grinned, "but I once heated up one of his swords. Gave him heartburn!" He burst into a high-pitched guffaw.

"He ain't tellin' the truth," the tall one said and jabbed at his partner. "Lies all the time. Fried his brain years ago."

"You boys got anything to set up?" said Cannon. He glanced at Vernon, then back at the carnival men. "Don't think the sheriff's got time to spend listening to you."

"We do have to go," said Vernon. Loman shifted from one foot to another.

"Two tickets, our compliments," said Cannon as he handed a pair of tickets to each of us. "Catch these boys early, and you'll get a good act."

We walked away wondering why the later act was not so good.

"Look like drinkers to me," said Loman. "Get drunk, puncture your gut with the point of a sword. Now wouldn't that be a show."

"You'd have to drink a little to swallow knives all your life." Vernon waved a truck through the gate. It was pulling a cattle trailer with a white Brahma bull inside. The animal's wild eyes peered through the narrow gap between the ceiling and wall of the trailer and exhaled like a giant balloon losing air.

I turned round to watch the truck edge between huts and tents and make its way to the bull corral at the far end. Just as it passed the carnival area where Sword and Fire were unpacking a box, I saw Cannon sitting atop a portable ladder, unfurling a canvas banner that proclaimed *Zigfield's Little Clowns*. One tall cartoonish man stood over four tiny men, all decked out in red noses and theatrical makeup.

"Well, I'll be!" I said. "The clowns are midgets."

Reality wasn't part of the act in a carnival sideshow. Perhaps we couldn't actually stand what was beneath the grease paint and happy antics. I didn't know. I'd never been around performers, especially not back stage. It was their responsibility to fool the public.

But killing was a different kind of act, even if cover up was still the requirement.

CHAPTER 3

The building is all soft pastels of dusty rose and beige, spread out in angles that appear to rise out of the landscape. Green leaf azalea bushes grace the outside of long, thin windows that reflect the November southern sun onto late model cars in the lot. It's silent here, a building constructed to fit the territory, a beauty combining the architect's clever design with an innate desire to find serenity.

The building is a liar.

Inside, the quiet is the death that lies upon steel tables, the soft click of the microscope focusing on minute particles scraped off clipped fingernails. The nails are black from days in a humid grave where her killer tossed her torn body, thinking it would rot before the boys in badges came along and pulled up the putrid flesh and laid it out for white coats to poke and gouge until she tells them who got her this way.

Down a long white hallway, behind doors with peep-hole windows, sit sculptors, redoing what some killer has undone. The artists, ladies in lab coats and shower caps, dabble in clay, making faces where only bones sat a few days ago. In the next room, the body bones lie on tables, their symmetry placed together like some decaying jigsaw puzzle.

"Are those the bones I found two years ago?" I followed Marshall Long's broad bottom into the inner sanctum of the state crime lab. Even the central air vents couldn't hide the earthy smell of dug-up materials.

"It's the young lady you located on that ledge in Palmetto Springs." He jabbed a puffed-up finger toward the table where he, or someone, had laid out a few bones to form part of a rib cage, one arm, the pelvic area and one leg.

"Where's the skull?" I rested my hands on my hips, the only sign of disgust I could muster when I saw, where the head should be, a giant yellow smiley face drawn onto cellophane.

"Reconstruction work," Marshall said and pointed to another door. "We put this off too long. Then along came two bodies, and we think she could be part of the pattern."

"Pattern?"

"Two sets of female bones found in water, one near Pensacola, the other in Madison. Guess where we are?" Marshall picked up a medical prod and tapped the top of the section of backbone that lay above the ribs.

"In between," I said. "But we found these bones two years ago and they could have been underwater longer than that."

"So could the others, but we don't think so." Marshall leaned over the table. He pulled a ceiling light toward the bones and focused it on the neck area. "We don't have much neck bone to go on here, but there is a tiny nick on this fragment." He looked up, his three folds of jowls slightly bouncing with the motion. "If you get close, you might see what I'm talking about, Luanne."

I stepped forward and bent over, our heads nearly touching. "Here, you hold the magnifying glass. Now focus your eyes just there." He pointed again to the top bone in the neck.

I moved the glass until I had the edge of the bone in view. The whiteness was still there, the color that had surprised me when I discovered the bones in the Twiggins case. We'd found two others, part of a misfortunate trio of women who ran into druggies at the wrong time. But this skeleton wasn't part of that. Dental records couldn't identify her, and she hadn't panned out in the missing reports. The poor girl with the shiny white bones had been in a lab drawer ever since.

"Looks like something nicked the bone."

"Exactly. And, guess what? This nick looks a whole lot like the nicks in the other two neck bones."

"Who found them?"

"Cops went looking for missing girls, I guess. Ask Tony." He took the glass from me. "Want to see the art work now?"

Marshall turned around and edged his white-coat-covered bulk between other bone tables to the closed door. He shoved it hard with one hip and let it swing back toward me. I followed him through, scowling at his bouncing lab coat.

"This is Luanne Fogarty, Sara." He nodded toward a woman wearing a white coat that nearly reached the floor. Her dingy red hair was pulled back with a purple headband. She wrinkled her forehead as though she had a perpetual headache.

"Ms. Fogarty," she said, keeping her frown and directing her eyes to the clay-covered skull in front of her. "I've heard about you, your diving and all that." She patted the wig on the head, sat up straight and turned the face towards me. "You found her, right?"

I stared at the light brown curls that surrounded a youthful face, one with chubby cheeks and a cute dimple in the chin. The teeth, all there, shining as white as the bones. The eyes haunted me, and no matter where I stood, they followed. Blue glass. That's all they were, but they stared, almost gleamed with life. She was a cutie this one, if indeed she really had looked like this. I shuddered. She had been nothing but fleshless bones on the ledge of a deep limestone cave when I first saw her.

"She's white?"

"Yes. That was easy to determine. So was her sex and

approximate age, as Marshall will tell you." She finally broke her frown and smiled in Marshall's direction. Did I detect familiarity? Her thin short body up against Marshall's elephant bulk? I brushed it off to momentary hallucination. "Not so easy the face, but I've got indications of things, and measurements."

"Even the dimple?"

"Well, that might be a little embellishment, but with her type cheeks, it's certainly possible." Sara wiped an invisible smudge from the clay cheek.

"Young, white, cute, and throat cut," said Marshall.

"Are you sure?" I tried to imagine the horror on this face when a knife came round and began to slice away her life.

"No, but enough of the 'could be' to get detectives working in that area."

"Can't you get DNA from a tooth?" I asked.

"Done that," said Marshall. "But we got to have someone to match it to, like a family member."

"And you don't know who her family is," I said and leaned down, eye-to-eye with the reconstructed face. "What do you call her?"

The moment of silence lasted long enough for me to turn around to Marshall.

"Luanne," he said. "We call her that because you found her."

"So Vernon and I are to search the area again, after two years?" I stood on the floating dock near the glass bottom boats. I had dived off this dock two years ago to search the deepest spring caves in the world, looking for bodies. Palmetto Springs Park had shut down then, the entire water system a crime scene. "We're not likely to find much, and I don't like sifting through sand and stirring up murky waters. Too dangerous."

"I know what you don't like." said Tony Amado. "In light of the new find near here, we've got no choice."

He, with Sergeant Loman and Vernon, had driven through heavy swamp from Tallahassee to meet me at the Palmetto Hotel. It wasn't the tourist season this far north like it was near Miami. North Florida cools down in the winter, sometimes freezes at night. The frigid spring waters only felt good when the humidity hung in ninety degree air. The few guests that did come in November tended to be from colder European climates.

I glared at Tony. We had an on-going respect for disrespect. I knew the caves and could dive them, had done it since childhood. He knew I knew them and needed me, but it hurt to hire a female. He would rather have asked my former lover, Harry MacAllister, but that didn't often happen now. Harry, wounded from a cave blast on another case, had a bum leg. It had broken when he was flung from the cave entrance and never healed correctly. He could still dive; it was walking above ground that hampered his movements.

"Just so you know." I looked at Vernon, he of the wide grin that sent shivers over me even in a hot Florida summer. He and I had been lovers and friends for the entire two years, a comfortable situation for our forty-plus ages. We often played dodge-the-deputies with our antics, somehow avoiding office gossip. He had pulled a wet suit over his bathing trunks.

"You ready?" He said. He picked up my tank and hoisted it onto my back. I locked the straps over my wet suit.

"Am I wearing the microphone?" I held up the full face mask. I could talk underwater and let Tony know what was happening.

"Both of us are," said Vernon and donned his own face mask. "I'll drop the flag."

We rolled off the deck into water that was nearly too shallow for divers. For a year, the region lagged behind in normal rainfall, causing lakes and ponds to dry up entirely, and springs like this one to drop their levels near shore. Beyond that, the caves, fed by centuries old aquifers were just as deep and just as cold.

We swam toward the far end of the spring where both the bottom and the temperature dropped off suddenly. Just above the cave entrance, Vernon let the buoyed flag bounce on the surface. We turned downward. I could feel the currents against my fins as I pushed toward darkness. When we entered the cave's narrow door, we needed the head lamps.

The entrance allowed for only one of us at a time. Vernon shined his light inside first, then motioned for me to stay put until he got through. He slipped off the tank, keeping the mouthpiece in place, and held it in front of him. With his upper body nearly as rigid as the tank, he gave a couple of kicks and moved through to his waist. Two more kicks and he disappeared from my sight. I swam to the entrance. From there, I could see his head lamp and not much else. I slipped off my tank and pushed through, following him into the watery bowels of the ancient earth.

Darkness ruled here, along with cold currents. Our narrow lights bounced off white limestone as long as it was a few feet from us. Beyond that, pitch blackness took over, and it was only with a little faith and lots of practice that made us swim through it.

We had found the bones on a sandy ledge, part of the slanting side of the open cave. I remembered schools of catfish around the bones, like they had found some morsels left to eat. I led the way.

"Tony, it's nothing but white sand from where I am. We'll have to sift." I spoke into the face mask. Shining my light about the ledge, I sensed a futility in finding anything. The ledge ended abruptly a few feet below us and darkness took over. This cave went deep into the earth, not a place we would go just to find more bones.

The cave divers who dared trace the origin of the waters had gone down there, and some had never returned.

Vernon took hold of his evidence sack and pulled out a hand sifter. I did the same. He started at one side of the ledge, I at the other, to avoid creating a blind with too much debris in the water.

Sand separated and filled the spaces where our lamps lit up the darkness, like a giant snowy paperweight turned upside down. I slowly filled the sift with sand then bounced it gently in the water. Nothing settled on the bottom.

We kept up the sift and bounce until we had nearly run out of time. "I'm going to feel underneath with my hand," I told Tony and replaced the sifter. I turned toward the bottom and edged along the drop-off, dragging my hand through the sand as I went. A stream of white disappeared into darkness.

"Paid off!" I said as my hand hit something long and smooth. "Looks like a leg bone. Foot is not here." I placed the bone into an evidence bag attached to my gear, then moved toward Vernon who was touching something in the bottom of his sifter.

He nodded to me and pointed to his evidence bag containing what must have been tiny bone fragments. He gave the motion to head to the surface.

I removed my tank and edged out the entrance, then waited for Vernon to follow. Going out took little effort as the current pushed against us like two uninvited guests. We ascended slowly and swam to the dock. The water warmed slightly, and our gear became heavier. We finally handed over the tanks and climbed onto the floating dock, where Loman threw us towels and handed over orange sodas.

"That's about it," I said as I watched Tony open the bags and peer inside. "Probably the rest of her is down hundreds of feet along with mastodon skeletons."

The springs and its maze of caverns hid centuries of secrets—bodies brought down by cataclysmic episodes or Indian war parties, and most likely alligator leavings. More than one human killer had deposited his victim here. Over the years, we've found mafia hits and foolish northerners who think they can learn to dive in a swimming pool then go into great depths and come out again. One wrong turn and the caves get you, hold you in a lock-up so that you panic and die on the spot.

"There's a peculiar thing about those bones being in that exact location," I said.

"Bones in caves is no peculiarity around here," said Vernon. He dripped water from his mask onto my forehead.

"The currents," I slapped him on the leg with my mask, "go out of the cave entrance. Remember how hard we had to swim to get in, but how easy it was to get out?"

"Yeah," Vernon sat beside me. He winked, "Go on, Lady Sherlock."

"You know, Tony is rubbing off on you," I scowled. "The body had to have been placed there deliberately, because it wouldn't wash with the current into that cave entrance."

Vernon nodded, then shrugged. "She's right, Tony. Somebody who dives would have placed her there."

"Unless," I hesitated.

"What?" Tony paced the dock, the perfect creases in his pants in my line of vision.

"Unless there is another entrance somewhere." Before Tony could ask for an investigative dive, I added, "I'll ask the NSS cave divers if they have a map."

"We'll get these bones to the lab," said Tony. He made a grunt, so slight no one else seemed to notice, that expressed disapproval. His thick, groomed black hair hadn't moved an inch in the breeze

that blew across the spring. He wore suit and tie, the expected uniform of a sheriff's detective, only his looked like he had just bought
it off a mannequin at an exclusive men's store. When Loman
scratched a mosquito bite, he threw his tie to the side of his neck
and pulled one corner of his wrinkled shirt collar away from the
jacket; Tony managed to carry an invisible iron.

"Think you ought to tell me about the others you found?" I
looked up at Tony. He hated being on the spot, but I'd developed a
sort of blackmail with him. I may do his diving jobs—though I'd
often threaten not to—but I'd give him hell about it if I didn't get
my way. It wasn't the traditional tears-and-pout female way of op-
erating, but it worked with him.

"Two women," he said as he rocked back and forth, heel to toe,
and causing the floating dock to slosh in the water. Loman grabbed
at air, his center of gravity hanging over his belt. "Got two young
women found in water, their throats cut. No motive that we can
find, and no connection to each other. And there is the one you and
Pasquin found, the bikini-top woman."

"But the same killer?" I watched Vernon slip off the wet suit.
Strong legs with curly blond hairs stood between me and Tony.

"Seems so," he said. "And the way these things go, your lady
could be in the same company."

"My lady," I grinned at Vernon who had begun popping me
lightly with his towel. "I own a corpse?"

"A cold water corpse," said Vernon. "The first two were found
in pond water. Rotted in no time."

I jerked a hair on Vernon's leg to stop his towel popping. Tony
frowned and turned his back to us.

"Doesn't matter," he said, his head turned upward as though
looking to the heavens for guidance. I'd seen this too many times
before. It was his superior mode, one that didn't allow him to

succumb to delight around a crime scene. "Both of you dive in all kinds of waters." He didn't wait for us, but jumped the foot-long span across to the concrete dock and headed for the patrol cars. Loman followed with the bag of bones.

CHAPTER 4

"It's fair week," I said. "I volunteered to work in the sheriff's booth. Isn't that enough?"

"You've dived in Doe Lake before," said Tony. "Follow me."

"Tony," I stopped inside the sheriff's department hallway, a medicinal place of ecru walls, gray floors, and a steel chair outside each door. "Doe Lake is dry."

"Yeah," he nodded. We ended up in a large room that had been set aside as a place to focus on finding the person who liked to nick at young ladies' necks. "Start here." He pointed to a row of photographs, some I had seen in the crime lab with Marshall. Close-ups circled tiny cuts on bones.

"Mine," I said and proceeded to the next group. "Not so pretty this one." I stared at bones lying in muddy shallows, the flesh and clothing still there in shreds, one not distinguishable from the other.

"Found in a holding pond outside Madison. Gone missing maybe three weeks before construction workers dug up her shoes. Take a look at the last photo." He pointed to a closeup. Fingers held the bone while another hand pointed to the tiny cut visible only to someone searching for a cause of death.

"This looks like throat slashing," I said as I read the statistics. "Seventeen years old, runaway, blue eyes, brown hair." I let my eyes drift upward where the full face photo of a teen-aged woman smiled at me. "Wanda Truman." I stared at the smile. Could this beautiful human be the same as that decimated mess in the first photo?

"Go on," said Tony who leaned against a desk.

"Sue Simpson," I whispered when I came to the smiling snap of another beauty with teeth that could have made it in a dentist's commercial. Her alive picture sat pinned at the end of a row of others that showed mutilated bones in a fish pond and another hand pointing to nicked bones.

"So our—your—bones are about the same age, and the nick, or half nick, in a tiny piece of neck bone, plus finding her in water, makes me want to assign the same person as her killer." Tony tapped the bone photo of Simpson.

"Anybody dive in the holding pond or the fish pond?"

"They're both out of our county, but yes. Sheriff's departments there searched both." He moved to another photo, one set apart from the others. "And this is the one you and Pasquin found. Autopsy report isn't in yet, but the signs are the same." He stopped, stared, then turned toward me. "We have somebody who likes killing and dumping."

"Killing and dumping young women who run away from home?" I shuddered at the thought of another serial killer in our area. Ted Bundy had scared hardware stores out of lock supplies some years back.

Tony glanced at me, then shrugged. "No assumptions made yet. The runaway part could be just convenience for the killer."

I stood for a moment longer, taking in the awesomeness of life torn apart and treated like garbage, of young women so tormented at home where they should be content that they exposed themselves to the dangers of the road. "So what's Doe Lake got to do with this?"

We drove across Tallahassee and turned on two wooded roads before pulling to a stop in a grove of trees. The leaves were turning already, casting a burnt umber and pastel hue across the woods. We would have an abnormally cold winter in the sunshine capital this year.

"Looks like the burn boys are still here. Good." Tony stood staring over a vast, smoking lake bed where tough gray and green grasses had taken hold and matted against each other. Doe Lake, usually a picturesque fishing spot with a sloping hill on one side and high banks circling around it, was nothing but a pasture of choking weeds now. "Nearly got the stuff burned off, when they found something." He pointed to one end where the crime lab trailer had backed into the boat ramp.

"Will they stop the burning?" I asked. Smoke rose from spots in the foliage like the bottom of Hell. There were no visible flames. The grasses were too close together; the lake could smolder for days and sometimes mix with morning fog, causing near zero visibility on the surrounding roadways. As a child, I stood in the fog many mornings, waiting for a late school bus that groped its way from stop to stop.

"Not entirely. But they'll stop burning until we finish." Tony motioned for me to follow him down a muddy path and around an arc in the shore. He nodded to Marshall whose dirty running shoes struggled to encase swollen feet. He had no shoe laces.

"Man in charge uses a Marsh Master," said Marshall as he pointed to a short, stocky man in green overalls. "Says he can ride you onto the lake if you want to go."

"You been out there yet?" A hint of a smile appeared at the corners of Tony's mouth.

"I don't go on boats, and I don't ride tiny tanks through the mud." Marshall raised himself tall, patting his stomach that threatened to rip open the buttoned shirt. He had discarded the lab coat, tossed it across one tire on the evidence trailer.

"Let's see this," said Tony and started to offer me a hand. Instead, he gestured to follow him down the bank.

The grass, thick and dry in spots, grew out of cracked, dry earth. But even in the cracks, Florida mud oozed to the surface.

"Walk at the markers," yelled the man in the green overalls. "You won't bog down there, and you won't fall into a sinkhole."

"Oh, joy! Why am I here, Tony?"

"You know this lake, right?"

"When it's full of water, and deep. I went down in a few of the deep sinkholes once. Not safe down there, and I don't care to fall into a dry one." I stepped carefully behind him.

"We're not anywhere near them right now." Tony led me to the bottom of a steep bank where the earth had eroded into a gash nearly five feet high. Yellow crime scene tape blocked off a portion of thick grass. Uniformed deputies and white coated lab techs stood around the top of the bank. One slim man, half my height, bent over something.

"Take a look." Tony pointed to the object of the man's attention. Among sooty grass that had only partially burned, something gray took shape. "See a body?"

"It looks like a man," I said. Like a painter who adds subtle colors to suggest a message, the picture revealed itself. A form lay in the grass. Some strands of red hair blew slightly away from matted black strands; features coated in soot formed a face; a plaid shirt tartan stood out in blackened squares.

"Fire wasn't hot enough to burn a body," said the small lab tech. "Grass keeps the oxygen smothered." He bent toward the end of the shirt sleeve. With an instrument he pulled from a kit, he gently scraped a finger on one hand. "He's sooty, but underneath, most of the flesh hasn't turned black yet."

"What happened to him?" I tried to focus my eyes to locate a wound, but the soot and grass were good camouflage.

"Try the neck area," Marshall called from the bank.

The man's head turned slightly to one side. Below his chin and one ear, the soot seemed blacker, almost smooth. "Throat cut," I nodded.

"Seems somebody tossed him over the side in this gash in the bank," said Tony. "Looks like he was rolled over to the edge and shoved in, maybe meant to go into the sinkhole."

"But there's no water," I said. "This lake has been dry for months. And I doubt the body would stay like that for months."

"You're learning, Luanne," said Marshall. "Couldn't have been more than yesterday that this fellow got rolled."

I took another look. The man was at least six feet, slight build, but he couldn't have been light. "If he was put in here just yesterday, then how come the grass is covering most of him?"

"The grass was higher," said the green overalls man who had positioned himself between Marshall and Loman at the top of the bank. "It's been smoldering all morning. Didn't find the man until I came over here to try and get this stuff to burn better." He popped two hands on his hips and rocked back and forth on heavy boots.

I nodded and stood up straight. "Okay, Tony, why am I here? It's not like you to just clue me in on stuff for the fun of it."

"We got to search the whole area, and you know those sink-holes." He pointed to the middle of the lake.

"I told you. I know them wet, not dry. You need dry cavers for that."

"And we've got them. NSS is helping out. But the one at the bottom, just at the edge of the body, has water in it."

"Just a minute! I'd have to descend a dry cave to get there first. I don't do dry caves, Tony."

"It's not even thirty feet down. Mr. White has ladders to get inside." Tony pointed to the man in overalls. White brushed at the label on his bib. I couldn't read it, but it must have spelled out the name of the company responsible for burning off dry lakes.

"Ma'am," he said, "we use the ladders to get equipment that falls in, even people sometimes." He grinned, showing rows of tiny, child-like teeth.

"And the water?"

"About ten feet deep. The biggest hole done plugged up with debris and filled up to about that point. Hot and slippery down there, but safe enough." He slipped his thumbs into the straps on his bib and rocked from heel to toe.

"And the scuba gear?"

"Just tie it on a rope and lower it over," he said.

"It's diving, Tony. I don't dive alone."

"In only ten feet of water?" Tony leaned over beside Mr. White. The two men, one tall and crisp with dark eyes and groomed hair, the other short and sweaty with faded blue eyes and ruddy skin, competed for space near the edge of the bank.

"Get Vernon," I said. "And I need to know about these walls. I've never crawled in a sinkhole like this."

"Come on the Marsh Master and I'll show you what you're in for," said White. He jabbed a finger in the direction of a machine sitting at the edge of the lake. There were two seats atop rubber treads that reached from the front to the rear of the vehicle. It would climb over the lake bottom the way a war tank traversed enemy terrain. Equipment—shovels, buckets, and rope—rested in secure areas behind the seats.

I followed White down the embankment, sliding part way in crumbling earth.

"This thing won't sink into a muddy spot?" I asked as he helped me into the passenger seat.

"Made to float on water, cross mud and grass." He climbed into his seat and turned to flash his baby teeth at me. "Has been known to hit a big hole and fall in, but hadn't lost anybody yet. Always got somebody to pull you out." He started the engine.

The machine reminded me of an elephant ride I took once at an amusement park. First the back hips rose on the right, then on the left, making me sway from side to side and hold on for fear of sliding off. Dry, partially burned grass, crackled as we edged to the sinkhole.

"Now if you look from here, you'll see how it slants downward." White gestured toward the bottom of the hole. "You'll see a milky substance toward the bottom. That's the water. We climbed down there couple of days ago to measure the refill. Going to take a hurricane or two to get this lake back where it ought to be."

"The sides of the cave are solid?"

"Solid, but slick and nasty. You got to watch where you step and where you put your hands." He looked at me and let his eyes glance quickly down my front. "You afraid of critters?"

"Not too fond of live snakes and alligators," I said and stared down his front in return.

"All kinds of things wash down there when the water drains out. Dead fish all over the place and the smell ain't nothing to wear to the ladies' circle."

"I don't plan on going to the ladies' circle. What kind of ladder do you use?"

"Up there," he pointed to the top of the bank where some men unloaded a metal ladder. They roped it section by section.

"And that's going to hold?"

"Has so far."

White backed the Marsh Master to the bank and waited until I climbed out and cleared the way for the men to place the ladder on the vehicle. He pulled away again and positioned the ladder at the point where we would climb down.

On the bank, I waited for Amado to return from the dive trailer a few feet away. Vernon had arrived with the equipment. He carried two tanks, while a uniformed deputy hauled the box with fins and masks.

"The water will be the easy part," I said as I checked the gauges.

"You ready?" Vernon winked at me.

Thank God I trusted him body and soul. I had never dived this kind of sinkhole before, but I had heard about how these lakes go dry. In Lake Jackson, a huge body of water on the other side of town, there was a giant sink that let go every few years and drained the entire lake. As the water gushed down unplugged openings to its journey to who knows where, turtles could be heard clacking against the walls, their fleshy feet grasping at slimy walls in an effort to save themselves from the black hole.

"Vernon," I said in a low voice, "is there any chance the hole at the bottom of this sink will unplug and suck us into oblivion?"

"Probably not," he smiled, but it wasn't a teasing one. "Cavers and engineers think its plugged up for a few years now."

"Scientists?" I shrugged. If I got jerked into a black stream on the way to the Gulf, at least Vernon would be with me.

"I know, not too practical, but their opinion is all we've got."

White called from the edge of the sink that they were ready for the tanks. Two of his men lowered them to the ladder where they tied them with cable rope. Vernon and I moved to the dive trailer and slipped on wet suits. We didn't need them for the cold, but no one knew the kind of bacteria we'd be swimming in. We secured the fins around our waists and rested the masks on our foreheads.

"Okay, what are we looking for?" I asked Tony.

"A weapon maybe, or anything that might have rolled off the body and into the sink. It looks like whoever tossed him down this embankment meant for the body to roll into the hole and never be found."

Vernon and I descended the bank, sliding part way down and climbing aboard the Marsh Master one at a time. When White had dropped both of us at the edge of the sink, his men lowered the ladder.

"I'll go down first," said one. "You two follow. Then these fellows will lower the tanks. Not much more room down there for anybody else." He stepped toward the ladder and hesitated. "Oh, yeah. When you go down, try not to touch the walls. They're slick with the white stuff, sticky, nasty-smelling, snotty stuff. Same at the bottom. Watch your step when you plant your feet on the ground."

"This is going to be fun," I said and moved toward the ladder.

"Let me go first," said Vernon.

Even as my diving equal, the man who had no qualms about my ability and never questioned my decisions at great depths, even he had to be the gallant Southern gentleman. I stepped aside and let him put his foot on the ladder.

I watched as Vernon's bald pate covered with a face mask descended into the depths. He yelled up once that things "stunk pretty bad." When he gave the all clear, I followed.

The wet suit grabbed at my skin. It was made for cold waters, not the humid air of this hole. At places, the sink wall grazed my knuckles as I grasped the ladder, and the white substance stuck. As I descended, the odor of rotting reptile and fish along with accumulated burning smells from the grass filled my nostrils. I would welcome the scuba tank air. At the bottom, I stood atop leaves, grass, turtle shells, flattened frogs, and things that could have been reptile skins or discarded pieces of tarp. The same would be plugging up the hole, like nature's bathtub filling up; only this plug had no chain. When it gave way, the water disappeared.

"Better ease in," said Vernon as he helped me with the tank. The sides could be fragile, not to mention the junk at the bottom.

I looked over the irregular oval of water. Along the edges was the same nasty white substance that loosened in the water and turned it milky for a couple of feet. After that, the water was dark, but seemed clear.

With our backs to the water hole, we pushed gently into the pool. This was not the deep, cold water of Palmetto Springs. There were no aquifer sources here to shoot up pristine water to form a new river. It was warm rain water, accumulated into a dirty hole. With the diving lights on, we swam past the white area and began to search the sides. It sloped in places; rotten vegetation clung to the wall, so thick in places that it obliterated the surface behind it.

I gently lifted strands of debris, searching for anything that may have come off a body or a weapon used to kill a man. Vernon worked beside me as we made our way around one side of the hole. Ten feet was no deeper than a swimming pool, but this one was dark and unpleasant, the slightest ripple causing a twig to tumble toward the bottom. We found nothing on the side, and at last reached the mound of debris at the lowest depth. This was the plug, the stuff that kept the two of us from taking our last trip to the ocean together. We would disturb only the surface material.

Finding nothing in the depths, we made our way up the other side. It sloped more here. Anything heavy may have slid when it hit. Or an open knife could hit blade first into the soft wall. If nothing came down to loosen it, it might remain there until the soil softened.

I signaled Vernon and pointed to the short, fat handle whose end rested on a bulge in the uneven wall. The blade tethered it to the soil, barely exposing the metal. He nodded and produced an evidence bag. I gently pulled the handle. The knife came loose, followed by a stream of dirt and white stickiness. The blade was short and curved and looked sharp.

I let my hand brush the wall as I swam to cover the rest of the area. I hadn't expected to find anything, when suddenly a sharp edge ripped over my fingers. I jerked my hand away and watched a stream of red filter through the white water. Vernon covered my hand with his and made the upward motion.

"Piece of glass sticking in the side," said Vernon. He had pulled it out before we surfaced. "Better get a bandage for that. You had your tetanus shot?" I nodded, and wrapped a towel around my fingers. The cut wasn't deep enough for stitches but the mineral in the water made it sting. Back on the edge, we brushed away the substance that stuck to our suits and took a whiff of rotten air when we shoved off our masks. I felt like we had dived in a garbage dump.

"There's one reason it stinks," said the man who had waited at the surface. He pointed to a rotting alligator skin in one corner. A baby, it was only three feet long and in a state of nearly skin and skeleton. "Got trapped when the water went down, I guess."

Topside, Vernon handed over the knife and glass to Tony. He glanced at my hand and ordered a tech to bring some Band-Aids.

"What's that nasty stuff all over your suits?" said Loman. He backed away from us.

"Scientists say it's got bacteria in it," said White who had a camera in his hand. "You divers stand right here. Guys get in beside them." He looked around and grabbed Loman's arm. "When I get lined up, you take the picture."

Loman scowled but took three shots of Vernon and me in

dripping wet suits standing next to White and his crew.

"Okay," said Tony, "get the body out of here." He waved to the men who would crawl down the embankment with a wire basket, secure the body, and haul it to the waiting coroner's wagon at the road.

"Is that what was used on him?" I asked as Tony turned over the knife with gloved hands.

"Could be. The point on the curve looks like a good nicking device." He dropped it into a paper evidence bag.

Inside the trailer, Vernon and I stripped off the suits. In my bathing suit, which was still dry and clean, I felt filthy. "Let's get to a shower," I said.

Vernon handed me a towel. "Here, brush off your face." He whispered, "Your shower or mine?"

"Mine," I said and stepped outside the trailer. From our position apart from the investigation scene, we watched the cops and civilians surround the yellow tape. In the distance, far up the bank and at the edge of the trees, people had emerged from hidden cabins and from cars parked on the shoulder of the lake road to see what kind of disaster had disturbed the cool November air.

One woman shoved two children together and began to walk toward the patrol cars. The kids started to follow, but she turned around and shouted at them to stay put. She came closer, her slip-on shoes forcing her to stumble across the foliage. She reached the coroner's wagon and stopped.

"Who's that?" she asked.

"Stand back, ma'am." A uniform deputy put his arm out as a barrier.

"My husband ain't been home for two days." Her voice shook as she attempted to pass the deputy. Her hair, a smutty black from a homemade dye job, hung in straight strands to her shoulders, and an oversized shirt covered a pair of jeans. She couldn't have been long out of her twenties.

"I'll take your statement, ma'am," said Tony and motioned her to the side of a car. He nodded for the men to move the body away.

"If I could see…," the woman said as she stared at the wagon. She turned to face me, and possibly seeing a friend in one of the few women at the scene, she took off across the few yards. "Ma'am, can you tell me who that is?" Her frightened Bambi eyes pleaded with me. "We live just beyond those trees, and my husband ain't reported for his job, you see…." She took a deep breath, shrugged and gave up.

"What makes you think that could be him?" I said and pointed to the coroner's wagon that headed away from the lake.

"He's got a job with the fair. We travel around, you see. He's a carnival worker and tries to go where they go. But they say he didn't show up yesterday, and if he don't work…" She fanned her hand toward the two kids standing at the edge of the trees.

Before I could say anymore, Tony joined us. He scowled at me from behind the woman. "And you think he ended up in the lake?"

The woman jumped, her thin arms grasping each other. She turned to him and nodded. "At least he could have. He's been known to put away beer by the six pack and he'd gone out with some buddies."

"Does he get into arguments with his buddies?" Vernon leaned against the car. He glanced at me, a signal not to let on that the man had been murdered.

"Don't know these buddies. We just got into town last Thursday. Settled the trailer in the park back there." She pointed again to the row of trees. "He finds friends at the fairgrounds and around." She frowned so hard I thought she might cry. "You don't think one of them tossed him in there, do you?"

"Ma'am, you better come with us," said Tony and took her elbow. "I'm Sheriff's Detective Amado, and you are?"

"Marie Beaufont," she said. "My husband is Rennie Beaufont."

"Cajun name," I said to Vernon. "Probably follows the carnival circuit around the southern states."

"Or the beer joints," he said and took my hand. "Let's find a swamp house."

CHAPTER 5

Vernon drove through Tallahassee, dodging the main roads near the government buildings, and headed for the paved road to Palmetto Springs. I lived in the swamp between the glass bottom boat park and the tiny town of Fogarty Springs where my ancestors set up a general store for the river boat people. According to my grandfather, they built a landing where the workers on the big cotton and corn barges could come ashore for fresh biscuits and fat pork slices and leave with cans of sardines, crackers, and illegal moonshine. The store carried a few dry goods, and medicines for cuts and rope burns, along with peppermint and pickles. But it mostly served as a talking house, a place where men off a shrimp boat could swap river haint stories with those off a lumber raft. Haints, of course, were ghosts, demons that came from the underwater caves or out of tall cypress trees, even a snake-gator, a half alligator, half water moccasin that was not only poisonous but preferred human flesh to deer meat. I suspect a few girlie stories got told, too, but Grandfather didn't reveal any. It took Pasquin to do that.

Dorian Pasquin, my octogenarian swamp neighbor and surrogate guardian, knew the river and the swamp as well as he knew the lines in his own face. And he knew Cajuns, being one himself, a sort of bastard one, as he put it. "Got too many Protestants hanging around the back of the barn," he'd often say.

Pasquin sat on my front porch almost as much as I did. And there he sat when Vernon and I pulled off the dirt road and parked under the tree. My family house had been renovated for a couple of years now, and already the swamp had placed its mark on it. The fresh paint darkened in places where moss and mildew graced the edges.

"Been waitin' for you, ma'am," said Pasquin. He fanned away swamp bugs with his straw hat that needed re-weaving. He had teased me as a child by calling me "ma'am," and the address stuck. "What you done to them fingers?"

I held up three fingers, each with a flesh bandage wrapped around it. "Mischief," I said.

"Believe it," Pasquin chuckled. "What you planning to do about your shift at the booth?"

I groaned. Tomorrow was the first day of the fair. I had promised to go directly from teaching classes in social dialects to practicing them in the booth. My shift as cashier and order taker would be from six to eight at night, or until the "closed for food" sign got hung on top of the menu sign.

"Sit a little longer on the porch, Pasquin. We'll be out when we get Hell grime washed off."

Vernon followed me in the house. He kept a few sets of clothes in the spare closet, and he had a key. Our lives had turned into a comfortable familiarity without the proximity of marriage to cause collisions. It had worked so far. Pasquin never approved, but he knew to keep quiet except for the occasional, "When you gonna tie the knot with that deputy and have a couple of young 'uns?" In our midforties, we weren't likely to produce any young 'uns now.

The closest thing to it was Plato, a stray I had rescued from a nasty poisoning attempt. His siblings didn't know better and ate the bad food. A light brown mutt, playful and loyal, he had a wild streak, a real puppy of the swamp. Content to guard the house for only an hour or two at a time, he roamed the river edges and climbed through the viney vegetation during the day. I had long given up worrying about a gator grabbing him for dinner. He sensed their presence, and often stood back from shore, barking at two eyes staring atop the water. Plato, no dummy, came around for meals in the morning and at night. If I needed a friend during the day, I could stand on my porch and give a loud yodel, "Platooooooo!" Eventually he would drop out of a bush and into the scene, his coat full of burrs or soaked with mud.

"Did you see Plato?" I asked Pasquin as we moved inside.

"Was sitting right here till I showed up. Licked my hand and took off down the road."

Plato had learned how to open the screen door on the porch, from both outside and inside. And he knew the woods and its perils as well as Pasquin. He also knew its delights, and they pulled him for romps on a routine basis. In a rainstorm, he high-tailed it back for shelter.

"Turned over the guard to an old soldier," I said.

"That dog ain't no fool." Pasquin crossed his heart with his hat, mimicking the military stance he had never taken. "You planning on going to the fair tomorrow?"

I pushed open the front door and entered the cool living room. Afternoons still grew warm and humid, though not with the vengeance of summer.

"I suppose I'll go after my last class, why?"

"Guess Edwin and I might want to see some of the sights, ride the Ferris Wheel." Pasquin was asking for a ride. He used his boat to travel distances in this swamp, but it couldn't take him into Tallahassee. His usual was to ask me first, and if that didn't pan out, to head for Fogarty Spring and catch a ride from anyone going that way. The return trip was not a sure thing.

"You and Edwin on a Ferris Wheel?" Edwin, a younger and not

so smart version of Pasquin, had joined in the swamp folks' social group. They met for a little "brew and bragging" as Pasquin said. The bragging came after a great deal of brew had been sipped, straight and often from the bottle. On the surface, they were simple people who lived close to nature, but in a bind they could be called upon to rescue just about anyone on the swamp floor and sometimes on the water.

"Let me take a shower and talk about this in a little while." I headed upstairs, Vernon behind me.

"Don't know what you've been doing, ma'am, but it don't smell too good."

The white goo stuck until I scrubbed it off with a cloth. The bandages came off my fingers in the water. The cuts weren't deep but they had drawn blood and could harbor germs from the rotting cave debris. After the shower, I poured peroxide over them and put on new bandages. "If I get some rare and fatal disease, I'll sue Tony."

"Better have a blood test," said Vernon. "Don't know what that stuff will do to your innards, but it sure does stick to the skin." He brushed at the little hair that remained on the sides of his head. He was bald on top, something that added to rather than detracted from his manliness. I had been taken from the beginning by his easy attitude. It still thrilled me.

"What's amusing you?" he said as he saw me looking at him in the bathroom mirror.

"Female thoughts," I said and patted his rear.

He grinned back and said, "Get rid of Pasquin."

Pasquin had leaned back in a recliner inside the living room and snored when we joined him. His hat rested in his lap like a revolver waiting to be grabbed in case of an intruder.

"Guess we'd better discuss tomorrow's agenda," I said out loud.

"Been waiting for that," said Pasquin without opening his eyes.

"You're just like a cat," I said. "Looks like you're sound asleep, but you know every move made."

He sat up. "Ha! Not every move." He nodded upstairs, his way of teasing me about Vernon's presence in the house.

"What are you going to do at the fairgrounds tomorrow night?"

"Me and Edwin want to go see the side shows. He says there's this one called Snake Boy. You know Edwin with his snake skin belts and all that stuff he's got hanging off the line in back of his house."

I'd been to Edwin's only once when Pasquin needed to stop there and give him some tomatoes he had grown in his little back garden. The house, a converted trailer with two add-ons, sat in a grove of low hanging oaks a few feet away from the river's edge. Edwin had propped the whole business up on several layers of cement blocks to avoid flooding in a rainy year. The front steps were more blocks piled in a terrace arrangement. We walked around to the back where Edwin worked at a picnic table. Several knives, their points affixed into the wood as though thrown there, stood at attention at one end. He had stretched a wire between two trees. Long snake hides hung drying in the heat.

"Oh, my God!" I said as I took a whiff. "A snake man."

Edwin had grinned like he was embarrassed and shoved a sleeve across his forehead. "Got an order to make some belts," he said.

"Creepy," I whispered to Pasquin.

"Every man's got his talents," Pasquin said and sat the bag of tomatoes on the table edge.

"Ya'll want some tea?" Edwin's silly grin reminded me of a not-too-bright inmate. I knew better. No one could tell you more about swamp snakes than this man.

"None for me," I said and backed away from a cage full of live slithers and hisses.

"Got to get to those," he said and resumed stripping the guts from a muddy colored snake that had been pinned to the table top at both ends.

"Is this legal?" I asked.

"Swamp legal," said Pasquin who didn't ask those questions. "He deals with the poisonous kind. No friendly snakes in that cage."

"Doesn't harm the friendly ones," I muttered and took up a position near the corner of the house. Edwin lived with snakes outside, and I wasn't sure what slept inside with him. I didn't want to know. Anybody who called himself Snake Boy would be an attraction to him.

"When I finish up the class, I'll need to hurry to the grounds. Can you and Edwin take the boat to Palmetto Springs? I'll pick you up there."

Pasquin nodded. "We'll be waiting."

"And make sure Edwin doesn't bring any of his slinky friends with him." I shuddered to think of a bag with a live moccasin writhing in the back of my '84 Honda.

The night looked promising, lots of leisure time to lie around my swamp with Vernon. We had never let the relationship grow stale by living in each other's pockets. He didn't move in, but he stayed over just enough to put an exciting touch to the place.

I popped a couple of chops onto an indoor grill, while Vernon chopped lettuce and carrots. We ate simply here, opting for the heavy fried fish and grits at Mama's Table in Fogarty Springs.

I poured red wine in my glass and cola into his. He had long since conquered a drinking problem by ignoring the stuff. We sat at the small breakfast table that faced the back yard—if one could call it that. It consisted of a tiny patch of grass that didn't get enough sun to grow tall, lots of oak trees, oleander bushes, and general swamp scrub. I had opened the back door, leaving only the screen door to ward off biting bugs; a light rain fell and made soothing purring sounds in the vegetation.

"I love November," I said. "Cool enough to turn off the air conditioner, but not so cold we can't open up to the elements.

"Good sleeping nights, too," said Vernon. He cut his pork and refused to look at me, a smile twitching at the edge of his lip.

"Sweet dreams," I said and raised my wine glass. His boyish teasing still charmed me, and I considered myself one lucky swamp woman.

Later, after we had moved in rhythm with the night songs of katydids, frogs, and screech owls who thrust their voices into the calm of the darkness, we rested in the soft breeze that came through the screened windows. Even as a child, the night sounds had soothed me, a reminder that no matter the food chain, life continued.

The phone rang.

"Don't you just love police work," I said as I rolled to one side of the bed and stretched for the phone. Vernon grunted.

"You awake?" It was Marshall Long.

"Yeah," I whispered, not willing to lose the moment. "What's going on?"

"You always go to bed at nine?"

"Not always. Did you call to find out what my sleeping habits are?"

"You got that deputy there with you, don't you?" Marshall let out a phony cough. "Sorry. Got a peanut stuck in my throat."

"You're going to get something larger than a peanut stuck somewhere else if you don't get to the point."

Vernon laughed and raised himself on an elbow.

"Okay, Luanne—the skeleton, not you—she ain't complete after all."

"Meaning?"

"Meaning that long bone you found in the cave isn't human. Most likely from a deer. And those tiny fragments your deputy picked up look like broken pieces of animal bone. Remnants of alligator feasting, no doubt." Marshall took a loud slurp through a straw.

"Don't do that!" I said and stuck a finger in my ear.

"It's my job. I'm supposed to find out where bones come from." He took another slurp.

"No! Stop slurping. The phone magnifies the sound and it's disgusting."

"Okay. You got that about the bones?"

"Anything else?" I stroked Vernon's arm. He lay face down, hugging my waist.

"The knife you found in the sinkhole, it's most likely the weapon that killed the man—and it could very well be the same weapon that killed the girls."

I sat up. Vernon groaned into his pillow.

"A serial killer?"

"Tony thinks so, and there's more." I heard another slurp, away from the receiver this time.

"Marshall, go on!"

"That woman, Marie Beaufont, identified the man as her husband, Rennie."

"Got himself murdered while out with his drinking buddies?"

"Don't know, but that's what the wife is saying. She's a ranter and raver sort. Got Tony hopping mad most of the time."

Silence set while Marshall played his games with me. "And you called at nine to tell me all this?"

"Oh, yeah. Tony says to meet him at his office first thing tomorrow morning and to bring your deputy with you."

"Diving?" I looked at Vernon who had sat up and placed a pillow over his lap.

"Could be, and I think he needs a woman's touch."

I sighed. Tony, who would opt for a man any day, never hesitated to use me if it suited him. I wasn't a deputy, only an adjunct diver on the books, paid good money for dangerous work. He had often called on me to explore the caves I've known since childhood. And lately he had pulled me in to deal with situations he felt none of his deputies could handle. At least that's what I chose to believe. Being short of staff was more like it.

"I've got a class at eight. Tell him I'll get there by ten."

"Seven," Marshall said. "He's starting the meeting at seven."

CHAPTER 6

"I'll be there at ten," I said as I watched Vernon go out the door with a coffee cup in hand. I refused to bow to Tony's demands. If I showed up at seven, I'd never make it to my class on time.

There is an impatient air about universities in November. It's almost over, almost time to pack up and head for cities where Mom once more lays dinner on the table. Meals of ordered-in pizza and canned sausages end for a few weeks. And exams have been passed—or failed for those who won't be returning. November is also football wrap time. Vans go flying by campus with banner flags hooked to the roofs. If a group of them end up at an intersection, honking horns lead the cheers. It's not a good time for The Great Vowel Shift in linguistics.

The morning had turned brisk, the first cold snap of the season. By the end of the week, farmers expected a freeze and would have to cover plants during the night. In my rush to make the class, I dropped my lecture note pad at the entrance to the gothic brick building that housed the linguistics department.

"This yours, Dr. Fogarty?" The department chair had followed me inside. His leather sandals over socks squeaked on the dark floor. He had found a niche of survival in this world, a remnant on a pile of useless bureaucrats. He had published brilliant works on South American Indian dialects in his youth when he had traveled throughout the Amazon in sandals not much different from the ones he wore today. He wore his hair long then, hanging loose on shoulders clad in muslin shirts. The thick, dark locks had faded to dirty gray, and the growth on top no longer existed, but the ends were still long. He pulled the thin strands into a pony tail and held it there by what he said was a treated llama umbilical from his Peruvian days. He still had the gaunt body of a vegetarian who occasionally smoked his dinner through rolled paper.

"Thanks, Manny," I said and took the notes. He had changed his first name to Manuel during his time near the Amazon. "Easier for the Indians than Holister," he said. He kept the Greenberg family name.

"You're almost finished for the semester?" He gazed at me, not an inquisitive look, not even a bored small-talk look, but a glazed stare. I figured he'd puffed on a joint along with his bowl of granola.

"Yes. This is the last week." I stared back. Wouldn't he know that?

"You have the Winter schedule?"

"You said you'd have it soon, Manny." I stopped but he stared in silence. "Don't you remember?"

He jumped, like someone had poked his ribs and reminded him of the current century. "Good," he said and walked past me. "See you after the holidays."

I watched the man turn down another hallway, and listened for his sandal squeaks to fade away. "Lost in the sixties," I said and opened the door to my classroom.

Students squirmed in their plastic chairs, reviewing what they knew about how the phonetics of Middle English had changed to Early Modern about the time Shakespeare wrote his plays. The next time we met would be finals, and they expected to regurgitate what I had given them. I tried to hint that I planned to introduce a "what if" scenario and have them write about the outcome based on their semester knowledge. By the end of the class, I had run out of invented situations and sent them home to hours of concentrated study. The worse to come was for me—grading the blue books.

The scene in Tony's office hadn't changed over the years I had known him. The clutter of files and evidence mingled into a system only he knew how to decipher. Behind his desk, a bulletin board threatened to topple off its one hook.

"You need to fix that thing," I said. "One slam of the door and it's on the floor."

"We got a problem, Luanne." Tony ignored me. "You said it's not possible for an animal or human to wash into that off shoot cave because the current is pushing against the entry." He leaned over his desk, his Cuban black eyes staring at me. "Then how did a deer leg get there, and how did this girl get there?"

I shrugged. "The girl could have been taken there, although that wouldn't be easy. Two divers would do a better job of it. Doubt any diver would drag a deer leg inside—unless they wanted to rattle a sheriff's detective, drive him crazy trying to figure it out."

"Cut it out, Luanne!" Tony's jaw clinched and worked back and forth. "How can you explain this?"

"Tony, I didn't do it. I don't have to explain it." I held up my hands in mock defense. He wouldn't yell at a man like this, I told myself. Ribbing him was a delight.

He breathed deeply, and in a calm voice asked, "Can you find an explanation for such a phenomenon?"

"Most likely there is another entrance that flows with the current. I'll get hold of the NSS divers and find out." I whispered the answer and turned to leave.

"Not yet! I got another thing I want you to do." He offered me a chair, without removing the files.

"Shall I sit on top or just swipe them to the floor?"

He crossed in front of the desk, grabbed the bundle and slammed them behind his chair.

"Marie Beaufont is in a conference room. She's hysterical one minute, terrified the next. We can't seem to get much, and my females aren't available."

"Your females? You have a stable now?"

Tony scowled and refused to answer. "Talk to her, Luanne. We got a problem and a half here. The knife you found was used on the girls and on her husband. All found in water, or where water should be. Just talk to her, will you?"

"Tell me about the knife."

"You saw it. It's got a curved blade. Mostly used to slice linoleum, tiles, and such. Anyone can buy one."

"And it makes a characteristic nick in neck bone?"

"Yeah. And the same nick has shown up in too many necks."

"I've got another class today, at two. Take me to her."

Tony led me down a gray steel hall and turned a corner. He knocked quickly, then opened the door. Loman sat with Marie Beaufont at a square table, both sipping colas. Marie wiped her eyes with a ragged tissue. She had the appearance of a depression-era mother who hadn't eaten for days.

Tony introduced me and nodded at Loman, who seemed gleeful at the thought of leaving. He jerked his head toward me as he went out the door, indicating he'd listen and watch through the two-way mirror.

"You was at the site," said Marie, an eager expression on her face. "I saw you in a suit."

"I found the weapon," I said and sat next to the woman. "When did you last see your husband?"

"He went off two days ago to sign up for the fair. We follow it, you see. From New Orleans to Miami, we follow carnivals and he gets good work there."

"Enough to support you year round?" To my knowledge, carnivals were Autumn affairs.

"He gets other work during the off months. Construction."

"Where do you live?"

"We got a travel trailer. Get places in parks and things. Kids don't like it much. They have to keep changing schools."

She dabbed at her nose with the torn tissue. I whipped out a cellophane package and offered it to her. "I sent them to their grandma in Live Oak," she said and tore into the package. "Don't want them listening to talk about their daddy's death."

"You said at the site that he often drank with buddies. Did he drink with them two nights ago?"

She looked at the tissue for too long, her bottom lip trembling. "I don't know. He didn't tell me when he went drinking. Just did. That's what I thought happened. Got signed up at the fairgrounds, then found somebody to drink with. But he usually comes home the next morning, all hung over, but he does come home." She stopped, looked up at me, then back at her hands. "He didn't come home this time."

"What will you do now?"

"I always get a job waitressing when we're on the road. I got something lined up at a truck stop. If I had any sense, I'd go home to Live Oak, but I need to settle a bit before facing them people."

"Your husband's people?"

"Oh, no. He's from New Orleans, and I don't guess has any people. Brought up in an orphanage. I met him at a diner in Pensacola about 1989. Handsome dude." She smiled.

"Would you care to tell me how the marriage went. I mean…."

"I know what you mean. He did his best, but he had this habit of going off to drink. Never came home mean or anything, just spent up all the cash on beer." She looked up suddenly. "Grouchy, but ain't never hit me, or the kids."

"Other women? Sorry, but I have to ask."

She didn't say anything. She shook her head like it was something she couldn't possible know.

"The sheriff will be checking into his contacts at the fairgrounds, and he'll want to ask more questions about your travels. You'll stay in the trailer park?"

"Yes," she whispered. "Do you think I could talk to you instead of that man?"

"The one sitting in here with you, Loman?"

"With the creepy eyes, yes."

"I suppose so. I'll speak to the detective in charge."

I left Marie in the care of a uniformed officer who would drive her home. There would be no funeral arrangements until the coroner released the body.

"You heard her, Tony," I said as I prepared to return to my teaching job. "She wants to talk to me instead of Loman."

Tony nodded, shot Loman a nasty glance and told me to stay in touch. I told him to show up at the booth tonight and sup on gator tail.

After ending the lecture on human phonemes, I tossed my book bag into the Honda. From the back seat, I pulled a knit jacket. The night temperature had dropped further. "Lizard cracking weather," my daddy had called it. Folks for ages claimed that a lizard caught outside in a freeze would crack open, make a sound loud enough to think somebody had jabbed a block of ice. And we did hear cracks in the winter. Still do. But I never found evidence of a cracked-open lizard. "Birds eat 'em," said Daddy.

When I pulled on the jacket, I saw a figure several car rows away. He appeared lost, or searching for something.

"Manny?" I called out, but the chair continued looking over the tops of the cars. I wound through the rows until I could touch his elbow. "Have you lost something?"

Manny turned round and stared at me, wrinkling his brow. Slowly, his eyes focused on me and recognition hit. "Luanne! Can you help me find my car? I forgot where I parked it."

"In your marked spot, isn't it?"

"Marked spot?" He frowned again.

"Are you all right, Manny?" Maybe the acid and marijuana mix had finally fried his brain.

"Yes. Oh, yes, I must have parked it in the…" His voice trailed off as he looked in the direction of special parking assignments. "It's not there."

I gazed around the lot. Only the expensive model belonging to the new dean sat in the marked spaces. "Can I give you a ride?" I winced, thinking of rushing to Palmetto Springs for Pasquin and Edwin, then on to the fairgrounds.

"Maybe you could drop me at the bus stop?" He pulled out a handful of change. "Oh, look! Bus tokens." He looked up at me and realization gave way to embarrassment. "The bus, Luanne. I've begun taking the bus. Didn't even drive today." He slapped his palm against his forehead. "Is this age or what?"

I smiled and said to myself, "Probably 'or what'."

"I can drop you by the big bus stop. It's on my way."

"Thanks, but it stops right outside the gate. I'll see you later, Luanne." He turned on his sandals and strode out the parking lot gate and crossed the street. Sitting on a bus bench, he seemed lost in the hustle of the twenty-first century.

Pasquin and Edwin rested in wooden chairs outside the swimming area at Palmetto Springs. It was too cold for swimmers to splash around in the already frigid spring water. In the distance, the hydrilla grass-pulling machine paddled around the cypress islands, yanking out the intruding grass and piling it atop a conveyor belt. Edwin grinned when he saw me walking across the lawn.

"Got my camera," he said and held it up like a child.

"Are you sure Snake Boy allows photo shoots?" I asked.

Edwin frowned; a pout formed on his face. For a moment I thought he'd cry.

"He'll let you take pictures, even if it's only outside," said Pasquin and pulled on his friend's sleeve. Edwin smiled again.

We drove down two paved roads before hitting the highway for the fairgrounds. This would be the first night for the public, the one that allowed free entry to school children.

I pulled into a spot reserved for personnel at the delivery end of the grounds. Already, cars lined the streets, waiting their turn to be waved into a lot.

"Meet me at the sheriff's booth before eight," I said. "And don't bring any snakes with you!" I shook a finger at Edwin. His laugh was high pitched and he gulped with excitement.

"How come they don't have any more girlie shows at these things?" said Pasquin as he led Edwin in another direction.

"Try the Jubile and Julene show," I said. "It's the next best thing."

The deep fryers were nearly heated up by the time I pulled on an apron. It was to protect me from cooking oil stains and to give me pockets to fish out change for kids whose parents handed them twenties. Mama and Harlie swirled around grilling burgers, toasting buns, and filling batter dishes, having no time to quarrel.

"Gator plates will be ready in ten minutes," said Mama. She grabbed a handful of cubed gator meat, rolled it in the batter and dropped it into the deep fat. It sent up an aroma, appetizing and beguiling.

"Two burgers up!" Harlie smiled my way, holding two plates with hamburgers, loaded with grilled onions, for me to pass to the eager faces across the formica counter. The entire booth was raised off the ground at least a foot, making the counter about nose high for average people. For the two preteens who waved bills, it topped their heads.

"You paying separately?" I asked. They nodded. "Two dollars each." I gave them each change for five. No time to think or to look into the faces that shouted orders.

"I'd like some gator tail, ma'am," said a voice that spoke around a tobacco plug.

I looked up to see a man who resembled a cowboy, a small-built man who had developed his biceps to the point that they threatened to topple him onto his stetson hat. The hat was too large. It covered his eyebrows, but let him peek under the brim with washed-out blue eyes. A thin, reddish-brown mustache attempted to grow across his upper lip.

"Gator for the cowboy," I shouted.

"You arrest people?" He smiled, the plug tucked firmly out of sight.

"Not me. I'm just a deputy's helper," I said.

"You'd look great in a uniform, big green hat and all," he continued to grin.

I tried turning my attention to the man behind him, but he wouldn't let go of the moment.

"Chawbutt Nixon, ma'am." He held out his hand. I reached

across the counter and shook it.

"Chawbutt?"

"Not my real name, of course. The fellows gave me it sort of as a title. I chew up bull butt real quick." He thumbed in the direction of the bull riding arena. "Come around in the evening and watch. I got all the best bulls lined up."

"I'll bet you have," I nodded, "Chawbutt." I grabbed the fried gator basket from Mama and handed it across to him. "Chew on a little gator tail for now."

He pulled out a money clip and slipped off the two dollars. "Now you be sure to come over and see me sometime during the week, hear?" He tipped the large hat with one hand, took the gator tail with the other and smiled all the way through the crowds.

"Think he's sweet on you, Luanne," Mama giggled. "Somebody named Chawbutt is sweet on Luanne."

My feet and back ached after an hour of picking up plates, passing them over the counter and collecting money. The faces multiplied until there was a sea of pimply preteens wanting greasy burgers and, only for the daring, cubes of fried gator. In the brief interludes between waves of adolescents, the lights on the carnival rides blinked and glowed, while barkers offered visitors the thrills of a sideshow that could only be seen on the circuit. Somewhere out there, Edwin would pull Pasquin into the Snake Boy show more than once, until the old man said "no more" and headed for the coffee and beignet stand.

Vernon came by once and let me know he'd be questioning Cannon at eight. I would meet him near the delivery entrance.

"And leave us to clean up this mess?" Mama yelled from behind a deep fryer.

"Got deputies to help you, Miz Mama," said Vernon and whopped her behind.

"Hey!" I said. "That's my prerogative."

CHAPTER 7

"Sit here with Mama. I'll come back for you," I said to Pasquin and Edwin. The two men plopped on stools behind the booth and helped themselves to a stack of leftover sliced tomatoes.

Cannon sat in half trailer that served as his office on wheels. Two armed patrol officers rode on horses at the perimeter of a series of trailers, watching cash boxes arrive at intervals from the various side shows and carnival rides.

"You people caught me at a busy time," said Cannon as he took a metal box from a booth clerk going off duty. "I got money to count."

Tony wasn't impressed. "This won't wait," he said and placed a foot on the step up to the door. Vernon and I followed him inside.

"You won't find this any too comfortable," Cannon said. He scraped some clothing from one chair, lifted advertisement fliers from another. Vernon found a crate and sat on top. "Watch that!" warned Cannon. "It's got clown props inside. Dumb asses left it outside where anybody could have picked it up." He sat down hard in his folding metal chair and rested his arms across the cluttered desk. "What's up?"

"Ever employ anyone named Rennie Beaufont?"

Cannon glared at Tony, his curly hair and beard surrounding a face that could have forced thunder. "You're asking me to look through files, right?"

"Not if you know the guy."

"Don't. That means files." He gestured to some metal drawers behind him. Stacks of papers teetered on top, and from the looks of Cannon's expression, just as much confusion reigned inside.

"You need help?" Tony nodded toward me and Vernon.

Cannon held up a huge hand like a stop sign. "Let me try." He opened the middle button on his shirt and scratched his chest. "Got any idea when I was supposed to know him?" He raked through the stack on top of one file, then began the other.

"Maybe your most recent fair, or carnival."

"Just came from Dothan, Alabama. Did a small fair over near Panama City." He dug into a cabinet drawer. "Yeah, luck is with us. Beaufont. Paid the guy for booth maintenance. Did all right. Got a note on here he wants to work in Tallahassee. Not sure he ever showed." He passed the paper to Tony.

"Any ideas about his social life?"

"I don't socialize with these people," said Cannon. He sat down again in the metal chair. "You might ask around the booths. Lots of workers follow the shows."

"Do the performers fraternize with the laborers?" I asked.

Cannon stared at me. "Not usually. Different sort of people there, but you'll find exceptions. We got one old coot who hangs onto his job by riding along with the performers. Try Snake Boy. He's got one more show. You've got time to catch it."

I held onto Vernon's arm. Close proximity to performing snakes wasn't my idea of an exciting evening. I offered to sit it out, but Tony insisted. "You're part of this investigation now, and I can't afford to leave anyone out. You'll get your pay."

We skirted back around the sheriff's booth where deputies packed away sodas and cooking oil and paper plates. Edwin and Pasquin had a conversation going about which stars appeared in an Autumn sky, when I asked them if they could stand another display of Snake Boy antics. Edwin jumped up, knocking over the trash can full of hamburger papers.

We waited outside the canvas draped structure for the teaser on the small stage. A man in a leopard skin cape, small enough to be a boy but pushing sixty, appeared with a wooden cage. He made a grand motion of undoing three padlocks with separate keys. He stood back and slowly opened the lid with a long, curve necked stick. Nothing happened for a moment, then a huge brown rectangle of snake head darted outward. The crowd gasped and made a little jerk backwards. The huge body slithered onto the stage, stretching several feet from the box in front of the short man. He bent over and raised the snake to the "S" position, the striking stance, and looked it squarely in the face. All the while, exotic Indian flutes played on a boom box, and a barker yelled over a microphone about how many natives the demons had squeezed to death, and how Snake Boy could calm even the most lethal cobra with his stare.

"It's a brown python," said Edwin. "Grows to be as long as I am tall." A teenager turned round and stared at him, then giggled for her friend.

"I got the tickets," said Tony. "Let's go."

Inside, we stood behind ropes that separated the skittish audience from a small platform. At the back of the structure, thick curtains fell before cages, not quite hiding the edges. Most assumed the snakes were inside and Snake Boy would pull them out, draping them about him while close to the stage rim. People who wanted to be thrilled took places close to the ropes. I stood back. I had seen what a cornered snake might do and planned to be no part of a carnival accident. Tony and Vernon stood on opposite sides. Their demons were human.

Snake Boy appeared on stage, this time with a microphone

hooked over his head, like Madonna in concert. He still had the cape draped over his body, but when he hit center stage, he whirled it off, dressed only in a leopard skin loin cloth, to reveal a boa constrictor wrapped around his oiled torso like a grape vine. The snake's head swayed near his neck, the tongue darting. Snake Boy began to talk about being abandoned in the jungles of Borneo, how this snake and that one eventually came to be his friends. From the rear of the stage, he pulled out snake after snake, all colorful reptiles that must have been well fed and possibly drugged. By the time he finished the show and lecture, he was draped in snakes. They wound around his arms, legs—shins and thighs—his torso, neck, and even formed a turban on his head.

Edwin clapped in delight. Pasquin looked at his simple companion and chuckled. I cringed.

"This is the biggie!" warned Edwin.

We heard a click from behind a curtain. A golden head, larger than Marshall Long's tennis shoe, shoved from underneath the curtain. Snake Boy didn't seem to notice as the reptile crept up behind him. The audience squirmed and squealed. The snake didn't end. Much of its body was still concealed by the curtain. When its head found the Boy's heel, he edged up the leg, winding over the snakes already there. Climbing until he reached the man's neck, he encircled the human body, coiling, coiling, until the tail exited the curtain and joined the rest of the length draped around the performer. He stood, as he said, with nearly five-hundred pounds of snake on his body.

I shuddered when the front curtain finally called a close to the slinky event. Were helpers back there unwinding and recaging the things?

"Wait outside for us," I said to Edwin and Pasquin. "We have to talk to this guy."

"You're going to talk to Snake Boy?" Edwin turned and pushed himself next to me. "Can I go with you?"

Pasquin chuckled again and pulled him along. "Maybe Luanne will get his autograph."

"Yeah, maybe I'll have him sign it on his favorite rattler."

I joined Vernon and Tony behind the stage area. Handlers moved the cages away, their inhabitants back behind bars. Snake Boy rubbed himself with a cloth.

"You can't come back here," he said, but stopped when Tony flashed a badge. "Okay, what's going on? I got the proper licenses for these monsters." He gestured toward the cages. "Even if Sylvester acts up now and then." He gave the finger to the giant gold python who hissed at the two men carrying his cage.

"I'd respect those things, if I were you," said Tony.

"Yeah, well you ain't me. Damn things get cheeky some nights, squeeze me a little." He rubbed one arm. "They get fed enough to behave."

"How did you get that big snake to crawl right up to your body and climb it?" I asked.

"Sorry, artist's secret," he said and scraped shiny oil from his chest.

"Cannon said you might know somebody we're inquiring about," said Tony. Vernon stood behind, surveying the back room. I kept my distance. A room full of snakes was never my cup of tea.

Tony asked about Beaufont. Snake Boy shook his head, but one of the handlers heard the question.

"I knew Beaufont from one or two jobs. Good man."

He strode forward, wiping his hands on a cloth pulled from his back pocket. He wore a jeans and tee-shirt, and had the muscled arms of a laborer who lifted things.

"You ever go out drinking together?"

The man shook his head. "Don't think Beaufont ever went out

drinking. Said he preferred to find a quiet place to read."

"His wife said he liked to hang out with the boys after hours," said Tony.

"Not when I knew him. That's why I remember him. Stayed to himself a lot. He did show me pictures of his kids. Seemed proud to have them."

Vernon joined the other handlers in the back and asked around, but no one knew the name. If Beaufont had been the drinker his wife said he was, he must have been a quiet one. I decided to make Edwin happy.

"Could you sign this for a friend who likes your snake show?" I thrust a flier toward Snake Boy, making sure my hand didn't touch his.

"An autograph?" He took the paper, borrowed a pen from the handler, and leaned over a crate. "First time this has ever happened."

"Believe me, it will be appreciated," I said. The man was no taller than my chest and he stood too close. I backed away with the signed flier, thanking him as I left the area.

We drove toward Palmetto Springs in silence. Pasquin's night out had tired his old body, and he dozed in the seat beside me. Edwin sat in back, opening and closing the signed flier and grinning to himself. I figured he'd build a cypress wood frame for the thing.

"You get any photos?" I asked.

"Yeah, out front. They wouldn't let me shoot inside. But I got that big brown python all right."

"And your autograph."

I felt slinky things around my feet until we pulled into the boat landing. Pasquin grunted, slapped his hat on his thigh and said his good nights.

"You'll be okay on the boat?"

"Never been anything but okay on a boat," he said. "You be ready around two to go for more gator meat tomorrow. Come on Edwin; let's get you home."

I waited until he started the motor and watched the boat light move out to the middle of the river. Pasquin moved slow and steady, and he had navigated this river most of his life. By the time I dragged into my rutted road drive, he would be snoring in his swamp house. Edwin, I figured, would stay up half the night reliving his snaky thrills.

I would be alone tonight. Vernon had duty and would end up at his own place near another lake.

Around midnight, I heard the whine. Plato had arrived from his night on swamp town. He scratched against the front door. I opened it to face a dog full of burrs. He twitched and bit at himself in between tail wags.

"What am I going to do with you?" I said and joined him on the screened porch. The weather had turned downright cold. I heard the heat pump click on to force warm air into my redone swamp house. "Come here." I held him down and with an old towel, began to pull the burrs from his short fur. He let out a yelp or two when I had to yank hard, but finally, a pile of hair filled burrs lay on the porch floor. Plato rolled around, stopping to scratch himself with first one hind leg, then the other. "You got into something, didn't you?" He wagged his tail but cut that action short to scratch some more.

I sat on the porch for over an hour, watching the poor dog rid itself of misery. When he finally settled down, he rested his head on the top of my foot and sighed relief. I let him stay and looked over the forest. In summer, the humidity would gather round me, bringing with it the bugs that no screen could keep away. Tonight, I tightened my sweater around the flannel pajamas. In the distance, I heard a boat in a slow putt around some cove, its light too far away to see. The temperature dropped until I saw my breath in the dim light from the living room. At the side of the porch, I heard the first crack. Two more followed a short distance away. Plato jumped at all three, but then relaxed and laid his head on my foot again.

"Lizards," I whispered to him. "Cracking lizards."

CHAPTER 8

"I've got one exam to give today. After ten, Pasquin and I go down to the alligator farm. At six, it's back to the fairgrounds."

I spoke to Vernon on my cell phone as I drove to the university. He wanted me to join him and Loman to question the Beaufont children in Live Oak. "We need a woman's touch," he said. "We can stop for lunch next to the Suwannee River. A deputy can fill in at the booth until we get back."

Sleepy-eyed students wandered into the classroom, pulled out blue books and either began to describe the dialect problem I gave them, or sat staring at the blank pages. One even put his head down and napped. Went he awoke, he wrote in a fury, like he had dreamed the answer. At the end of the two hours, I collected the books and headed to my car. I'd have to find time to grade them between collecting gator meat and talking to fatherless children. Down the hall, I passed Manny who stared straight ahead. He didn't acknowledge my hello. He still wore sandals, in spite of the cold, and today he didn't have on socks.

"Losing it," I whispered to myself.

"Cold season coming," said Pasquin at the edge of the landing. He waited for me to haul myself from the car, stack blue books on the porch and join him. "Probably won't use the cooling any more this year." He wore a heavy blue jacket that encompassed him. His white hair, covered with the tattered straw hat, stuck out at the neck like a bald eagle.

"Army surplus, right?"

"Best warm stuff around." He revved the engine and we headed down the river.

"What happens if you fall overboard in that thing?" I asked as we turned onto the final water lane to Rinks' farm.

"It'd float, I think." He ignored me and slowed the engine. "Just round this bend."

We tied the boat to the dock, next to a late model speed boat. No one worked around the gator cage, and no one came when Pasquin gave his, "Whoweeeeee."

I held the boat as he climbed out, then followed him onto shore. When we passed the gator cage, two of the beasts who lay next to the fence raised to their feet and hissed in a reptilian baritone.

"Acting like they ain't been fed," said Pasquin. "Wonder where that man is. Mama done paid for that meat." He strode away from the cage to the back entrance of the barn.

I watched two gators get into a short tussle in the crowded cage. The one time I'd been here, they were docile and half-asleep. When I looked up, a young man hardly out of his teens, in a hooded tee-shirt, walked rapidly toward Pasquin. For a moment, I thought he was going to jump him. When the man saw me, he stopped.

"You people got business here?"

"Came for meat ordered weeks ago," said Pasquin. "Rinks around anywhere?"

The man shoved the hood off his head and looked behind him. "Had to go up the river for something. Don't think he'll be back soon." He put his hands on his hips and stood directly in the middle of the path.

"Just look in the refrigerator," said Pasquin. "I believe he wrote Mama's Table on her stuff."

The man hesitated for a moment, the pointed to the path. "Stay here; I'll check."

In less than five minutes he returned with a large box marked for Mama's Table. "I'll take it to the boat for you." He followed us to the landing and placed the box inside the cooler. "Don't think Rinks will be back soon."

"We got another order to pick up," said Pasquin. He tapped the hat on his thigh and chest, his way of becoming irritated with the man.

"Yeah, okay." The man stood back on shore and waited for us to pull away from the landing. "I'll see what's up." He stood there until we turned the bend and could see him no more.

"Wonder if Rinks knows his help ain't feeding his livestock," said Pasquin.

When we reached my landing, Pasquin and I carried the cooler to the front porch. Plato met us and jumped about sniffing and growling at the cooler.

"Funny," I said. "He never commented on gator meat before."

"Hope it ain't gone bad," said Pasquin.

"Tony says to let them talk. They know about the murder, likely to be traumatized." Vernon drove an unmarked car, its heater blasting dry air into the front seat. The frigid night and morning lingered into the afternoon. I huddled into my oversized sweater, the blue books resting on my lap. Loman dozed in the back seat, his occasional snort waking him up to ask if we were close yet.

"Will the grandmother be there?" I asked. I sent a red mark clear through two sentences of nonsense.

"Name is Mrs. Kelly, a widow. And Marie will be there, too," said Vernon. "She came down last night. Says today is her day off, and she needed to be near her kids."

"Anyone check out the domestication of Rennie?" I made a large X across a paragraph.

"Seems he was an ideal young father. No violence. Only problem is coming home late."

"Lots of fathers come home late." I slid the red pen through three lines, skipped five, and slid over two more.

"You like doing that, don't you?" Vernon nodded at the blue book in my lap. "You're way of killing someone—slash with a red pen."

I sighed. "Yeah, and this kid needs a little blood-letting." I made a huge question mark over the last page of gibberish and closed the book. "He attended class about twice, and had the audacity to take the final." I marked an F across the front of the booklet.

"Hope they all won't be like that." Vernon squeezed my knee.

"Me too."

We pulled into a fast food restaurant alongside a car full of boys in football jerseys. Their radio blasted as they argued about who would go inside to get what. We couldn't compete with the noise; we climbed out and headed inside for coffee and burgers.

"You gonna call to say we're in town?" Loman unwrapped the burger and bit into it twice before coming up for air.

"No," said Vernon. "They are expecting us. The woman knows she has to have the kids there."

"Are you expecting anything unusual?" I asked, tossing the half-eaten burger into its wrapper. "Cold meat."

"Let's head out," said Vernon, grabbing his coffee.

Loman looked at him like a wounded bird, his last bite of bun and meat still in his hand. "Gotta take a leak." He pushed the remnants into his mouth and headed toward the back of the room.

The teens were still booming over the parking lot. Horse play began inside and jerseys were flying. Vernon and I sat in the front seat, waiting for Loman, when one of the boys pushed his shoe against a window. A crack appeared and yelling got louder. Vernon honked the horn once. When the boys looked his way, he raised his badge and smiled. All noise stopped. Before Loman returned, the teens had started the car and headed for some other diners to disturb. "Future of America," said Vernon.

We drove past the line of fast food spots and car dealerships on the main highway until we came to the outskirts of the city. When we turned onto a residential road, we traveled back in time. The tidy wood frame homes with trimmed hedges and mowed lawns gave off an aura of peace. But these were the foolers. Beyond them, on other roads where the pavement needed resurfacing, we encountered the inevitable trailers, lined on cluttered streets where the moss hung over the structures and caused moisture to accumulate. The trailer tops had begun to rust.

"She lives at the end. A double-wide."

Inside, we could have been at a funeral parlor. Marie Beaufont's mother kept the room darkened, and with the olive green furniture and dark paneled walls, it gave off a depressing aura.

"Keeps it cooler in the summer," the elderly lady said, her back rigid and her nose in the air as though she dared anyone to criticize the queen's realm.

Doesn't do much for the winter, I thought.

With everyone seated in a recliner or on a sofa, Marie entered with the two kids. She had them sit in dining chairs at one end of the circle. She stood behind them.

"René, Jr. and Sally," she said. "Twelve and nine."

The moment was awkward, too stiff to get anything of value

from the kids. Vernon stood, pulled a straight chair to one side and sat near the staring children.

"You do have an idea why we're here?" he said.

They nodded. "You want to know about our daddy," said Sally. Her feet began to swing in the air.

"He was a real good daddy," said Marie. She touched her daughter's shoulder, and the girl's legs ceased moving.

Vernon glanced at me. I stood and asked Marie for a glass of water. She hesitated, shot a look at her mother, and headed into the tiny kitchen. I followed and leaned in the doorway.

"Tell about his habits," said Vernon.

Loman sat near the grandmother, occasionally looking up from his notepad to smile at her. She stared at his sleepy eyes and frowned her disapproval of the genetic pool that caused them.

"He worked a lot," said René, Jr. "But we went lots of places."

"Like?"

"Fishing. Sally didn't like that much, but I did."

"And what did Sally do with her dad?" Vernon smiled at the girl.

"Daddy, his name is Daddy, not Dad." She straightened her back.

"Daddy. What did you do for fun?"

"He plays games with me. We got a deck of cards. And he helps me make some beads. He's real good at that." She pulled at a glass-beaded necklace. "He brought me a bead box once."

Vernon reached toward the necklace, touching it softly. "Very nice," he said. "Do you have a lot of these?"

The girl nodded, her smile revealing pride.

"He helped me make my wrist brand," said the boy and held up a rawhide band, carved with vines.

"Talented man," he said. "Was your daddy away a lot?"

Both kids nodded.

"Can you tell me where he went when he came home late at

night?"

"He had to work a lot. Mama says he had to work late to bring home money for us." René pulled himself tall in his seat. In two years, he would be six inches taller and speak in a lower voice. The awkward signs of approaching teenage-hood showed in the wiggling of his arms and legs.

"Were you ever awake when he came home?"

The children were silent until René looked around for his mother. She hadn't returned to his back. "One time I heard him come in. He was kind of dirty and he had a white thing wrapped around his hand. He'd cut himself at his job. Mama was asleep, so I helped him put a bandage on it."

"And how did he treat you?"

The boy looked bewildered for a moment, then shrugged and looked at Vernon. "He said I was the best son any man could have." The kid's eyes watered.

"Both of you know what happened to your daddy, right?" Vernon's voice lowered.

"A bad person killed him. Probably somebody at his job," said Sally. She quickly bowed her head. Her brother looked away, biting his lip.

I watched the children during the session, sipping on the water their mother gave me. She stood against the wall with me, her hands trembling slightly. Brother and sister appeared sincere and had no bruises or tell-tale signs of abuse.

"Can you show me the bead box he gave you?" I asked just as both children looked as though reality had clobbered them with a block of cement.

Sally beamed and slid off the chair. She ran to a back room and returned with a ragged box that had seen too much use. Its hinges threatened to give way.

"See! It's got compartments for all these beads. They're glass." The girl held a few colored objects in her hand and lifted them toward me. "And I've got lots of needles with plastic line to string them together." She held the package of needles with the other hand. "They're different sizes to fit different size beads."

"Very clever," I said, taking some of the beads into my palm. "Is this the box that came with them?"

"Yeah. Daddy was going to change it to something prettier, but," she shifted her head in a coy fashion, "I found the gift before he had a chance."

"You found it?"

The girl nodded, but her mother stepped into the conversation. "Run put it away now. I've got to get back to Tallahassee before too late."

The boy joined his sister at the back of the trailer. His mother turned to me. "Somebody at the fair gave Rennie the box a few years back. He stuffed it under our bed, but Sally found it. Rennie told her it was hers, that he was saving it for her birthday." She sighed. "Now, I don't know if that's the truth, but Rennie never scolded the kids. He turned a potential disciplining into something nice. He was like that."

"Seems to have worked," I said. "She'll have good memories of him."

Vernon gave both children business cards and told them to call him if they wanted to tell him about anything else. This intrigued them. They had seen the cop shows, and now they had a cop card of their own.

With the children out of the room, Vernon turned his attention to the women. "You've told the other detectives that your husband treated you well and provided for the family." He directed his words to Marie.

Marie nodded and took one of the chairs vacated by her children.

"Huh!" came a grunt from the grandmother, who up to now, said nothing. "Provided by dragging them all over the country. Never a settled home." She shifted her body. Her grayness enveloped her and she seemed to disappear into the darkness of her room.

"But he did his best, Mother," said Marie, her voice weary.

"Could have worked right here. Had the job once. Quit. Can you imagine? Stable job. Company he worked for is still in business and would have taken him back in a second."

"And what did he do here?"

"Flooring," said the old lady. "Laid tile, linoleum, carpet, you name it. Was good at it. But he had to run off and follow them carnivals."

"He laid linoleum?" Vernon asked and Loman sat up straight.

"Laid that stuff right in there." The woman pointed past her daughter to the white floor in the kitchen.

As we rode back to Tallahassee, the sun set and the air darkened, like the dimness of the old lady's trailer was following us. Loman began to whistle lowly.

"You feel like singing?" said Vernon who smiled into the rearview mirror.

"Nope, just thinking." He leaned forward. "You got this good father who seems to like his family. Yet he chooses to be an itinerant worker of sorts. And he's good at laying linoleum."

"We knew that," said Vernon. "Tony got the low down on his odd jobs and carnival work."

"And the weapon that killed him was a linoleum knife," I said.

CHAPTER 9

When we reached the fairgrounds and the Sheriff's booth, Pasquin had the money apron tied onto his front and was taking the last of the orders from an eager group of women.

"Ladies' night out!" He grinned when he saw me.

"Who roped you into this?" An octogenarian behind the busy counter didn't seem to bother anyone but me.

"Mama said the deputies ran short of men. Got a ride into town and here I am." He held onto the bottoms of flimsy paper plates, balancing burgers with grilled onions slipping over the edges of the buns. "They ain't the gator-eating crowd," he said and smiled as he took dollars and gave change.

"Where's Harlie?" I asked. The surly man's apron rested over the back banister. Mama stood over his burger grill.

"Got called away. That stupid Snake Boy lost part of his act." She ripped open a bag of buns and flipped them onto the edge of the grill to warm. "Better not find that long thing in my booth."

"A snake got out?" I shuddered. Snake Boy didn't deal with poisonous reptiles, but he did have long constrictors. I thought about Plato running about the swamps. Would he know how to dodge a python?

"Edwin nearly went crazy," said Pasquin. "He's got his boat ready to search the sloughs and ponds." Pasquin chuckled as he tossed some napkins onto the counter. "Can't imagine what that boy would do if he came face to face with Sylvester."

"Sylvester? That's the extra long thing at the end of the act, the one that drapes over the man and all the other snakes."

"Big thing," said Pasquin. "They closed the act."

"Couldn't have gotten far," said Vernon. "I'd make a bet it's going to turn up in somebody's tent or trailer."

"Or maybe the prize chicken hut," I said. "When it eats a few of some kid's blue ribbon roosters, it'll crawl somewhere warm to digest it all."

"Gonna scare somebody out of his skin," Pasquin laughed out loud.

I stepped inside the booth to help put burgers together. Each time I pulled out another supply of buns or napkins, I did a quick eye search for a snake looking for a warm spot. Instead of a snake, I spied Chawbutt Nixon in line again.

"You catch me on Old High Bottom last night?" He grinned, this time not hiding the edge of his tobacco plug.

I shook my head and moved quickly to help pile burgers onto plates.

"Won the pocket book," he beamed. "You ever go out to dinner?"

I shot a glance in Pasquin's direction. He chuckled but took the hero stance.

"She ain't been dismissed from this job, son. You run along now and let the lady work." He nodded toward the bull arena.

"Just a burger first," he said, grinning as though no scold from an old man could spoil his glory. "Served by the lady, of course."

Vernon and Loman headed back to the sheriff's office to do their report on the visit to Live Oak. It was up to me to drive Mama and Pasquin home, then find my own peace in my swamp house for a few hours. Tomorrow was another exam. I planned to take the rest of the blue books with me and grade while the new group took their tests.

By the time we packed up the food in the trailer and loaded the Honda with Pasquin and Mama, who ran an on-going fuss about whether or not a python would eat raw gator meat, it was nearly midnight.

The roads, two paved ones and a sandy lane, were nearly deserted as I headed away from the dimming carnival lights to the stretches of dense forest. Even in a drought and the extra cold winter, the foliage threatened to engulf all evidence of life.

Pasquin snored in the back seat, Mama in the front. Like children, they awoke groggily when I pulled up to the side of Mama's Table, her riverside cafe in Fogarty Spring. She lived in a small house a few yards away, but she stored the food inside the cafe kitchen.

We worked without comment until Mama locked the cafe door and strolled toward her house. There was a narrow lane between palmetto bushes. The only evidence of a house was a yellow porch light that glowed within a grove of oaks.

"You want me to walk with you?" said Pasquin.

"No, old man. You'd just get in the way if I had to throttle a beast." Mama ran her hand over the expanse of her hips and headed home. She carried a baseball bat. "For the big snake," she said and waved back at us.

"We're going to run a photograph of the reconstructed face in the newspapers," said Tony. "Maybe somebody will recognize her."

We stood in Marshall Long's office, crowded amongst boxes of slides and folders. Marshall had summoned us with evidence taken from the bodies of the two women from Pensacola and Madison.

"Both victims were in shallow water, but we got semen from one and a pubic hair from another. The two samples are from the same person. Now you fellows find the person."

A photographer joined us and we moved to the room where the clay head of the girl I had found two years before sat staring from the artist's table. Sara had placed a poster board behind her for the photograph. We watched the man take five shots.

"Okay," he said. "I'll get these developed and put your notice in the paper." He saluted Tony and left.

"Your fingers healed yet?" Tony asked. I did a double take. He usually wasn't much interested in my health.

"All back together." I held up the fingers where only faint red scars told of an underwater cut.

"You got cut on a beer bottle shard, it seems. Broke when some-body tossed it in the hole. Can't find any relation to the deceased." He nodded at Marshall who nodded in return.

"That hole is full of beer bottles and other trash."

"Wish I could toss in a few of exams," I said. I had suffered through another morning exam, when a message on my cell phone had ordered me to the crime lab on the double. Tony was pushing for an all-out investigation, because he suspected someone con-nected to the traveling fair shows.

"Cannon's records are sloppy. He knows he paid Beaufont a few times for work as a handler, but he doesn't have specific days and hours, only dates." Tony's jaw clenched. He shot me a dirty look, his way of saying he didn't like waiting for me to talk about my real job.

"What's a handler, exactly?" I asked.

Tony shrugged. "Does about anything the boss says, I imagine. We do know he was in Pensacola and Madison around the time those two killings happened."

"You think maybe he knew who did them and got silenced?" Loman asked, messaging his thumb against his fingers in a money hungry fashion.

"Could be." Tony leaned over his desk in an animal ready-to-attack fashion. "And I'll do a DNA test on everyone of those drifters if I have to."

Marshall groaned. "Fair ends Saturday. You better get started."

I headed home to my cocoon in the swamp where I metamorphosed into something a little nicer, just like the caterpillar. Vernon wouldn't join me tonight. He had people to watch, and I needed to mark the booklets and turn in final grades. The next morning, with no final on the agenda, I planned to make one last gator meat trip with Pasquin.

Tall pines swayed above the spreading oaks, and they in turn towered above the thorny brown scrub and sticky palmetto as I turned onto the rutted dirt road that led to my family home. I had renovated it from a termite banquet to a livable white house, complete with central heat and a dishwasher. The screen porch still stood as a monument to Old South, and I sometimes longed for the days I spent rocking there, chatting with Pasquin or just listening to frogs and katydids sing. Humidity was just part of the scene then; now it turned into pure misery on the hottest days.

But today wasn't hot. A cold front swept down from Canada. Citrus growers farther south started the smudge pots. Locals covered up sensitive plants and let the pipes drip to prevent freezing. And Plato greeted me on the front porch.

"Too cold, huh?" I scratched his ears. He moaned in ecstasy and shook himself violently. "You planning on sleeping inside tonight?"

As though he understood, he pawed the front door. Inside, he planted himself in front of the fireplace.

"Okay, I know what you want. It's not a bad idea." I tossed the booklets onto the floor beside the sofa and headed for the log pile. Plato rose and sniffed at the blue books.

"Don't you pee on those books," I said. "Well, one or two would be okay, but not right now."

Plato lost interest and trotted off to his water dish in the kitchen. I built the fire and rested my back against the sofa for a moment. When I was small, my grandfather stood here, his backside to the fire. When that got good and hot, he'd turn around and warm the front. Women forsook all decency when they needed to do the same. Most would back up to the fire and hike their skirts. No one could see anything but the embers, but everyone knew and said nothing. Funny how they never turned around and pulled up the front of their skirts.

I hit the sofa, jerked out the red pen, and concentrated. If I let nothing interfere, I knew I could finish the grading in a couple of hours.

Plato whined for food about the time my neck cramped. He had to go out, but was scratching to come back in within twenty minutes.

"Must be damn cold out there," I said, and stepped outside the kitchen door. Icy dry air surrounded my skin. "If some snake is loose, he's hibernating. Pythons aren't used to this." I imagined Sylvester huddling behind someone's stove, scaring their hair white when they bent over the oven. "Don't you get eaten by some big snake, you hear?" Plato wagged his entire body. He submitted to my hugs and cuddling. Most of the time, he just wanted a good scratching and a few kind words. "Want to go with us on the boat tomorrow?" I asked.

The next morning a frost hit the area like a northern snow storm. Everything went white. Plato did his business and demanded to come inside. He decided to stay where it was warm and didn't ride to the end of the road with me to get the paper.

I sat at the table, drinking coffee and reading, and cuddling a cold dog in my lap. "You should see this, Plato. Looks just like a real face." I stared at the photograph of the clay model. There was nothing in the article nor in the caption to say it wasn't a picture of the actual face. It also said nothing about a dead girl. Just asked if anyone recognized her.

Pasquin yelled from the landing. He hated early mornings, and I didn't want to make him any grouchier than he already was. Plato followed me to the boat.

"Colder than an iron sow's teat," said Pasquin, his army coat engulfing him.

"Isn't that balls on a brass monkey?"

"Take your pick. Too cold to run down a river." He revved the engine. "Old Plato got the urge to be with people today, I see."

We moved down the river in silence, our collars turned up around our ears. Plato sat on the bow and let the air blow his ears around for a few minutes, then huddled next to me. I liked the warmth of his body.

We met no one on the river. The white frost eventually wore off in the morning sun, but the frigid air still surrounded us. My legs began to ache, reminding me that I was no young chick. In the back of my mind, I thought about diving and wondered how much longer I could last. Harry MacAllister, my sometime diving partner and former lover, rarely went down these days. Besides the pain of his bum leg, he had developed a fear of cave walls crumbling down on top of him.

"Too quiet," said Pasquin as he neared the bend to Rinks' landing.

"How would you know?" I asked. "It's always quiet here." I sat up straight. Plato was already up and sniffing the air. He began to whimper softly.

"Something smells," said Pasquin. He edged the boat slowly around the heavy oaks until we could see the landing. Something floated just below the surface.

"It's the motor boat," I said. "It's partially sunk."

Plato howled once and moved back and forth in the boat. Pasquin put his hand on the dog. "He smells it, too."

We moved closer, and the stink hit me in the sinuses. "Got to be dead meat around here." I tried to see the gator pen. "Move a little closer," I said.

"Not going near the landing," said Pasquin. He took an oar and paddled us within a few yards of the sunken boat.

The enclosed gator pen looked no different, except the gators weren't moving. Not even a squirm.

"Too cold?" I said.

"Maybe, maybe not." Pasquin reached below his seat and pulled out a shotgun. "Just don't like the looks of this."

"The door to the barn is open," I said. It stood ajar, something Rinks never allowed because of the cold storage inside.

"You bring your pistol today?" asked Pasquin.

"Yeah. But it was for a big snake."

We sat still for a while, feeling nauseous from the putrid smell of death that wafted from shore. Plato continued to shake and pace.

"No one is here. I'm going to look around." I picked up the other oar and rowed to a spot where I could jump ashore.

"You be careful, ma'am." Pasquin pulled the shotgun into shooting position. "Take the dog with you."

Plato wouldn't go. He stood on my seat and yelped a few times, and kept an eye on my movements.

I drew the pistol and headed for the gator pen. No starving reptile stood on all fours and growled. None could. Each gator had a nasty hole in his head, like someone had systematically blew them away, execution style. The smell from the pen gagged me.

I moved to the barn and looked inside, my hands around the pistol. The place was empty. Inside the industrial refrigerator, no meat package marked *Mama's Table* lay ready. When I stood quiet for a moment, silence prevailed.

"No one around, but someone killed all of Rinks' sales for several years."

"Wonder where Rinks is?" Pasquin didn't let go of the gun.

"Let's get the sheriff out here." I squeezed Plato who wagged a reluctant tail. He sniffed my coat, then decided I was okay and lay his nose in my lap.

CHAPTER 10

"A missing gator farmer?" Tony mocked my words over the phone. "First a giant snake gets out, now a man who sells gator meat is gone. Who's next?"

"The gators are dead," I said.

"So maybe he shot the product and headed out of town. Could be up to his snout in debt and decided to slither away."

"You're not funny, Tony. Better find Rinks. You, after all, are selling his meat."

"Guess we'll have to take the sign down," he said.

"I'm on my way to Mama's Table now. She's not going to be happy about this."

"This is going to be a matter for Fish and Game right now. If there's more to it, they can call us."

Tony hung up, leaving me holding the receiver to my ear. "Jerk!" I folded the cell phone and tucked it into my coat pocket.

"Let's get some brunch," I said and held on while Pasquin moved the boat uncharacteristically fast across the cold river.

"You mean I don't have to wrestle with that nasty man today?" Mama poured steaming coffee into heavy mugs. We buttered hot biscuits and thawed out.

"Not unless you want to help him with the burgers." I warmed inside and finally slipped off my coat. "This weather better not hold all winter."

"Won't." Pasquin loaded his biscuit with fig preserves. "We'll be hot again next week. Be crying for a cool breeze."

"You see the paper today?" Mama placed the front section in front of us. "Looking for that girl you found in the cave."

I nodded. Mama and the public weren't supposed to know the girl was a mere skeleton, but the swamp vine worked too well. Even Edwin would know it was a clay reconstruction.

We nibbled on biscuits until Mama's assistant cook brought out a plate of sausage, hot and spicy and made right on a local farm. I stabbed one with my fork.

"Eat like a lady, Luanne," Pasquin said without looking up at me. "Use your knife."

I smiled and put the sausage on the plate. Pasquin had been a surrogate father and friend for most of my adult life. He chided me on occasion about not marrying and having a boat-load full of swamp babies, but mostly he accepted me as is.

"I hear tell that widow's got a job at the Interstate truck stop," said Mama. She sat a plate of beignets in front of us. Pasquin perked up and gave her a complimentary grunt. He reached for one of the sugary treats and ate it slowly, along with loud sips of strong coffee.

"You mean Marie Beaufont?" I asked. "How would you know that?"

Mama laughed, shaking her blond curls, tight from a new permanent. "The owner is an acquaintance of mine."

"Any word on what kind of worker she is?"

"Shaky, so I'm told. Especially when the place crowds up, but then the woman's husband was murdered. Who wouldn't be shaky?"

Pasquin licked his fingers of sugar. "Maybe she thinks the killer is coming after her."

"Now, who's got bad manners," I said and passed a paper

napkin across the table. "Sheriff has checked out Beaufont's deal-
ings in his jobs. Doesn't seem to have any enemies."

"Just got robbed, if you ask me," said Mama. She rested one
hand on the back of a chair. "Meanness is all over, and some people
will slice your throat for three dollars."

I thought about this for a moment. The cops had found Rennie
Beaufont's wallet in his pocket, at the edge of a sinkhole. No money
was found, but it didn't seem disturbed.

"If anyone took money from his wallet, they replaced it carefully," I said. "Wouldn't a random robber just grab the wallet and
run with it?"

"Seems like it," said Pasquin, "and he wouldn't stay around to
roll him into a dry lake."

The scenario bothered me for a few moments, until Vernon
called and asked me to drop by the sheriff's department. They were
getting calls about the girl in the paper.

"You're just in time," said Vernon as he hurried me into a conference room. "This old man just walked in with a photograph. Spitting image of that clay head."

Vernon and I sat across from a man who hadn't shaved in a
couple of days. He identified himself as George Newberry.

"Been on the road for nearly five years now," he said. "Weren't
no life for a young girl." He shoved the photo into the middle of
the table. The tattered edges and broken lines attested to a life inside a pocket that often slept on the ground.

"That's Gaylin," he pointed to the girl in the photo. Her smile,
ethereal, almost Mona Lisa, and the wide eyes, made her seem older,
beyond the estimated early twenties. "She joined me when she turned
eighteen. Got waitress jobs sometimes, while I got construction or

farm work. Mostly we just moved around the country, sleeping in shelters." He stopped and breathed deeply. The man's gaunt appearance and sunken eyes told of heavy smoking about to foster emphysema. "I been in a hospital down in Gainesville. That's where I saw the newspaper."

"How did you get to Tallahassee?"

"Hospital worker gave me enough for a bus ticket. I showed him the picture. Said I needed to get here."

Vernon picked up the photo and passed it to me. The hair, naturally curly, was a lighter brown than the one the artist used on the clay head.

"Tell us about her."

"We been traveling around, maybe two years, working, like I said, at odd jobs. Got rough sometimes. Other men on the road like to get sweet on a pretty young girl. But I always protected her. Didn't nothing ever happen to Gaylin on the road." He breathed deeply and coughed.

"Would you like some water?" I asked.

The man nodded, and I went into the hall cooler. After drinking down the entire cup, he continued.

"She got tired of not having a permanent place to sleep. Said she was going into Tallahassee to get a job and a place to stay. We were sleeping in a park close to Wakulla, back in the woods."

"Can you tell me exactly where?" Vernon leaned forward, forcing the man to look at him.

"Probably could show you, but don't know exactly. Stayed too many places in the meantime. They get to looking all the same."

"Go on."

"Gaylin went off like this every once in a while. She never stayed away. Came back in a couple of days and we took to the road again. She had these things, see. Stuff she brought from home that was valuable to her. She always left them with me. That told me she was coming back." Newberry hesitated, looking into the table. He raised his eyes, haunted and sickly, he said, "But this time, she took her stuff. Even her bead box. I knew then she wasn't going down the road with me again."

"Bead box?" I nearly rose off the chair.

He nodded. "Raggedy thing she got when she was little. Built it up over the years with lots of colored beads and string and needles." He smiled. "Made bracelets and stuff. Gave them to other people on the road, especially if we came across any children."

"Do you have any idea where she stayed when she left you?" Vernon placed a hand on my arm.

"No. Just knew she wasn't coming back. I took off in three or four days. Went down south. Been between the Keys and Orlando near 'bout three years now, 'til I got this stuff." He tapped his chest with a fist. "I'm a vet, you know. Had to find a vet's hospital."

Vernon called someone and arranged for George Newberry to stay in a motel. As soon as the man left the room, we nodded to each other.

"Tony's going to have to tell him the truth. The poor man will have to identify the clay head."

"And give a blood sample?" I asked. "Can't they match the tooth DNA with his?"

"Most likely," Vernon nodded.

"There's something else," I said. "He's going to have to identify the bead box."

We sat is silence, until Vernon rose and said he had to report the interview.

"Vernon," I said, "if Beaufont had Gaylin's bead box, even gave it to his own daughter," I stopped. "Marie said her daughter found it under the bead, that her father really hadn't meant it for a gift."

"And you're saying?"

"I'm saying that maybe Marshall ought to try matching Rennie Beaufont's DNA with the semen and hair found on the other two victims."

CHAPTER 11

"This will take some time," said Marshall. He sat on a rolling stool that was invisible underneath his spreading hips. Vernon, Tony, and I surrounded him in his crime lab office.

"Just do it," said Tony. His agitation revealed part excitement about a break in the case, part irritation that this was my idea. "I need to get Newberry in here now to identify the clay head. You got it presentable?"

Marshall nodded. "Put a drape around the neck, got the backdrop up. Man could still faint. I've seen it happen. People think it's the real head and just drop right down. You better stand behind him." Marshall leaned over, supported himself on the edge of the metal desk and stood. His knees cracked.

"You planning on getting those fixed one day?" I said and pretended to lean over and stare at his legs.

"Just need oiling," he said and led us to the room where sat the clay image of someone who had been nothing but white bones in an evidence drawer for years.

Vernon nodded to Tony and went to retrieve Newberry.

Marshall, Tony and I waited. We stood around the clay head like sentries guarding a corpse. The room, with its pots of clay and artists' instruments packed into the background, sat silent and waiting.

Vernon led Mr. Newberry inside the door. "It's in here, sir. Just a clay reproduction." He motioned us to step aside.

Newberry stood for a long moment, staring at the head. His eyes, watery and frozen, told us the end of the story. "That's Gaylin," he whispered. "What happened to her?"

"What happened, indeed," I said as we huddled inside Marshall's office.

After Marshall took a blood sample from Newberry, a uniformed officer drove Gaylin's father back to the motel. The man was offered a counselor through his veteran's benefits, but he said he needed to be alone. As he left, he mumbled something about protecting his daughter.

"It seems," said Tony as he glanced at me, "that Beaufont could have robbed the girl of the bead box, or found it somewhere, or," he hesitated, "killed her for it."

"Or," I added, "killed her and took it as a trophy."

"I didn't want to hear that," he said. "If that's the case, we've got a serial killer roaming around."

"Not got," I said. "Had—Beaufont is dead."

Tony twitched in his chair. "You got word on that cave entrance, yet?"

The thought of contacting the NSS cave diver unit had crossed my mind several times since Vernon and I last dived, but I had not done it yet. Tony would dwell on this, not on the bead box revelation.

"I'm off now." I rose before he could say anything.

The National Speleological Society is mostly dry cavers, but its cave diving unit is a brave one and has done much of the mapping in our springs. I drove to their offices at the edge of the university and sought out the clerk who no longer went down in any kind of cave.

The man could have passed for a gnome in a British garden. His short, stuffed-sausage-link body was topped by a head full of red hair and a thin red beard that reached nearly to his navel. He had a sweet, kindly smile, and I wondered why he wasn't telling stories to children in their section of the bookstore instead of dealing with people who liked dark places.

"Here's a map of that cave area," he said. "I'll get someone to talk to you." He disappeared behind a door and returned with a thin man whose pale face told of too many days inside the earth.

"You were here, right?" He pointed a finger at the place where we entered and the ledge where we found Gaylin's bones. "If you travel on through the big section of this cave, you'll finally see a dim light over here." He traced a thin finger through the water to the opposite shore of Palmetto Springs. "The bottom rises gradually, almost unnoticeably, until you start to feel warmer waters. If you follow the light up, you'll feel the currents running against you. You'll end up in a mass of lily pads and grass. Right here." He poked a finger tip to the shore, a place at the end of a small peninsula of land.

"So someone could walk out on the land, toss in an object, and let it take the current to the big cave?"

"That would happen," he nodded, "if the object were heavy enough to drop down into the current. A light object might stay close to shore."

"A human body?"

His eyes darted toward mine. "Yeah," he said, "that would drop into the currents."

I drove back to the sheriff's department. Everyone had gathered there, leaving Marshall to his DNA tests.

"Just to be sure," said Tony, "I want you to go down again."

Vernon stood close to me, knowing he'd be along for the swim.

"This cave is more a cavern, Tony," I said as I pointed to the massive circle on the NSS map. "It's too deep. There may be a part of Gaylin Newberry in there, but it would be so far down, we'd be risking our lives to find it."

Tony paced, his hands behind him. His olive skin, usually pale against the black hair, tinted red. He hated to be told no.

"This man—killer—dumped the women at the edge of watery places, places frequented by gators. Seems like he might be trying to dispose of the evidence two ways, water and food for reptiles." He turned round to face me. "You don't have to go down to the bottom, just search along the edge, where he dumped her. Can't you do some kind of current thing, find out where the body could have drifted when it went off the shallow shelf at the edge?"

I shrugged. "Searching that area is easy enough."

"And I need that bead box," he said. "You and Vernon can drive to Live Oak again."

"I'm not a deputy. I've got papers to grade, things to finish up for the end of the semester." I stood before Tony, feeling open and vulnerable.

"Find time. You'll get paid." He waved me off and turned to give directions to other detectives.

"Good thing this isn't a stress dive," I said as I slipped the tank straps over my shoulders.

Vernon and I sat on the sandy soil near one end of the peninsula where we thought Gaylin was dumped. The shallows were covered in lily pads, eel grass, and the dreaded hydrilla grass. I hated this. It wasn't dangerous like deep cave diving, but at least the water in the caves grew no grass. I had once seen a long moccasin swim a few yards from me. At first he looked like a hyacinth stem or a vine, but when he poked his head above the surface, I backed off. In a search like this, I found myself with one eye on possible evidence, the other on reptilian alert.

"You start at that end; I'll start over there," said Vernon. "We'll meet in the middle."

"I'm screaming bloody hell if I see a snake."

"Who'll hear you?" Vernon grinned then covered his face with a mask.

I swam to the outer rim of the shelf. It barely reached four feet below water in its deepest places. Below it, the abyss. I began an eye and hand search, wearing gloves this time. My fingers wouldn't get sliced again. Feeling first the edge of the shelf, then moving above it and back again, I looked for anything that might have been bone or an object carried by a human. To anyone on shore, I must have resembled a catfish, pushing forward, spitting out useless debris, backing up, doing it all over again in another spot.

"There's nothing here," said Vernon. "Been too long, and there may have been nothing left of her the moment she went into the depths."

"Besides, the guy doing the hydrilla removal has been through here plenty of times in the past two years." I pulled onto the bank.

We changed at the bath house, made our report to Tony, and headed for my swamp house. We had little time before I needed to be at the fairgrounds. Vernon would have to question Cannon again, trying to trace Beaufont's movements.

Pasquin and Plato sat on the front steps. The weather had warmed, and he fanned himself three times and Plato three times. The dog threatened to bite the hat brim each time it swung his way.

"Fish and Game called the sheriff," he said. "They done had a big robbery out to Rinks'. Seems a bunch of people ransacked the place, took all the money and a few machines, and killed the gators."

"And Rinks?" I asked.

"Can't find him; sheriff thinks he may be dead."

"Why are you here?" I scratched Plato's ears; he whined in animal joy.

"Sheriff said you and me got to make a statement. They'll take it at the fairgrounds. I'm riding in with you."

I looked at Vernon. We both shrugged. Another quick moment of passion stolen from our best intentions.

The blue books sat on my dining table, a depressing reminder of where I really made my bread and butter. "Later," I whispered and waved them good-bye. I went to the kitchen and put on a kettle for tea.

"How come you know this weather so well?" asked Vernon.

"Been in my bones near 'bout forever," said Pasquin. "Turns warm just about as quick as it turns cold."

"How is Edwin doing with Sylvester?" I asked. The long python shook my thoughts ever so often, making the hair stand up on my arms.

"He and that Snake Boy been searching all sorts of places, mostly around the grounds. They don't think it's going to hurt anybody yet. Too cold outside and it had been fed before it left." Pasquin chuckled. "Edwin wants more than anything to find that monster."

"I'm with Edwin," I said.

My plan for a romantic hour or two had been bashed, and I just couldn't force myself to grade blue books. I sat at the dining table, drinking hot tea, and wondering how I would survive to retirement when I dreaded the work as I did. In the beginning, I had all the excitement of motivating my students to go about the neighborhoods in north Florida, taking down social dialects in phonetic script—a real Henry Higgins. When the novelty wore off, I delighted in sharing linguistic knowledge with students who "didn't know that" and sat bright-eyed in awe of my travels in France, the Andes, Los Angeles, wherever I could find peculiarities of language. Now, even that pleasure had worn down, and I longed to be away from it. Would I turn out like the chair, Manny Greenberg, aimless, forgetful? I watched Vernon stow the diving gear on the front porch. *Not as long as I can swim!*

"You just lost in thought, ma'am," said Pasquin. He stood over me with the tea pot. "More brew?"

"Who taught you to make this stuff?" I said. The aroma of cinnamon filled the air.

"Been knowing since I was a little boy," said Pasquin. "Put in a stick or two, add a clove, sugar, little cardamon, lots of milk." He sipped loudly from his steaming cup. "Cure what ails you."

"Reminds me of chai, Indian tea." I loved the aroma as I felt the steam hit my face.

"Got a little Pasquin in there with the Indian," he said.

Vernon joined us and winced when he took a sip. "You got any plain coffee?"

"Not your cup of tea?" Pasquin laughed at his own joke.

The phone rang. Tony asked to speak to Vernon, whose forehead wrinkled all the way to the bald pate, then opened up in awe.

"You got to be kidding," he said.

When he replaced the receiver, he took a deep gulp of the sweet tea, and smiled.

"Okay, you've kept me in suspense. What's going on?"

"What do I get if I tell?" He teased me by whispering in my ear.

"A sock in your chops if you don't tell," I said and poked his rib.

"Now, now," said Pasquin, "not in front of the old man. Might give him ideas."

"You poked Mama lately?" Vernon grinned in the old man's direction.

Pasquin chuckled. "She's likely to punch me clear cross the river."

"Vernon!"

"Okay, okay. Tony said Marshall called. The DNA tests aren't complete but it's looking more and more like the semen and hair are a match for Rennie Beaufont. Tony preferred to tell me." He winked. We both knew Tony's problem, that he valued my input but wouldn't give me the time of day if he could.

"If Beaufont's DNA matched the samples, then he raped, and likely killed, those two girls. Since he had the bead box, he likely killed Gaylin, too." The warmth of the tea turned to cold.

The three of us sat in silence for a moment.

"So who killed the killer?" I asked.

CHAPTER 12

"We've got a search warrant for the man's trailer." Tony nearly danced in his anger. "Why the hell didn't we do this sooner?"

"No cause," said Loman, his sleepy eyes focused on a blank note pad page. "Who would have suspected the dead man to be a killer?"

"We could have searched in order to find his killer," Tony chastised himself until he saw me leaning against his office door. He straightened up, tightened his face, and make a pronouncement.

"Get the warrant, Loman. Luanne, you're coming along. The Beaufont woman seems to trust you. Just don't get in the way."

"Like I got in the way when I said you should compare the semen and hair against Rennie Beaufont's DNA?"

He turned sharply toward me, his eyes blazing, like he wanted to spew out a barrage of antifeminist slurs. Vernon had stepped behind me. Tony glanced his way and went back to his desk to answer a call.

"Man's a walking bomb," I said. "I'm the catalyst." I burst into a smile. Vernon squeezed my waist. "He likes me; he really likes me!" I aimed that remark toward Tony, who shot me a sneer as he spoke to the sheriff about the warrant.

Marie Beaufont wept openly at her dining table. She could not fathom her husband, the good father, being a killer. When Tony tried to give her the search warrant, she waved it aside and buried her face in a dish towel. I placed a hand on her shoulder, but she brushed it away. Anger wracked her bones as much as the shock of the whole affair.

"I planned on burying him the first of next week," she said amid gulps of anguish. "How do I tell his children?" Her voice raised a couple of pitches.

No one had answers for her. Killing had been a private thing with her husband, it seemed.

"We'll start in the bedrooms," said Tony, and waved Vernon and Loman toward the rear of the trailer. "Luanne, you stay here with Mrs. Beaufont." He mouthed, "Watch her."

"I can't be called that anymore," said Marie. "I'll have to go back to Kelly, my maiden name. Change my kids' last name." She stared at nothing. "Oh, God! He can't have been a killer, a murderer of women?" She looked up at me.

"I don't have the answers, but it will work out okay. You have good kids."

"The papers…"

"They don't know anything yet. We aren't sure about your husband." I knew nothing could calm her; it wouldn't calm me if I had been in her shoes. For a moment I felt a cold wind on my heart when I imagined someone telling me Vernon might be a killer. "Can I make you some tea?"

"Just a glass of water," Marie said and grabbed the dish towel again, pressing it into her face.

The men put me here to comfort her, but I felt awkward, useless at trying to help someone who had just told her children their father was brutally murdered and dumped into a dry lake bed and now has to tell them he has been raping and killing women.

I managed to take her the water and let her drink it in silence.

The tiny kitchen was neat as a pin, embarrassing me for having a much larger cluttered one. Not a speck of breakfast grease or a cereal box, not a piece of cutlery left in the drain board. There was no automatic dishwasher, but Marie seemed not to need one. I scraped my fingers across the counter top and smelled them. *Bleach.* I slipped a finger under a drawer and pulled it open. Inside, the family silver, a cheap set, sat neatly arranged, each in its on bin. Behind the plastic organizer a row of steak knives lay blade to blade. I opened the next drawer. Heavier knives sat here, a big butcher and small paring, and a pair of poultry scissors. The bottom of the drawer had recently been papered with kitchen utensil theme paper. Its newness gave off a plastic smell.

"Are you looking for something?" Marie said. She stood at the sink, refilling her glass.

"No, of course not. I'm not much help to you, am I?"

She glanced at the drawer, and for a moment, I thought I saw defiance, a look of *get out of my stuff.* I didn't blame her.

She glared at me, then softened. "Not too many people have been all these years."

"You'll miss having a husband around to do things." I winced when I said this. It was bait, not how I really felt. I wanted her to talk about the man.

"He never did things around here. I cleaned, cooked, painted, even did the lawn when we had one. Of course, we kept moving the trailer. I gave up gardening and did potted plants."

"Where do you put them?" I asked, looking around the room.

She sighed. "Don't have any right now." She glanced toward the window that looked over what should have been a front yard. "They all died."

Marie bit her lip. Her eyes flared an anger only she knew. Both of us jumped when the searchers came from the bedrooms to continue in the living room.

"Ma'am," said Tony, "have you cleaned this place recently?"

Marie nodded. "I clean for therapy. It makes me feel like I have some kind of control over things, my mother tells me. I even clean her house when I go to visit."

"You used a heavy cleaning product?"

"Bleach, mostly, but a piney thing on the floors. Why?"

"Just wanted to know what that smell was." Tony moved about the room, systematically rifling through drawers and boxes.

"We're ready for the kitchen," said Vernon and waited for us to move into a bedroom.

"This is Sally's space," said Marie as she remade the lower bunk bed. "Don't cops put things back?"

I didn't answer. "The kids never complained about the tiny quarters?"

"Of course they did. So did I, but he wouldn't listen. Said we had a good living, didn't get wet when it rained, ate well. So what if Rene, Jr.'s space was up there and Sally's down here. 'Some kids ain't got no space at all' he'd say." She sat down on the remade bunk. "In about a year we were going to have to find a better arrangement. Rene would be going into puberty, and he just couldn't sleep in here with Sally."

"What will you do now?"

She looked at me, her face hardened. "Stay here until I can save some money. The kids will do better with Mother for now." She took another breath as though she needed to say something.

"Rennie," she gulped at her own surprise at having uttered the name, "signed on with Mr. Cannon to work with his carnival shows. He must have put in some hours." Her eyes pleaded with me. "Could you ask him? I mean if there is a check, however small, I could use it." She closed her eyes and sat down again. The tears flowed silently this time, and she rested her head in the towel.

"I'll find out all I can," I said.

We left Marie Beaufont in the misery of her tiny travel trailer.

"Ironic how she can't clean up her life the way she can clean up that little rattle trap." Vernon held onto a bag. "Not much here. We found another bead bracelet under the mattress of the little girl's bunk."

"Are you going to talk to Cannon again?" I asked Tony as he headed for his car. "There's more there than he has told us."

"You know that for a fact?" said Tony, his voice sending out the don't get too smart tone.

"No, and neither do you," I said. "If you won't talk to him, I will."

"Now just a minute, *Ma'am*," he mocked Pasquin. "You can question only with a detective there, and you'd better let the detective take the lead."

"See you at the fair," I smiled, knowing he'd be right behind me.

"All his co-workers are suspects," said Vernon as we drove to the fairgrounds. "As far as we can tell, the girls were strangers to him. Runaways, loners who left their families. And the families have checked out. Not likely they had any idea Beaufont had killed their daughters—not that they cared that much."

"Are there any more bodies out there?" I rested my head on the window and watched the capitol building grass and other neatly trimmed government lawns turn to low-lying structures that housed mechanics' shops and beer joints. When we crossed the hill, the span of the fairgrounds lay before us. It wasn't dark yet, but already cars stacked up in the lot and along the shoulder of the roads. Handlers scurried about, preparing the bulls for the riding competition, repairing tents, and, I suppose, searching for Sylvester. The preacher had taken up his spot near the gates and shouted into the street at teens and elders alike.

"A killer like that—likely there are more bodies. Maybe not around here, but we'll look in other places he has worked."

I shuddered. To live beside someone, feed him, care for his physical needs, have his children—and all the while his greater need had to be cared for by strangers, girls who gave it all to Rennie Beaufont's passion for a strange kind of pleasure.

"Marshall Long is contacting his counterparts in a few other cities and states." Vernon talked on about how the FBI and other police forces had been notified, how someone like Beaufont would eventually fit one of the profiles behavioral scientists had researched since Ted Bundy crossed the country, tricking women into cars and clubbing them in their sleep.

"Lots of these men have girlfriends and wives who don't have a clue what they're up to," I said. "A man like Beaufont works in the company of other men—drifters and freaks—people who wouldn't necessarily be around his wife. I'll bet there's something here." I let my voice drift off as I glimpsed Chawbutt Nixon, garbed in a plaid shirt, cowboy hat and spurred boots, check out a bull pen. He turned and spat sticky brown tobacco on the ground. When we drove past, he stared into the car, his eyes like those of a dumb animal that couldn't comprehend the world beyond the corral.

"There's Cannon," said Vernon as we parked behind a trailer. "Hanging around the bull ring. I thought he was the carnival man, side shows and all that." He nodded to the man as we got out of the car.

"Sir," said Cannon, offering a nicotine-stained hand to Vernon. "You like bull riding?"

Tony pulled up behind us, got out of the car, and stared at the heavy fencing that would herd a frightened brahma bull into a holding pen where cowboys would goad him into a frenzy. One would finally get on his back and dig his heels into his sides. When a rodeo clown opened the gate, the bull would dash into the arena, doing his best to shake off the intruder who dug into his sides and twisted his balls in a rope vice.

"At least the beast comes out alive," I whispered.

"You got business in this sport, too?" asked Tony.

"Nah," said Cannon. "Just curious about how they do it."

In the distance, Jubile moved his bulk around the side of a trailer. Julene joined him, holding his hand and guiding him to the outside table for their evening meal.

"Now that's what I'd like to see riding a bull," laughed Cannon as he nodded toward Jubile. "Like to see a two-ton beast shake him off."

"Can't see how he'd ever get on," said Tony. "You got a minute, Cannon?"

Cannon stared a second too long at Tony. "Something on your mind, sir?" He never moved from his stance against the bull fence.

"Something like that."

Cannon moved back, smiled and shrugged. "Come to the tent. It's not too cold to sit outside."

I followed Tony and Cannon to a small tarp roof that had been set up near the trailer where he did business. Four plastic chairs cluttered the tiny space. Glancing toward the food table, I caught sight of Jubile shoving a glass toward Julene. She shook her head until Jubile slapped her face. In an instant, she grabbed the glass and drank. Her eyes blinked from the pressure of the big man's hand, but she didn't cry.

"Did you see that?" I said. "He slapped her face."

Cannon shrugged. "They got their differences sometimes. Show people are like that." He rested his heavy arms on the plastic chair.

"But he's such a huge man to be hitting that little woman." I sensed abuse and a rage began to build inside me.

Cannon chuckled. "You wait. You'll probably see her go after him like piranha on a whale. That little Julene can take care of herself."

Jubile used chunks of bread to sop up stew from a large bowl, sitting in silence across from his partner. They seemed at a truce for the moment.

"Now, sir. What is it you need?" Cannon stared at Tony.

"It's Beaufont," said Tony, leaning toward the man, his jaw grinding, a sure sign he was determined to get his way. "We got reason to believe he was involved in a crime, and we need information."

Cannon sighed. He gazed into the distance as though he'd give anything to be watching bulls toss cowboys than to be answering business questions. "I never keep records too good," he said. "Sometimes I just hire somebody, put them on the job, and pay cash at the end of the job. I forget if Beaufont worked here or not, but he could have."

Tony sighed. "I need to ask around. You'll set up a place for your people to meet me?"

"Between shows," said Cannon. "I'm not pulling anybody out of a show."

Tony nodded. "Any problems your employees have with women?" He glanced toward Jubile.

Cannon tossed back his head and laughed. "Any of them without problems with women?" His laugh broke into a cough. "Sorry, but that's a joke. Most of the show people been married all kinds of times."

Tony stood up. "See that you line up all your acts for questioning." He glanced around at the make-shift patio. "Find a card table and set things up right here." He nodded to me, and I followed him toward the patrol car. We passed Sword and Fire who argued in loud voices about who would go first and who took the longest on stage.

"Might be good if I asked around while I'm working the booth," I said.

"Stay out of things, Luanne. This isn't diving." Tony didn't look at me. He would never consent to my nosiness, but he loved it when I found out things.

CHAPTER 13

The poor junior rank deputy that had substituted for me was ready to hang Mama and Harlie by the time I arrived to do my duties.

"They threatened to use mustard on each other," he whined. "I had to rescue the bottles from them for the customers." He picked up a squirt top yellow bottle and waved it in the air.

"Three burgers up!" cried Harlie. "You still working here?" He leaned toward me like I had taken a nap break.

"Gator meat!" Mama's unusual use of a high-pitched shrill was a clue that things had not gone well.

"What were they fighting about this time?" I asked the deputy as he pulled the apron off and handed it to me.

"Just got in each other's way, over and over again. It's not safe around here with all that hot oil and nasty temper. Like threatening moccasin territory." He motioned toward the line of hungry teenagers waiting to give food orders, then hurried down the back steps. "I'd rather chase a gunny any day."

I pulled out the pen and order slips and began taking the requests for two orders of fried gator, two cheeseburgers, and lots of soda pop. Harlie grumbled in the background as he tossed in a package of frozen french fries. "Grease needs changing."

"Change it then," said Mama as she ladled out gator cubes into paper plates. "Don't know why you got it so hard. I clean my frier every morning."

He sneered in her direction and made a gesture that said, "Well, la-dee-da!"

"How come you two don't hit it off?" I said. I handed over the gator plate to a pimply faced boy who had yellow dyed hair and a ring through his lip.

"Oh, I can hit it off him all right!" said Mama. Her eyes darted fire in Harlie's direction.

"Tried enough times," he murmured under his breath.

I turned around when most of the line had been served. "I get the feeling there's something else here besides cooking territorial rights."

Mama and Harlie stopped and glared at each other. One held a grease ladle, the other a long spatula, like weapons in a duel.

"Huh," said Mama and went back to her cooking.

Harlie needed hamburger buns. I knelt to help drag out new bags from below his cooking table. "Okay, Harlie, what's gone on between you two?"

His knees cracked when he knelt down beside me. His middle-aged bulk stretched the uniform pants to their limits. "We used to be an item. Years ago. Before she got hips like a holstein." He sighed and his eyes took a faraway gaze. "Great two years. Then she got jealous. Said I two-timed her. Been fighting ever since." He grabbed bags of buns and tossed them on the table. His knees cracked again as he stood. "She ain't no forgiving woman, Luanne." His eyes darted toward Mama again.

I slipped over to Mama's side and arranged some paper plates. "Go easy on Harlie, okay?" I whispered. "You can straighten him out later."

"Later?" Mama's word came in a hiss. "I don't see that man later."

I wanted to know the background, to hear how this long ago

romance had turned to sour grapes that kept on souring into retirement age. Before I could ask, three Fish and Game men walked up to the stand.

"Any problems?" Mama asked.

"Lots," said the one with a chewed-up toothpick hanging from the side of his mouth. "We got problems right here on the grounds with a missing snake."

"Sylvester from the Snake Boy act?" I cringed just thinking of that thing wrapped around some kid's body.

"Yeah. Hasn't been found in any of the usual places it might have gone. Now we got to search the produce tents and warm places." He pulled the toothpick from his lip and scratched the inside of his ear, shoving the wide brimmed hat to one side of his head. "Like those shelves you got under your work tables." He turned to the other two men. "I'll start here and work down this way. You go the other direction." He pointed to one man. "And you head across the front." The third warden's eyes widened, and from their water, I suspected he was frightened of finding the quarry.

"So you think it's still on the fairgrounds?" I asked as I stood back and let him poke behind packages of buns, plates, and cups.

"Pretty cold for a snake to be roaming about. We figure he's got him a nice little corner to curl up in—take that back—nice big corner where it's warm. Gets hungry, he'll go after dogs, chickens, anything he thinks he can squeeze."

"That thing is big enough to squeeze Harlie," said Mama, who had taken up a stance on the stairs. "I'm killing it if I see it."

"Don't get in no fight with it, ma'am," said the warden. "It could give you a nasty bite. Snake Boy says it's kind of temperamental." He finished the shelves and did a quick glance into the corners of the booth. "Better go see if it likes cotton candy better than fried gator," he said. He glanced at the battered cubes of gator tail and turned up his nose. "If you could see what that thing eats, you wouldn't be serving it."

I passed Mama on the steps and ran after the warden. "Have you guys found out anything about Rinks' Gator Farm?"

"Looks like somebody had it in for him. We figure either he owed somebody money, or he was giving somebody too much competition. We're bettin' on him being scared off. Probably find him hiding somewhere until things cool down." He cleaned under one fingernail with a toothpick.

"They shoot all his gators, ransack his storage shed, and disappear?"

"Something like that. Good way to scare somebody into paying up, don't you think?"

"I've never heard of rival gator farms." I watched the man use the toothpick to clean under another nail. "You know, we've got extra toothpicks on the counter."

"Thanks. This one will do fine. He shoved it into the corner of his lips, smiled and headed for the cotton candy booth.

Back in the sheriff's booth, I picked up the order pad again. "Man won't eat gator, but he'll use the same toothpick for all his bodily functions," I said.

"Men are like that," said Mama, loud enough for Harlie to pick up the sarcasm.

When the crowds thinned out, we put away the supplies. Mama and Harlie stowed the perishables in the trailer coolers. The last crumb swept from the wooden floor, Harlie pulled down the tarp that would close up the ordering area. In the distance, the ferris wheel continued to turn and barkers yelled out the last shows for the evening. The bull ring had loaded up its fearsome cargo and shoved wounded riders into medic vans. The only thing left was the stench of bull droppings. I headed toward the Jubile-Julene sideshow.

Cannon stood out front.

"Keeping guard?" I asked.

"Waiting for money," he smiled. "Want a corn dog?" He had two fried hot dogs on a stick in his hand.

"Enough fried stuff for one evening," I said.

"Mmm," he stuck one of the dogs into the mouth space surrounded by hair.

"No chance I could see their last show?" I motioned toward the tent where the line had been escorted inside.

He held the corn dog with his teeth, shrugged and pulled aside the flap. Nodding to the ticket taker, he pointed for me to join the others.

I stood on one edge of the crowd near the back of the tent. A canvas flap shut off the view of the dressing area. An announcer with a slick purple suit and greased back hair stood on stage. His speech resembled that of a holy roller preacher who emphasized with emotion and rose up and down on his heels and toes.

"See how the miniature world can conquer the giant!" He harped on and on about how Jubile had been tamed by the little beastie woman, Julene.

"Yeah," I said under my breath, "only in a carnival show."

I slipped further back and parted the flap slightly. A few feet away, two laborers played cards on a storage crate. Their attention was strictly on the cards each one slapped down, then cursed, then slapped down again. I eased into the space and let the flap fall gently into place.

Though separated only by canvas, it seemed another room far from the gawking crowd and the greasy barker on stage. I edged my way beside the men playing cards. They didn't see me until I was within inches of touching one sleeve.

"Ma'am?" said one who looked startled and gazed around to see how I had entered the area.

"I'd like to ask you something," I said, holding my voice to a whisper. "I've been looking for someone who used to work in a job like this."

"Got a name?" said the other man who deliberately moved back to get a full view of a female body.

"A Cajun, Rennie Beaufont."

They looked at me for a moment. The first one shrugged. "Yeah, he works in carnivals off and on. He's got another gig, like we all do. Not too much steady work in this at different times of the year."

"When did you see him last?"

The second man smiled. "You hot for him?"

"Not hardly. You knew him, too?"

"Worked alongside him a few times. Man did his job. Didn't have much to say, but was a nice fellow. Seemed dependable."

"Hasn't been around here lately, though." The first one reshuffled the cards.

"Did he play with you?" I motioned toward the crate.

"Nope. Said he didn't like games. Said he had a family to run home to. I think I even saw his woman once."

The first man chuckled. "What do you mean you *saw* his woman?"

"Nothing like that," he laughed. "She looked okay. Might not have been a bad idea." He glanced toward me and got a look of shame in his eyes. "Think she was looking for him. Had an older lady with her."

"Her mother, perhaps?" Marie had never mentioned her mother joining them in the travel trailer.

"Possible. She didn't introduce us." The man slapped a card on the crate to signal a new game.

I moved into the shadows, and the men seemed not to care. I

eased back into the crowd in the show room.

Jubile had moved onto the stage, not seated in his usual chair, but by some miracle on all fours. A huge pink blanket covered his mass of a body. The sleazy emcee had moved to the back and called out, "Julene! Your baby has been bad!"

The emcee disappeared, while Julene appeared from one side of the stage. She wore the garb of a dominatrix and carried a black whip longer than she was tall. Her dark red lips cackled in a haunting, freakish manner. The crowed giggled, except for two men in the front row. Their eyes lit up and silly smiles appeared on their faces.

Julene tromped in metal-studded high-heeled boots toward Jubile. In a flash, she pulled away the pink blanket and tossed it to the back of the stage. Jubile, his flesh drooping and sagging with no discernible shape, wore a Sumo wrestler thong. He began to make crying noises, his big face whimpering and blubbering. "No Mummy, please no."

"Bad!" screeched Julene and let the whip rip onto one side of Jubile's buttock. It wasn't fake. A red streak appeared, and Jubile looked startled for a moment. "Confess!" she screamed and hit him on the other side. He pretended to bawl, and flinched every time she snapped the whip.

Julene continued to stomp around the bulge of a man, cracking the whip with the artistic skill of a cowboy. She nipped him in the sides with the tip, then turned it around and paddled him with the handle. When she finally wrapped the long end around the flesh that surrounded his neck area, people began to murmur and back away. Not the two men in front. They edged closer, smiling, their eyes half closed. One stuck his hand deep into his pocket.

I groaned and spoke to the woman beside me. She had turned her head away. "This is nothing but S and M," I whispered. The woman looked up at me, her face puzzled by the letters. I didn't explain but backed out of the front flap and nearly ran into Cannon. He was tonguing a pink cotton candy.

"You know, you've got your nerve offering an act like this at a family fair." I pointed inside where the cracking of the whip had been replaced by a shrill voice ordering Jubile to turn over. "Julene is nothing but a pint-sized dominatrix."

"Take a look on the ticket booth," said Cannon, the pink confection mixed into his beard. "Nobody under eighteen allowed to even buy a ticket."

There were the words just under the price of admission. "So you got a fat man and midget show that's really an S and M display. You know, there are a couple of men in there now who are going to ask to see Julene after hours."

"Not my business," he shrugged. "I collect for my time only." He pulled off a hunk of pink and crammed it into his mouth. When a man came out with the cash box, he tucked it under one arm, saluted me, and headed toward the clown tent.

"Are you sure this is legal?" I called after him, but he gave no signal that he heard me.

I had half an hour before I had to meet Vernon at the Sheriff's booth. He and Tony would be traipsing the grounds, questioning workers and performers about their knowledge of Rennie Beaufont. I'd had enough of side shows, so I drifted toward the display tents. From a few yards away, game wardens clustered around one end of a long tent.

"Found the snake yet?" I asked as I approached the same toothpick warden.

"Not yet. We're just going inside this poultry area. Nobody has complained of their prize chicken disappearing yet."

"Maybe it only eats the losers." I peeped inside. Young Future

Farmers were cleaning out the cages, trying to eliminate the smell of chicken droppings before the next morning. "Do those kids know they might run across a python?"

"Haven't told them yet," said the man. He pulled the toothpick from his lips to laugh. "One way to find the critter is to wait for the scream."

I gave him a sour look and stepped inside. The smell nearly choked me, and I knew why I never bothered with a chicken house as a kid. Various varieties of poultry cackled and fluttered as the kids cleaned the cages. Up and down the long row of wire, blue, red, and green ribbons hung in testimony of how each one had appeared in the eyes of judges.

Behind me, two wardens entered with long, hooked poles and flashlights. They moved about the rows, shining the lights beneath the cages and poking into darkness with the hooks. The kids stopped their cleaning to watch and wonder. When one asked, the answer came back, "rat snakes. They like to hang around chicken coops."

"Yeah, some rat snake," I said and backed into fresh air.

I figured the owners would be cleaning the cattle tents, too, and instead of inhaling more of the barnyard, I headed back to the sheriff's booth. Mama and Harlie had gone, getting rides from other people who headed to their sides of the county. The booth, darkened and covered, sat like a ghost to fairs past. Behind the booth, the trailer with the left-over meat sat locked, a cord hooked into an outlet to keep the refrigeration working. Other than a security light that put a dim glow over everything, the area was dark. I sat on the rear steps, hoping Sylvester had not decided to pick that spot to hide from the torment of stardom.

Near the road, I spied two men getting out of a pickup. One pulled an ax from the back. When it seemed they were coming right at me, I ducked into the shadows near the refrigerated trailer.

As they passed under the security light, I saw a familiar haunted look in the face of the younger one. His eyes darted first to the bushes near the road, then toward the closed booths on the opposite side.

"Think we'll find him here?" he asked.

The older man grunted and patted the boy's shoulder. He turned toward the bull ring, the younger man hesitating, then trotting to catch up. They looked to be up to no good. Having nothing else to do but wait around, I followed them.

When the men crossed in front of the animal tents, they stopped suddenly, the younger one nearly ramming his partner. Three game wardens stood around, making small talk, their hooked poles resting on the ground. The older man gestured for the younger one to follow him around the side.

At the bull ring fence, the young man stopped while the older one searched through the parked trailers. He checked the license plates on each one until he found what he was looking for. He called to the young man, pointed toward the tires, then drifted toward the other side of the arena.

The young man's eyes darted around him again. I sneaked behind the trailer pointed out by the partner and waited. He looked around again and lifted the ax. With one blow, he severed the back tire.

"Hey!" I said, a dumb move when someone was wielding an ax.

"What?" The young man stopped, his face turning to chalk as he realized he had been discovered.

We stared at each other until the blow hit the side of my head and the lights went out.

CHAPTER 14

"Luanne!" I heard Vernon's voice somewhere above me and wondered if he had been sitting in a tree stand all the time.

"Why are you up that tree?" I asked, my head nearly bursting apart.

"Why are you on the ground? What happened here?" Vernon slipped his hand beneath my head to hold it off the dirt. When my eyes focused, I realized he wasn't in a tree at all, just kneeling and looking down at me.

"The tire," I said and managed to point to the trailer.

Tony stood beside the trailer, talking into a cell phone.

"We're calling the medics. Looks like somebody tried to sabotage this unit."

"Why?" I raised up and immediately fell backwards. For some reason Chawbutt's face flashed before my eyes.

"Just stay put. You've got a nasty bruise on one side of your face." Vernon brushed my hair from my forehead.

"I think one of those guys hit me," I said.

"So do I," said Vernon. A uniformed deputy knelt beside him. He had a pen and pad in his hand. "Mr. Nixon here found you on the ground."

Chawbutt leaned into the light. He grinned from under his too big hat, the plug of tobacco bulging one side of his jaw. He tipped the hat slightly.

"Oh, God." I let my head rest heavily in Vernon's hand.

"Can you describe them?" he asked.

"Scruffy, like dirty clothes. One young, one middle aged. I think I've seen the young one before." A scared face stared at me from a doorway somewhere.

"Here, at the fair?" asked the deputy.

"Dead gators," I said and dizziness overtook me.

The hospital emergency room teemed with humanity, some sick, others waiting to see if somebody was sick. I sat in a hallway chair with an ice pack over the right side of my face.

"You'll have a bruise for a few days," said the intern, his eyes sporting bags to attest to the overworked state of the facility. "But no concussion or broken skin. Whoever hit you knew how to do it and knock you out."

"A professional hit man?" I couldn't resist, and the intern smiled.

"At least a practiced one." He handed a report to Vernon who would file it with the sheriff's department. "You can go home now."

Home in the swamp was what I needed. My face felt numb with a growing ache somewhere deep. Vernon drove in silence, squeezing my hand once in a while to see if I was okay. By the time we reached the dirt ruts that would lead to my little haven in the woods, my jaw throbbed.

"What were they up to?" I asked.

"Tony says it's a grudge thing. Must be some dispute between the men you saw and whoever owns that trailer." He smiled at me. "You'll take one of those pain pills and crawl into bed, right?"

I shrugged and let him lead me to the dark porch. On the steps, a disheveled Plato wagged his tail and barked once. He must have sensed something wrong. He brushed his body against my leg and whimpered.

"You're hungry?" I patted his wiry ears.

Vernon turned on the lights and turned up the thermostat. After feeding me a cup of hot tea and some leftover cornbread, he forced me to take a pain pill. Plato ate his own food then took up a stance at my feet.

"He'll stay around tonight," said Vernon.

The pill knocked me out for a while, but when it wore off in the wee hours, my face throbbed. Plato came to the side of the bed and licked my hand.

"You want out?" I watched his tail wag faster. Looking over, I saw Vernon in deep sleep. "Okay. I need to move anyway."

Feeling like my face would drop away on one side, I held my hand against it and maneuvered the stairs with the other hand. Plato trotted in front of me. When he reached the front door, he backed up suddenly, his happy pant turning to a low growl.

"What is it?" I glanced at the clock, four in the morning. The outside was dark as pitch except for one sensor light that had clicked on. "Maybe you better try and hold it for a while, Plato." I whispered as I peeked through the front window. The yard around the screened porch was illuminated for a few feet. Nothing stirred there. The porch itself sat in semi darkness. I flipped on the switch. Just outside the screen, where the porch met the steep steps, I noticed a round object like the top of the head. When it moved, Plato went crazy. He hit the door with his paws and growled and barked and spit dog venom as best he could. The head took flight. It had been attached to a body that hid in the shadows beside the steps.

"What's the matter?" said Vernon. He stood at the top of the stairs, a blanket wrapped around his torso.

"Somebody is out there."

"Let the dog out," he said.

"I don't want him shot." But Plato was going to ruin the door if I didn't open it soon.

When I opened the inner door, he nearly tore down the screen. On the steps at last, he bounded toward the dark swamp in chase of a phantom. In the distance, I heard a boat motor. No dog would catch the man now.

Plato had run into the night toward my landing across the road and a few yards to the river's edge. His barks echoed through the swamp now, shutting down the few sounds swamp critters made even in the cold of winter.

Vernon retreated to the bedroom for his pants and a flashlight.

"Nothing but a few footprints by the steps," he said as he returned from the landing, a nervous Plato sniffing the ground and the air. "Who's the enemy this week?"

"I saw that kid's face before his pal knocked me senseless. They looked like swamp people. You don't think they are…" I wanted to say "after me" but the words resounded in the quiet swamp and I whispered them instead.

"Tony is on the case. We'd better call this in." Vernon, Plato, and I returned to the living room. Plato took up a spot near the front door, daring anything from snake to fowl to mammal to come near. The hair stood up in a row along his spine.

The side of my head throbbed the next morning. The area near my ear was black, and the blue coloring extended as far over as the cheekbone. But the eye made me a monster. Somehow, the man had hit near the corner, causing the lid to meet the under eye bag and close it shut halfway over. If I gazed through the narrow slit next to my nose, I could see.

"People are going to report me for female abuse!" said Vernon.

His fingers came close to the bruise but didn't actually touch me.

"Sunglasses in the middle of winter," I grumbled as I fished out a pair from a drawer in the kitchen. "Guess I should be glad I still have my teeth."

With dark glasses and a sun hat, I headed out the door with Vernon. We had to meet Tony at the fairgrounds to make a formal report.

Before we got into the car, Pasquin showed up, his straw hat holding in imaginary heat. Plato greeted him with a tail wag and sniff, then headed into the trees and down the swamp Pasquin and I had trekked across to each other's house for all the years I had lived here.

"Heard you got roughed up a bit last night," he said. "Swamp vine is buzzing about it." He referred to the people who had lived for years in the swamp, who patrolled the river and its banks for rogue animals—human and otherwise. No secret like this would be kept.

"Mama's Table, right?"

"Already been over there for breakfast." Pasquin took off his hat and shaded his eyes from the bright sun that didn't seem to be able to warm up the forest. "Let me see that." He pointed toward the glasses.

With the hat off, I let Pasquin peruse the damage. He grunted, perhaps from knowledge or just from the strain of bending his old bones in an unnatural direction.

"Poultice 'll take care of that. No broken skin." He donned his hat again. "Give an old man a ride into town?"

With Pasquin in the back seat, we headed toward the fairgrounds. Traffic grew thick as we reached the city limits. State workers sat in snail-paced cars, their morning coffee in one hand. Tail pipe vapor floated upward in the cold air.

"Never could tell where all these cars came from," said Pasquin, a man who knew how to con a ride from just about anyone.

"And half of them don't know where they're going," said Vernon, his frustration showing as we slowed to a stop.

We made the turn into the grounds and wound through the mass of trailers, stands, and tents until we reached the bull pens. Patrol cars had lined up in front of the fence, their markings nearly as imposing as a brahma bull.

"You need to tell us just what you saw," said Tony as I opened the door. He made no comment on the condition of my face, as I knew he wouldn't. Sympathy was not a characteristic of this good ol' boy of Cuban descent.

"You have my statement," I said.

"Need it again, now that you're not in a hospital room." He stood aside as I pulled out of the car. For some reason, standing made my face throb, but the moment passed.

Loman poked around the axed tire of the trailer. "Sure meant to do this in," he said to no one.

"Whose is it?" I asked.

"Zigfield's private trailer," said Cannon who appeared from one end. His curly hair had not been combed and stood in tufts of kinks rather than one mass. He wore a jacket with no shirt underneath.

"Not the one with the clown pictures on the side?"

"He gets somebody to drive this one in behind the one that houses the clowns. Can't stand to live with the little guys, he says." Cannon laughed and tapped on the side of the trailer. "He wasn't here last night. Took off just after the last show."

"Where is he now?" asked Tony. He glanced around. The miniature clowns had lined up a few yards away. Without costumes, their faces took on dour, frightening demeanors. Some smoked. One sipped from a bottle in a paper bag.

"Been playing poker half the night," said Cannon, "according to his men." He pointed to the clowns. "He'll be in soon and is he gonna be pissed." Cannon laughed out loud. "Man's got a temper."

An officer donned a white coat and slipped on latex gloves. He went to work on the area around the trailer, hoping someone would have left a print before he took a swipe at the tire. He would check the ground and hole in the tire, but he didn't expect to find anything.

"She's your best bet," he said and pointed to me.

Pasquin moved closer to the trailer. He leaned over to look at the cut and nearly lost his hat to the ground. "Axed the tire," he said. "Sign of swamp revenge."

The deputy in the white coat looked up at him, sneering at the musings of an octogenarian.

"Seen it done many a time," he said. "Strand a man in the swamp if his tires are axed, or his propellers smashed or his oars floated down stream. Better be looking for what this man did to the one with the ax." He pointed to the trailer.

"Wish motives were that simple," said the deputy.

"Most are," said Pasquin as he backed away and donned his hat.

"Man's coming!" said Cannon who darted to the other side of the trailer.

In the distance, a lanky Ziggie took long, angry strides toward us. His baseball cap flopped away from his head as his pace moved his body up and down like a piston. At closer range, his unshaven bony face told of a night of card games and cigarettes. A butt dangled from one corner of his mouth.

"What the hell is going on here?" His voice sounded hoarse, like someone who had talked all night, in between smokes.

"Somebody doesn't like you much, Mr. Zigfield." Vernon stood before him, matching the man's height. They faced each other, two specimens, one healthy, the other a hardened sample of flesh in deterioration.

"What happened?" The cigarette butt dropped to the ground. Ziggie's eyes drifted toward the row of clowns. "If you creeps did something…" He gestured with his fist. The little men stared back with grim expressions.

"Take a look," said Tony, and motioned the man toward the tire with the hole.

Ziggie made an arc in his pacing around the damaged tire. In between frustrated sighs and under-the-breath curses, he kicked up dirt with the toe of a broken leather cowboy boot like some brahma bull ready to gore anyone who got in his way.

"Any idea of who wanted to do this?" Tony's jaw worked in a clinch. He was growing impatient with the man.

"None." Ziggie looked toward Cannon and frowned.

"Man on the carnival circuit, one who goes to all-night poker games, ought to have some enemies," said Tony.

Ziggie ignored him and bent over to touch the chopped ends of the gaping rubber hole. "Gonna cost plenty to replace this. Too big a hole to be repaired." He looked toward Cannon again. Cannon stood away from the trailer, his hands resting on his hips in a "dare me" stance.

Vernon touched me on the arm and nodded toward the clowns. The little men, now looking more like Billy Goat Gruffs, scowled in the direction of their boss. Vernon slipped behind the deputies and headed for their group.

From my viewpoint, I saw Vernon's back and his gestures as he asked the men who had a grudge against Ziggie. The little men broke into laughter and shook their heads.

"They said 'who didn't have a grudge against him' but they

wouldn't give out a name." Vernon said to Tony. "Maybe we better put out some watches."

That meant some poor uniformed deputy would sit near the trailers all night, maybe even two deputies given the number of vehicles that rested nearly bumper to bumper.

"For a while," said Tony.

"They didn't exactly come in the dead of night," I said. "The fair, at least the carnival part, wasn't closed yet."

Tony's jaw worked. He refused to look at me. It never ceased to grind at his gut when a female adjunct—meaning me—told him something he should have already known.

"Let's see if the riding patrol saw anything." He headed toward two uniformed deputies who sat atop chestnut horses. Both shook their heads.

When Tony returned to Ziggie, he called Cannon back into the group. "Look, the fair is going to be over this weekend. I don't want any trouble. If any one of you has a beef to settle, do it out of this county."

Cannon started to protest, but Tony held up his hand. "I mean that. No discussion necessary!" He turned to the deputy who was removing his lab coat. "Write your report." Then he spoke to Loman about putting on extra patrols starting before closing time.

I smiled and jabbed Vernon. If felt good to make Tony jump, even if my face still throbbed each time I turned my head.

"Fish and Game is turning this back to the sheriff," Loman spoke to Tony. We had been greeted by two wardens as we left the grounds. "Looks like somebody robbed and wrecked Rinks' gator farm, including the slaughter of the gators."

I looked at Pasquin. "Think they'll ask you to take them into the swamp?"

"No doubt, ma'am." He smiled and whipped at an imaginary bug with his straw hat. "Maybe they know the way but they're going to need us to show them what we first saw."

I sat at one end of Pasquin's boat. He steered at the other. We trailed behind the wake of Fish and Game and Sheriff's patrol boats. Before we made the turn toward Rinks' Farm, we saw the hydrilla grass boat with its paddle wheels pulling on a massive clump of the alien grass. White's company operated the boat, just as it did for the dry lake burn-offs.

"About time they got around to this part of the river," said Pasquin.

White himself handled the boat today. He waved as he shifted the noisy gears to pull the grass up the metal belt and onto a storage area in the back. Somewhere not far down the river, he'd have a dump truck waiting to load the stuff and haul it away.

"River's nearly clogged all the way to the middle," Pasquin said. "Done taken over the edges." He knew where to move his motor boat, when to raise the motor out of the water and use the oars to get around the invading grass.

Pasquin never hurried. We barely kept the others in sight as they rounded bends and cleared overhanging oak branches.

My face felt like someone had hit me with a hot iron. One of the deputies had made up an ice pack for me. I rested it against my skin. The river mist rose quietly off the surface into cold air. Even with the sun shining full blast, the temperature stayed at an uncanny low level.

"You seen MacAllister lately?" said Pasquin. He slowed and reversed the motor, unwinding a gnarl of grass from the propeller.

"No." I tried to add a little scorn to the reply. Harry MacAllister, my former diving partner and lover of long ago, had been Tony's favorite to call on when diving was needed. Even though he had "done me wrong" as the song says, I was over it. Vernon had filled the gap of bitterness and loneliness. But I still felt hackles go up when anyone tried to imply that I *should* be seeing Harry for any reason.

"Well, you're about to get reacquainted," said Pasquin. He tipped his hat to someone behind us.

I turned around. A boat had joined our little armada toward Rinks' Farm. Harry sat in the driver's seat of a small motor boat. His thick salt and pepper hair blew backward in the slight breeze kicked up by the movement of his boat. In the seat behind him, a space normally saved to stow scuba gear, sat a woman maybe half my age, a blond with a black turtleneck sweater and sunshades.

"What does Tony need with him?" I nodded toward Harry. Other than a slight nod in return, the girl in the boat didn't move.

"Got him a filly gator in the back seat!" Pasquin slapped his knee and laughed at his own joke.

The boats lined up around Rinks' dock like a parade coming to a stop. I stepped out of Pasquin's boat and joined Vernon on the landing.

"Tony!" Harry called out from his boat. Finding no place to tie up, he stopped the engine and sat dead in the water. "You got something you want me to look at?"

Tony smiled and motioned for Harry to pull alongside the patrol boat. I stayed put. At the landing, Harry looked up at me. "Luanne," he said, making a slight turn to the blond behind him. "This is Mitzi."

I nodded. "A diver?"

Harry laughed. "Not her. She can barely swim." Mitzi made no response.

Pasquin moved close to me and whispered, "bet she swims in the bare, too."

Tony pulled on the edge of Harry's boat, evening it with the dock.

"What's up?"

"Got some nasty events here at the farm. Thought you'd like to see."

"You've got a diver or two." He pointed toward me and Vernon.

I stepped close to Tony. "What's going on?" I tried to sound threatening.

"He needs to get back into the swing of things," said Tony. "I hear he's been depressed, not able to go back into the water."

"And looking at rotting alligators is going to change that?"

"Getting him interested in a crime," said Tony, "may help him dive again."

I stared at Tony. I never knew he cared that much about anyone and wondered if he would have done the same for me had I been the injured one.

Before I could think of a sarcastic retort, he pointed toward a noise coming down the river lane. White sat in the driver's seat of his grass puller, a thick man in a gray sweatshirt stood at his back. He moved the awkward boat through the middle of the river, sliding its flat bottom across the grass. The metal conveyors had been pulled above the water level and stuck out in front like a flat ended weapon. White couldn't move more than three miles per hour. His puller hadn't been engineered for rapid movement.

"Sheriff over there?" He called to anyone on shore. "We got a problem up the river there." White showed none of the cockiness he had the day we found Beaufont's body in the half-burned lake. He appeared unusually pale.

I followed Tony to the river edge, standing in six inches of cold water.

"Went to check out a section I pulled a couple of months ago. Grass has grown back but isn't to the surface yet. Thought I saw something that wasn't green." White took a deep breath. "Got my fork pole here and pushed the fronds around. Could swear there's a body down there."

CHAPTER 15

Diving in cold clear water meant pulling on a wet suit. Pasquin had turned the boat around, taken me to my landing where I loaded the gear, and returned to find another patrol boat waiting at the scene. Harry sat in his boat with Mitzi still on her seat. She had said nothing during all this, never even removed her dark glasses. White had moved his puller to the shore edge and sat in the high chair to watch the events.

"Ms. Fogarty," said the heavy-set deputy who manned the wheel of the sheriff's patrol boat, "Amado said to tell you to go down and see just what that is. Now don't stir up nothing, just see if it's real and needs the crime scene people."

I looked at Harry. He turned a sheepish face down toward his leg. It was permanently injured and caused a limp, but didn't interfere with diving.

"Does it hurt in the cold water?" I asked.

"No, not much." He shrugged, and for the first time ever, I saw the look of a coward in his expression. An underwater bomb had left Harry like this. I'd been there, too, but my injuries were lighter and I had forced myself to go down again and conquer the fears. If he didn't overcome this fear right now, he may never dive again.

"Tony would rather you do this. You know that, don't you?"

Harry shrugged again. "He knows you'll do just fine. You won't need a buddy to head straight down. He would have sent Vernon if

143

it was dangerous. We'll be watching you."

I pulled the tank straps over my shoulders and snapped the buckle in front. The wet suit gripped me tightly and would protect me from the frigid currents of the river.

Three boats made a circle around the location where I would dive in a straight line. From the top, we saw thick green grass. Whatever had been dumped there one day would have been covered over by growth the next. Only the wake of a boat or a sudden push of current parted the grass enough to see pink that could have been part of an arm. Whether real or a mannequin, it had to be checked.

Sitting on the edge of Pasquin's boat, I leaned over backwards and hit the water. Turning around, I pushed against a slight current and headed for the bottom. In spite of the suit, I felt the cold. The grass would prove a problem if I entangled myself in it. The roots were short and shallow, but the grass itself was strong as rope. Taking special care of the tank, I parted the fronds.

No mannequin lay on the bottom. Up close, the flesh on the limbs was pink in places, ivory white in others. Bloated, they were grotesque, bobbing about like overstuffed, tossed-out furniture. The face turned sideways, too far, in an unnatural position. But what was natural about lying at the bottom of the river? Straw brown hair floated around the head, neck and chest. With one hand, I brushed aside some hair. Only the left side of the face was visible, the other side buried in river sand. An eye, bloated and bulging, stared into the eel grass. The entire face appeared stuffed, blown up by death gases, yet somehow familiar. I moved the hair from the neck and found the gash. It began near the ear and most likely ran under her chin. The neck, however, had bloated around it. A bloated body in clear water should have floated to the surface by now. This one never would. Thick grass had grown around it like a green shroud, and the rope around her waist made sure the grass wouldn't lose its grip.

By afternoon, the game wardens were left with Loman at Rinks' Alligator Farm. Tony and crime scene techs along with patrol boats and deputies lined the river. On shore, a coroner's wagon waited. So did Marshall Long.

Vernon had joined me in the depths to take photos and help lift the body into its wire cage. We waited at the surface, decorated in green strands of hydrilla like watery Christmas ornaments. Once the crime scene people gave the word, the body was moved to shore. We followed.

"Female, youngish, maybe twenty-five or thirty years old," said Marshall. The giant of a man had squatted near the body to probe with a gloved hand. "Throat cut. Yes, let's see that again." He lifted the girl's chin with one finger, revealing a mass of torn flesh. A piece of eel grass clung to one section. Marshall pulled it away and passed it to a tech who stuffed it into an evidence bag.

"This cut looks mighty familiar," he said. "Curved blade, possibly. Deep. Have to get her to the lab to see if it's all the way to the bone."

"You think she was murdered and dumped?" said Tony.

"Looks that way. Have to check the lungs in the lab."

"You're saying this looks a lot like the other girls, the ones Rennie Beaufont is supposed to have murdered?" I said.

No one answered. Vernon nodded, then began putting away the diving gear.

"I've got something to say about that," I said. I waited for Tony to shut me up, but he just ground his teeth.

"Such as?" said Marshall. Two deputies helped him to his feet.

"The other girls were left in water at the edge for the elements or the gators or whatever. This one was weighted down with a sack of bricks. And, she was placed out there, not close to shore. No current would have moved her, not with the bricks holding her down."

Marshall looked at Tony whose olive skin had reddened. He slapped the detective on his arm and laughed. "She's got a point, again!"

Tony turned to face me. "You're an agent on this case, Luanne. Silence to all except those working specifically *on this case*." He strode up the bank and sat in a patrol car.

"He always has to tell me that," I said. "Like I can't remember who pays me pennies to splash around in cold water."

"At least it's not dirty water," Vernon laughed. He had a respected deputy-to-deputy position with Tony, but he wasn't beyond ribbing the man when the woman he loved got there first. "Hydrilla may ruin the ecology, but it keeps the water clean."

We were loading gear when the game wardens pulled alongside and deposited Loman on shore to speak to Tony.

"Has the marks of a payback," said Loman. "We asked a few people who live on the river in that area. Rinks had his enemies."

"For what?" said Tony. He stared at me when he realized I was within earshot. "There are no other gator farms in the area. No competition as far as I know."

"One neighbor said we'd better look beyond the critters. Said boats pulled into Rinks' landing by the dozens some nights. Figured he was running something." Loman raised himself on his toes when he gave out information, like a preacher convinced he had the truth for his flock.

"Drugs?" Tony's starched collar seemed to be choking him. We had all been a part of busting up a huge drug operation a couple of years back, when I had found the bones that turned out to be Gaylin Newberry.

"No evidence of that, but seems poker games could get out of hand down there." Loman stepped to his left and hit loose soil. He lost his balance and nearly tumbled down the bank. "Da-yam!" He scooted to the top where his footing would be more sure.

"Your scenario is that he did some cheating and somebody got back at him by destroying his business?" Tony nodded as though convinced he was right.

"It's been done before," said Loman. "But we won't really know until we find Rinks. He's got this boat house around the bend. Lives on a second floor. The place is so cluttered it's hard to tell if he's just a slob or somebody ransacked it. Wasn't locked."

"You searched without a warrant?" Tony's face reddened.

"Missing person, likely foul play. We were looking for a body—or someone in need of aid." Loman smiled slightly at the legal excuse.

Tony faced the river, his jaw working, his face fading from red back to olive. He stood with his hands on his hips, and if a fashion photographer happened upon the scene, he could have shot an immaculately dressed man. The dark suit, the crisp white shirt, the tie, all in place and creased in just the right spots. Tony could fall in the water and emerge looking just like he looked now.

"All right," he said. "All points out on Rinks. Find the man." He turned around and headed back for the patrol car. He would wait for the coroner to remove the girl's body. He had already radioed missing persons.

The sheriff's department had a standing rule that after a dive, a diver was entitled to rest. It rarely panned out that way. If other duties called, the diver performed them. The fair would have to be taken care of tonight, and Tony would release no one to take my place. Vernon and I headed toward my swamp house. A few moments of bliss and a nap, and we'd be on the road again.

"I've got to run by the university," I said. "I've barely finished the grades, but if I don't turn them in, my check may be held."

"Manny would do that?"

"He would have in the past. He's been acting strange lately." I'd nearly forgotten about the glazed-over stares, the lapses in memory. "Can drugs taken in the sixties affect you forty years later?"

"Don't know. I've heard LSD has latent feedback. You think Manny has a problem?"

"He's got a problem all right."

The weather turned colder, and the wind wasn't helping any. I huddled into my sweater as I ran from the car to the linguistics office. Most students had left by now, the parking lot nearly empty. Leaves fell off trees and fanned across the spaces, clustering in bundles at the base of the gothic brick building. Inside wasn't any warmer. I trotted down the dark corridor to the massive room that served as an office complex at the end of a row of classrooms. Other professors were huddled together in one cubicle.

"Luanne!" called a short stubby man who specialized in grammatical structures. "Did you hear about Manny?" He pushed his way through the group, his face bright pink as he gave me the news. "Got hauled off to the psyche ward this morning. He came in and had no idea where he was. Said he was running from some Indian tribe out to shrink his head." The man beamed.

"Why was he taken away?" I flashed the folder of completed grades to the secretary who had come from Manny's corner office.

"Tried to fight off everyone who wanted him to sit down and

take it easy. Used his totem as a weapon." The man pointed to the stone carved mass of ugly faces that Manny said was a gift from an Alaskan student twenty years ago. He had kept it on his desk amid cluttered papers.

I turned to the secretary. Her face looked exasperated. She shot the entire group of professors a dirty look. "He's at the hospital for tests," she said, taking my folder of grades. "Until then, I'll take your grades and sign them off." She stood before the group, the powerhouse now, someone who could hold up the much needed pay check. She held out her hand. "Anyone else ready?" Everyone moved slowly back to his cubicle.

"I'm off now," I said. "Will you have the January schedules out soon?"

The secretary smiled, and had I been a canary, she would have eaten me.

"There's no time to head back to the swamp now," said Vernon. "Might as well go to the fairgrounds and try to find a quiet place to sit."

"We could stay in the car until time," I said. "It's getting cold out."

"Haven't cuddled in a car since I was a teenager," he grinned. That grin had been my downfall. When I first saw the man, he was dressed only in a bathing suit, standing on the floating dock at Palmetto Springs. Tall and balding, he had the body of a strong swimmer. It hadn't taken us long to discover that we swam well together, in and out of water.

"Just our luck Tony would come along and tap on the window." I laughed. We had been caught before in a vacant office at the sheriff's department. Tony nearly split a seam over that event; no telling what he'd do for a car scene.

Vernon parked at one end of the lot that hadn't been filled yet.

I scooted over as he stretched out his arms—and immediately hit the gear shift. Moving one knee, I knocked the cell phone beneath the gas pedal. "Modern conveniences don't help much," I said. "What do teens do these days?"

"Stay in Junior's room. He's got it filled with equipment, spends long hours on the Internet. His parents don't ask what he's doing all that time." Vernon laughed and tussled my hair. We leaned across the gear shift for a passionate kiss. A tap sounded on the driver's window.

"Tony?" Vernon whispered in my ear.

"Cannon," I said. The man peered through the glass. His curly hair and beard trembled in the cold wind.

"Zigfield," he said as Vernon rolled down the window. "He's gone. His stuff is still here, but he ain't."

CHAPTER 16

The freezing wind blew shards of hay against my face. It felt like broken glass. Cold dust rose off the fairgrounds, filling sinuses and forcing cowboys to belt out he-man sneezes. Cannon had wrapped a dirty blue blanket around his shoulders. We followed him to Ziggie's damaged trailer.

Inside, the place reeked of stale cigarettes and unrinsed beer cans. Ziggie had left an iron out as though he had pressed a shirt then left things to cool down before putting them away. However cluttered the living and kitchen areas were with smoke and liquor, the rest was immaculate.

"Are we supposed to be here?" I asked Vernon.

He nodded. "Missing, we need to look for him." He pulled open a clothes closet to reveal several long-sleeved shirts in mustard and olive green. They had a sheen on them that would have matched the grease on a barker's hair.

The bed, a cot affair jammed against one wall, lay under a tussled mound of sheets and blankets. The linen had yellowed and gave off a human sweat odor mixed with aftershave. Vernon leaned over a green trash can. "Been up to something," he said as he used a pen to fish out a used condom. "Anybody seen that Yasmina woman since the day she hitched a ride in his car?"

Light hair, long and straight, flashed through my mind. "The woman in the river, Vernon." I had a sudden bout of goose bumps.

151

"She looked familiar, but I figured it was because she resembled the other victims. I'll bet my river house it's Yasmina."

"Virginia Jones," said Marshall, "that's her real name. Yasmina was the street—or shall we say 'roadside'—name."

Vernon, Tony, and I stood inside Marshall's med tech office. Impacted with files, books, and what seemed to be remnants of numerous lunches and midnight suppers, it barely accommodated four adults. Marshall, his bulk stretching against a tee shirt that read *Poe's Pathology* over a cartoon of a man holding a pen and a whiskey bottle, had chucked his white lab coat to the floor. It lay in a pile of two others, waiting to be taken to the laundry. Detectives had done their work and Marshall the autopsy. It wouldn't matter now if the woman called herself Virginia or Yasmina.

"She did her hustling in truck stops, places frequented by mostly men," he added. "Not part of my job, but Loman spelled it out for me."

"And cause of death was a slit throat?" Tony tried to move closer to read the print-out Loman had sent to Marshall. He nearly tripped over a box of supplies.

"That killed her, yes. But somebody had to conk her on the head first. From the looks of things, she put up a struggle."

"Any scrapings or semen?" Vernon retreated to the doorway and leaned against the jamb.

"She bit her nails, and even if she got anything under them, the water washed it away. No semen. Doesn't look like she'd pulled a trick for a while." He shot a glance toward me, remnants of the embarrassed Southern male who wasn't supposed to talk of such in a lady's presence.

"Anything on the bricks?" I tried to put him at ease.

"Detectives are trying to find their source. Rope, too. Both looked used."

"So whoever collected them could have, say, raided a building site?"

"More like a destruction site," said Marshall. "Lots of cement stuck to those bricks, chopped up like they had been knocked down with a sledge hammer."

"The other girls, " said Tony, "or victims, were runaways, women who decided living on the road was easier than in their family homes."

"Where did Zigfield pick her up?" I asked.

"Wish we could ask him," said Vernon. "His clown troop said it was at one of the truck stops on I-10, but they couldn't remember which. Seems they did a lot of beer drinking and card playing in the back of that trailer. Left Ziggie to his own pursuits of pleasure."

"One thing you got to contend with, Misters Lawmen," said Marshall. He picked up a photograph. "The slice on her throat was made with the same kind of knife as the others." He showed us a close up of Yasmina's gaping neck cut. "Not as swift and sure as the others. Lots of jagged cutting before they got to the artery." Marshall pointed to torn flesh at the edges of the cut.

"Perhaps a copycat?" I asked.

"Perhaps *copycats*," he said. "From the bruising around the arms, I'd say more than one person had a hand in this."

Vernon and I stood next to the bull riding area. Tonight would be the grand finale, the event that paid the biggest money to the riders. Contenders were arriving from as far away as New Orleans and Memphis. Big bulls were here, too, the vicious snorting kind with reputations as infamous as their riders. Chawbutt Nixon paced the outer rims, chewing his tobacco and spitting. He tipped his hat once, but the silly smile wasn't there. His anxiety fit him like the too large stetson.

"I get the feeling the answer to a lot of this is right here at the fairgrounds," said Vernon, "and if we don't find something out soon, the evidence is going away in an assortment of travel trailers."

"Why would a group of people attack and kill that woman, but there is no sign of rape?" In the distance, I saw Mama get out of a patrol car and begin setting up in the booth. "I mean, I know the rapist is dead, but wouldn't a copycat try to duplicate the crime?"

"If he could," said Vernon. His attention had turned to a couple of cowboys who were threatening to saw off each other's balls over who would have access to a particularly difficult brahma bull. He strode towards them. Chawbutt stood back and watched the action, then resumed his pacing.

I headed for the Sheriff's Department booth to help Mama. Harlie had joined her and was tossing packages onto the floor of the booth from the back of his pickup truck.

"Man! Watch where you throw that stuff." Mama held up a frying pan.

"You planning on using that on me?" Harlie stood up, put his hands on his hips and glared at the woman.

"You planning on hitting me with one of them fat fists?" She raised the pan higher.

"Please!" I said and stood on the makeshift steps. "Let's get through this one more night, okay?"

Before another threat could be made, Edwin scooted to a dusty stop from a full trot in front of the booth. "They ain't found Sylvester nowhere," he said. His eyes nearly popped out from the wide forehead, his hair standing on end. He pushed the palm of his hand against the hair and made it stand up even higher. "Game wardens looked all over this place and he ain't here."

"Anybody look in the water holes around here?" I couldn't imagine a giant python opting for the cold weather in the area, but Sylvester was a cranky snake.

"I got Pasquin checking some sloughs." Edwin scratched his head. "Snake Boy won't ever be the same without his whole act."

"Will you ever be the same, Edwin?" I tried not to laugh. "That snake is going to show up in somebody's camper and scare the be-Jesus out of some poor woman."

"Huh!" Mama said as she turned on the gas below the deep fryer. "Most likely that Snake Boy is hiding the critter till he can get insurance money."

Edwin gasped. He couldn't say anything, just shook his head in disbelief.

"Men do things like that, you know." Mama shot a glance toward Harlie. "Always thinking of themselves."

"Maybe you'd better tell that to Vernon when he comes by," I said. Mama's summation, however derogatory to men, rang true.

"Probably pull him out at the next carnival and say it's a new snake."

"Listen to the woman, Luanne." Harlie called from his position of stacking boxes on the floor of his side of the booth. "She knows about everything there is to know. Been around long enough."

"Old fart!" Mama spoke as she dumped a dab of cornmeal into the grease to test the heat.

I moved close to her, where Harlie couldn't hear me. "One day, I want to sit and have tea with you and you can tell me about this war that never ends."

"War?" she said. "It'll take something stronger than tea for me to talk about this little tussle." Mama smiled and turned up the heat.

Edwin grunted and ran off toward the Snake Boy tent. He was

a grown man, most likely in his early forties, but he seemed a child. He lived for his swamp critters and traveled by boat most of the time. His face had the demeanor of someone not quite there all the time, or perhaps it was all there, just not much of it.

"How does that man live?" I asked.

"Got some trust fund from his folks, so I hear tell," said Mama. "Money comes in once a month. He owns his place and doesn't seem to need much."

"No women?"

Mama stopped rolling gator cubes in meal and looked dazed for a moment. "You know, I don't think I've ever heard him talk about women. Saw him looking at a girlie magazine once, but he got so embarrassed, he slammed it shut and left it on the dock." She laughed. "Can you imagine some woman taking on that snake lover?"

"He doesn't always smell right," I said.

In the distance, cars began to park in rows, and carnival rides turned on their lights. A new group of riding patrols entered from a side gate, their horses rubbed down and shining. Patrol cars lined the highway. I recognized some of the men in plain clothes. They took up positions near the gates.

"More detectives than usual," I said.

"Hope they got somebody looking at Rinks' Farm, too," said Mama. "We'll have to go all the way to Georgia for gator next year if they don't reopen that place."

Harlie tossed onions on his grill and the odors filled the air. They coupled with the cotton candy machine down the way. Nostalgic scents from my youth came flooding back to me. My stomach growled.

"Tony needs us," said Vernon. He had rescued me from hectic duty at the booth. "They're questioning Mrs. Beaufont again, and she's none too happy about it."

"For what?"

"Just trying to see if there was a connection between her husband and Zigfield."

"What about her husband and Yasmina?" I had to trot to keep up with him.

"That, too."

I scrubbed my hands with a wet wrap towel as we headed toward the sheriff's office. I smelled of cornmeal and onions. "Just one more night of this booth stuff and I will be a trained waitress."

Vernon grinned. "Then you can go to work at Mama's Table and forget about student papers."

"Not a a bad idea, said the teacher with stacks of blue books." I sighed. The burden of teaching had become just that. "You know, I've got a crazy-in-the-head boss who has been carted off to the psyche ward. Why do I stay there?"

"Same reason we all do." Vernon squeezed my knee. "Money, security, familiarity. And if it gets to be too much, we can all take retirement in the psyche ward." He turned into the parking lot. "Looks like your lady is here." He pointed to a patrol car near a side door of the brick building. Marie Beaufont had climbed out of the back seat and waited for someone to follow her.

"And her mother?" I said as I saw the stern Mrs. Kelly emerge beneath the glare of the street light.

Inside, we met at Tony's office door. There was still no room inside his domain. Neat as he was in dress, he worked in chaos. Not even his own swivel chair was free of folders, some yellowed and torn on the edges.

"Vernon, you and Luanne will talk to Marie in the last conference room. I want to know just what she knows about Zigfield, Yasmina, and anybody else that happens to have a connection with the fair or carnival circuit."

He sent Loman off to interview the mother and took Cannon to another room for himself.

Marie, if possible, looked worse than the day we searched her trailer. She had lost weight, and her eyes seemed sunk far back into her face. She had pulled back her scraggly hair into a tight little knot. She wore no makeup, and her lips had begun peeling like they were chapped. Her late twenties had turned into early forties.

"I'm sorry about this, Mrs. Beaufont," said Vernon, using his Mr. Nice Guy attitude that was supposed to put her at ease.

Her back stiffened, then folded again. "I doubt that," she whispered. "And could you call me Marie? I'm kind of sick of the name Beaufont. And Kelly doesn't seem right, either."

Vernon nodded. "Marie. We need to know if you have any knowledge, however small or remote, about any of the carnival people your husband may have worked with. We've got reason to believe someone knew what he—your husband—was up to."

Marie's back stiffened again. She shook her head but didn't answer.

"You indicated once before," I said, "that your husband didn't run around with other women, but spent time beer drinking with buddies. But we can't find anyone he drank with." I waited for her to turn her eyes in my direction.

"I guess I was wrong, wasn't I?" She glanced at me briefly. "He seems to have been running circles around other women for quite a while. Or should I say stalking?" She took a deep breath and looked toward the door.

"Did he ever mention anyone named Cannon?" asked Vernon.

Marie looked back at Vernon. "I know who Cannon is. He gives out the checks. I've met him. Had to pick up a check for my husband on occasion."

"Why?" I asked. I figured a man who spent his money on beer wouldn't want his wife picking up his check.

She tapped her finger tips on the conference table. "Rennie—he sometimes went on to another carnival job, ahead of Cannon and the others. I had to get his pay. Cannon couldn't be trusted to mail it."

"Why couldn't he be trusted?" Vernon leaned toward her, forcing her to look at him.

She shrugged. "Actually, I don't know. It's just carnival people are so transient. And Cannon, well, he…" She looked toward the door again.

"Go on."

"He's been a little suggestive at times. I don't trust him."

"You mean a lech?" I squirmed.

"Just that. He never really tried anything. Just tried to put his arm around me once too often." She spoke to the table.

"And that's why you had to pick up the check? Couldn't trust him to mail it?" I felt something didn't ring right here.

"That's why I didn't want him bringing it to the trailer. I usually got my mother to come with me." She stared at me, and for a moment I saw anger burn in her eyes.

"Your mother lives in Live Oak," said Vernon.

"She visited often, especially when Rennie was away on a job."

Vernon sighed. "Let's go to Zigfield. Ziggie. Ever meet him?"

"He played cards with Cannon. Was usually around when I picked up the check. But he always took off when I arrived. I don't know him."

"Ever hear the name Yasmina?"

Marie's forehead wrinkled. She looked directly at Vernon, then quickly away. "No. Sounds foreign."

"What about Virginia Jones?" I asked.

Marie's face turned quickly to me. "Not that I can remember."

Vernon sat back and lowered his voice. "Tell us about anyone you knew on the carnival circuit." He rested his hand on a note pad.

Marie shrugged again. She rubbed her finger across her peeling lips. "Maybe the clowns. I don't remember their names, but they were little people who complained to Cannon a lot. They didn't like Zigfield. At least that's the impression I got. And I met the fat man and his little lady, but they really never talked to us much." She stopped and brushed something from her eye. "The two men with the swords kept to themselves."

"Snake Boy?" I asked.

"No. I knew about him, but never met him."

"And your mother," I said, "did she meet these people, too."

"Could have. She was with me at times." Marie twisted in her seat and clutched her stomach. "Look, I don't know anyone really. I've got to take an antacid." She leaned over the table.

"You haven't been eating," said Vernon.

"Can't. Not everyone has the burden of a husband who killed right under her nose."

"Have you told the children yet?" I asked.

She took a deep breath and folded both arms across her stomach. "They know," she said.

CHAPTER 17

"Marie knows a lot about Cannon," I said in the hallway. A female deputy had brought in a glass of water and a seltzer for Marie. "Does Cannon ever mention her?"

Before Vernon could answer, Tony joined us in the hallway. "Man admits to playing cards with Ziggie and—get this—Rinks. Most of the time the games were in somebody's garage here in town. But, sometimes they all headed out to a barn past the gator farm."

"Could be as simple as nonpayment of gambling debts," said Vernon.

"Did he say there were women at any of these games?" I asked.

Tony looked at me and frowned. "Why?"

"You didn't ask, did you?" I smiled and tasted the canary.

"No reason to." He glanced at Vernon who turned his face to hide the upturned corners of his mouth.

"You've got four dead girls, and you don't think there is a reason to ask if they played cards?" I raised my arms and let them slap against my sides. It had great effect on the Cuban Red Neck. He flinched, or at least blinked rather heavily.

"Is he still there?" asked Vernon, pointing toward the conference room.

Tony stared a moment then motioned toward the room with his thumb. "Have at him."

I started to fall in behind Vernon, but Tony, caught once, wouldn't allow his authority to slip completely away.

"Not you! You aren't a sworn deputy."

"Never stopped you before," I said. "Besides, he's not under arrest. This is just an interview, sir!" I saluted and tried to follow Vernon again.

"Stop!" Tony's face reddened, even puffed a bit over his collar. "You'll stay right here." He jabbed his finger downward as though fixing me to a marked spot.

Vernon disappeared behind the conference door. I put my hands behind my back and rocked on my heels, doing the toe-heel preacher movement I had seen Loman perform when he thought he knew it all. I stood only a few feet from Tony who wouldn't move even though he desperately wanted to be away from me.

"You and Vernon go back a-ways, right?" I asked. He hated small talk; it was a way to really fester an anger.

"Long ways," he said and glanced toward the room.

"Bet you know a lot about each other." I smiled.

"I know enough. He's a good man."

"Yeah, like you knew about his drinking problem some time back." I grinned when he couldn't find a retort. "You told me, re-member?"

"He told you, too."

"Yeah. He tells me a lot." I smiled again. Vernon had never told me anything about Tony that was just between the two. He did hint once that Tony overlooked a lot of Vernon's antics because of a big *faux pas* on a long ago case that Tony had made.

Tony paced a few steps one way, then returned. "What has he told you?"

"Lots," I said and shrugged. I moved away and leaned against the wall.

"Lots of what?"

"Stuff." I kept quiet.

"I see." Tony nodded and glared at me, then took off toward his own office.

I waited until the door opened to the room where Marie sat drinking her seltzer. The deputy who brought it to her met me as she left. "That woman isn't well," she whispered.

I nodded and sat down at the end of the conference table. Marie sipped the drink and moaned once in a while. She kept one hand across her belly.

"Is all this causing your stomach to ache?" When she didn't answer, I continued. "It would upset mine to no end. I once got into such a state of anxiety that my stomach twirled like a washing machine." I watched her finish off the seltzer. "It docs go away, however. Especially when the problem is resolved."

She lowered her head and hiccuped. When she raised her face again, she stared at me. "How do you resolve murder?"

"It's his murder, Marie. Not yours." I returned her stare.

She sat still a moment, then began to shake her head. She closed her eyes and a tear slid down one cheek. "I feel like I've inherited it." She pulled out a tissue from one pocket and dabbed at her eye. When she had dried it, she turned on the table, wiping up any evidence of a seltzer glass and any dust that may have accumulated there. She looked around for a trash can.

"I'll take it," I said. "They don't seem to have one in here."

"You people aren't too clean, are you?" She held up the tissue, revealing black dirt from the table top.

Vernon appeared in the doorway. "Tony's office." He motioned for me to follow him. A deputy returned to the room to sit with Marie.

"We'll meet in the anteroom," said Tony outside his office. He had assembled Loman and two other detectives along with Vernon and me. A secretary followed him with a box of papers.

Inside the conference room that had been used as the war room for the rape/murder cases, we took chairs around a table stacked with folders, some empty. The cork boards on the walls still held the photos of the victims and their bones.

"Loman will fill you in," said Tony. He took a seat in a far corner, but couldn't sit still.

Loman's body rose on his toes, and he began to read from a sheaf of papers.

"First three girls—Pensacola and Madison and Palmetto River—were young and ran away from home." He pointed to the photos. "First on the board, that is. The first to die was, of course, this one." He pointed to the photo of the bones taken from the Palmetto Springs Cave. "Gaylin Newberry didn't exactly run away from home. She ran away from the road, tried to make it in a world her life hadn't prepared her for." He took a deep breath, proud of his philosophy on the poor girl's life. "But the four have something in common, we just found out. They all had a job or two or at least proximity with a traveling carnival, and they all passed through a truck stop along I-10."

He turned toward a map that was ready to topple from its worn tape on the wall. "Now, this latest filly." He stopped and gulped, realizing his political incorrectness. "Latest victim. She's got a record all over the place at every truck stop across the top of the state." He pulled out a photo from his coat pocket and handed it to another detective to pass among us. "That's her gig, what she does for the customer, I guess." Loman wiped a fist across his mouth.

The photo showed a nearly naked Yasmina, dressed in what she must have thought was harem garb. She had sewed on streamers of fake coins to a scanty bikini top and bottom. Her long hair hung limp and sparse across her shoulders. With the help of too much lip color, she pouted.

"She danced for her customers?" I asked, nearly laughing at the grotesque image.

"Seems so," said Loman. "Out in the parking lot sometimes. Didn't get paid for it, but that was her tease, her lead to more profitable activities." He blushed and wouldn't look at me.

Loman's forehead dripped with sweat in spite of the cool evening. He started to say more but motioned for another detective to tell what he knew. The other man, a younger replica of Loman without the sleepy eyes, took the floor.

"We questioned lots of people at these truck stops. Seems Yasmina did her own tricks but was sometimes willing to get a few girls to help her out."

"Business was good," said Loman who tried to be funny.

"And, sometimes the customers were not only truck drivers. They were show people who drove their trailers on the circuit and frequented truck stops."

"That's not all," added Loman. He shoved his hand in the air to tell the detective to stay there and tell the rest.

"We got Cannon to confess he had seen her around the card games, and that Zigfield had availed himself of her services a few times." The man looked to Loman.

"And Beaufont?" I said from the rear of the room. I felt I had to comfort these men. In spite of seeing horrors on a daily basis, they still had trouble talking about seduction, rape, and pimping in front of a woman.

"Cannon thinks he might have come around a few times, but the man never played in the games."

"So Cannon does know who Beaufont is—was?"

"Seems so," said Tony who took over the front of the room. "And he was at the card games near Rinks' farm as far as Cannon can remember."

"Has anyone looked into Cannon's alibis?" I stared at each of the detectives.

"He checks out," said Loman. "We can't pin anything on him. Seemed genuinely concerned when Ziggie disappeared."

"I've got a question," I said and stepped closer to the front. Tony stiffened. "Did anyone ask Cannon about his involvement with Marie Beaufont?"

Tony smiled and relaxed. "Just did. He says the woman tried to come on to him a few times, but he never found her appealing enough to take the risk. Besides, he said it was for money and that's something he doesn't part with easily."

"I see, and you believe him?"

Tony tensed again. "Until we know better. Right now, we're looking for Rinks and Zigfield." He changed the subject quickly. "Loman is going out again to hit some of the truck stops between here and the Georgia border. Any of you got questions you want him to ask, say so now."

"Sounds like a circus act, all right," I said as Vernon and I drove first the paved highway, then the dirt road to my swamp home. I rested my head against the window and watched the darkness interrupted by a distant porch light or some pickup truck headlights far back into the thick forest.

The closer we came to my end of the swamp, the less lights showed through the trees. People lived back there, communed with an assortment of dangerous snakes, snapping turtles, alligators, and deer who ate their vegetable patches. Unless you knew them, you'd think it was all moss and undergrowth, and strange animal noises. Those people knew the swamp and could navigate it, like Pasquin, in the darkness.

"Rinks knows this area," I said and lifted my head. "He could hide in a thousand places."

"Or be dead in another thousand, like at the bottom of the river." Vernon squeezed my hand.

Vernon stayed the night as he often did these days. Our affair had become comfortable and familiar. Plato greeted him as readily as he did me. We nibbled on left-over ham and biscuits we had picked up from a fast food place. Then we nibbled on each other until exhaustion sent two middle-aged divers into oblivion.

Sometime between the passion of the moment and hazy after glow, I heard the crunch of footsteps somewhere away from the house. *Why isn't Plato barking?* When I nudged Vernon, he answered with the heavy breathing of satisfied sleep. I eased from the covers and tiptoed downstairs. Standing near the back door, I listened. Swamp critters made little noise in the cold of winter, but they were dead silent when something alien ran among them. I opened the door and checked to see if the screen was hooked. An outside sensor light had come on, but this was common in the swamp. Too many creatures roamed during the night. Cold air entered silently and engulfed me. For a moment, I thought this is what the tomb must feel like, presuming one could feel anything by the time he got to the tomb. Beyond the area of the light, pitch black took control. Maybe a deer, I thought. The crunch of the steps had an unsteady, almost uncoordinated gait. In a few moments, they faded into the distance.

"Maybe Edwin is chasing Sylvester," I said.

"It's down to twenty-four this morning," moaned Vernon. "Care for a dive?"

"It would be just like Tony to come up with one," I said. I handed him a cup of coffee. "Pancakes, eggs, oatmeal?" I shook a box of cold cereal in his face.

"You know the way to man's heart," he said. "Cook me up an omelet."

I poured the flakes into a bowl and passed him the milk jug.

"Wonder where Plato got off to last night," I said. "Pretty cold out for a swamp dog."

"Probably chasing a Florida panther," said Vernon as he scooped cereal into his mouth. "You know that hound could be some kind of swamp phantom for the life he leads out there."

"Not always around when I need him." I had abandoned the cereal for hot toast when the phone rang.

"Your college," said Vernon and passed the receiver. "I'm off." Vernon gulped his coffee and headed for his patrol car. "Got fair duty all day. Catch me there."

The phone call broke the peace I had planned for myself during the morning hours. There would be no cozy moment by the fire to read a book or an hour or two to make fudge. The dean was calling in the linguistics faculty for an emergency meeting.

I sat in the cold office, my down coat still zipped around me. "What's with the heat?" My voice blew mist toward my colleagues who huddled in their chairs like Eskimos in a drafty igloo.

"Turned off for vacation or not working at all," said the phonetics expert. She wore green and white speckled earmuffs. "Where is the man?"

"I'm going to use his phone and call maintenance if we have to sit in this cold chair one more minute." Another colleague who had just joined the faculty spouted off with his cock-sure threat. His hotheaded remarks had more than once offended some of his colleagues as well as the dean. No one expected him to last to full professorship.

"Sorry about this," said the dean as he entered. He wore a turtle-neck sweater that reeked of moth balls. Heavy winter clothing didn't often get aired in Florida. "We have to choose a temporary chair. Greenberg has some kind of dementia, maybe won't be coming back." He sat behind his desk and began to draw a file towards him. "I don't have time to take over his duties. One of you will have to do it."

We looked at each other. This meant deciding who would teach what and lots of other little perks that caused squabbles among department members.

"We aren't all here," I said.

"Three people headed out of town and won't be back until next semester. We can't consider them. This has to be someone who plans to stay around." The dean scanned a list before him. "Also has to be someone permanent."

"Interim won't do for me," said one man who had been there longer than the rest of us. "I'm off to Miami tomorrow."

Two others shook their heads. They were heavy into research and publishing, trying to survive in academia.

"Luanne?" The dean stared at me.

"Oh, no," I said. "I'm barely staying with teaching right now."

"You're into this law stuff, right?" The dean picked up a pencil and made some marks on his list.

"Big time! Making schedules and nursing fractured egos isn't my style." I felt panic rise in my throat.

"It's interim, and you're qualified." He pulled off his glasses and stared at me.

"Manny's secretary can help you," said one woman who spoke with a lisp.

"Sir!" I begged with my eyes, but the dean circled a name on his list.

"I'm appointing you, Luanne, just until we get a permanent chair. And that could be soon. You will, of course, sit in on interviews."

I shut my eyes and sighed. If I refused, the department could be in chaos and I would get the worst of the class offerings. I convinced myself that in spite of the work, I'd at least be in control. I nodded.

"Good!" The dean lifted a thick folder and placed it in my lap. "Greenberg's duties. Just get the semester started." He moved to the door and held it open for us. "Now let's all go home to central heat."

Life would not be good this vacation, I thought. Right now, chasing alligator assassins and serial killers in underwater caves sounded inviting. Pushing off first-year students to instructors who felt college should protect them from the inadequacies of high school teens but didn't, was a fate worse than a tub full of frogs. Manny Greenberg had turned into something that resembled a sixties drone trying to deal with it. Now his mind was nearly a mass of blank slate.

I sighed and hugged the folder against by chest as I walked through the cold air to the parking lot.

CHAPTER 18

"You're the new chair?" Vernon grinned and tussled my hair. I had stopped at the fairgrounds to give him the news and see if any progress had been made.

"Interim chair. Don't tease me. I'll be up hours trying to figure out the mess of next semester." I pulled my parka hood over my head. "Can't you find a warm place to stand?" We were in the middle of the booth area. Everything was boarded tight until the final evening after which the fair would fold its acts and roll away to some other city.

"We're waiting for Loman. He's been checking out backgrounds." Vernon's bald head was covered in a knitted ski cap. His gloved hands held a cup of coffee that had lost its steam.

The trailers that housed Snake Boy and Jubile and the other carnival acts, freak acts left over from the glory days of Lobster Boy and real Siamese twins, began to stir. Cannon had arranged for a coffee tent where a huge urn brewed up enough caffeine to wake a hermit. Boxes of doughnuts rested on a card table.

"Better get one before Jubile gets here," laughed one dwarf clown. He coughed violently, the morning routine of a lifetime smoker. His fellow clowns tumbled out of their shared trailer behind him and helped themselves to steaming cups and glazed breakfasts. They stamped their short legs to keep warm.

Julene joined them without saying a word. Her morning frown said, "Don't bother me." The clowns, out of costume, looking more like little trolls, stood aside and eyed her, but said nothing.

When Jubile showed up, he was dressed in a long kimono robe and thong slippers. He brought his own mug and filled his cup then found a wooden chair that would hold his bulk. Snake Boy edged into the group, filled his cup and stood aside with the clowns.

"Found that reptile, yet?" asked the first dwarf. He coughed through a sneering laugh.

Snake Boy glared at him and didn't answer.

"Gonna have hell to pay if it eats a kid," said another little man.

"Might even steal a baby out of its crib," laughed another.

Snake Boy turned toward the men, his eyes burning. "Maybe he'll eat one of you little turds." He grabbed a doughnut and headed toward his trailer.

The little men moved around to keep warm, jumping up and down occasionally. Julene pulled her thick sweater tightly about her and sat on the steps of a nearby trailer. Her face looked old, strained. She stared into blank space as she sipped the hot liquid.

Only Jubile seemed undaunted by the cold. He leaned back and the chair creaked beneath him. His robe parted up to the knee, revealing heavy flab intertwined with blue veins. He sipped, then closed his eyes in a succession of movements that shut out the world.

"I'd say they weren't a happy lot," I said. Vernon and I had been watching the scene.

"Don't care much for each other," he added. "I need to heat up this cup." He poured out his cold coffee, and we joined the troupe.

Vernon held out his cup without asking if he could drink from their coffee maker. One dwarf nodded. Everyone else ignored us. I took a styrofoam cup from a plastic bag and filled it. There was no cream or sugar on the table.

"Doughnut?" Vernon had lifted the box to an assortment of

glazed and iced confections. I pulled out a long chocolate thing.

We stood around, moving our feet to try and keep out the cold, our breath forming clouds as we exhaled. The little men glanced up at us but didn't talk. Julene was still in a trance, perhaps in a world where she cuddled grandchildren in a cozy farm house.

"Any sign of Ziggie?" said Vernon.

"Ziggie don't make signs," laughed the first dwarf. His coughing eased now that he was puffing on his morning cigarette.

Vernon smiled and nodded.

"Just what part does Ziggie play in your clown act?" I asked.

A stir began, not words, but a kind of mumbling and grunting. I looked down at the men. They shot guilty looks in my direction.

"He's the longlegs clown, the driver of the cart we ride in." The first dwarf said. "My coffee's cold." He head for the urn and re-filled his cup.

"So he actually puts on make-up and joins the act?"

"Of course. You don't think we just bring him along for the ride, do you?" Another dwarf with a particularly evil scowl finally spoke. "He's the normal-sized one."

"Who will drive tonight?" I asked.

No one spoke until the silence felt as though it would pop.

"We've modified the act. Cannon will suit up and drive the cart, but he won't do any of the silly stunt work." The first little man tossed his cigarette to the ground and stomped on it. He lit another.

"Cannon?" Vernon spoke into the air. He avoided direct contact with any of the men, giving the impression he would talk to them all equally. "Isn't he a little big for Ziggie's clown suit?"

"Got his own," said the first man. "Keeps it around for emergencies. And with Ziggie, you get emergencies every now and then."

"Heads off with a tart about every other week," said the scowler.

"Picks them up where he finds them. Wonder the man don't have AIDS." He gripped his coffee cup with both hands in a strangle hold.

"Meets them at carnivals?" Vernon walked to the maker and filled his cup another inch.

"Truck stops, carnivals, gas stations—you name it. Got to have his p…." The man stopped suddenly and glanced in my direction.

I shot a quick look at Julene on the stoop of the trailer. She seemed not to hear.

"Has the man ever taken off with one of his—tarts?" Vernon winked at me.

"All the time. Only," said the first dwarf, "we usually know. Things give him away. The girl is around his trailer. He's drinking a lot. He's got no time for the act. Next thing you know, he's off to some motel room."

"And this time?" Vernon sipped slowly.

"No signs. No girl. Just gone."

"I hear he likes to play cards." I followed Vernon's lead and re-filled my cup.

"Does, but he's never been on a three-day binge of card playing. Does it at night and comes back here to sleep until show time." The little man shot another cigarette butt to the ground and pulled out his pack.

A silence settled over the bitter cold morning. Only the stamping of feet and an occasional grunt from Jubile disturbed the moment. Then the first dwarf decided to talk.

"You want to know about Yasmina, right?" He stared up at Vernon and me, a look of fear behind the stream of smoke from his cigarette.

Vernon nodded.

"He met her over three years ago at a truck stop. She had this dancing act. Only it wasn't an act, just a treat before the bang, if you get my meaning." He glanced at me, but the guilty look had gone. "She came with us for a few days, then got dropped off at another truck stop or headed out with some carnival barker. We'd go for a few months without seeing her on the circuit. Then, pow! There she was in the trailer again, stinking up the place with perfume. She had this knack, you see, of getting real friendly with men. She even offered them another type of girl if they didn't like her."

"Another type?" Vernon stared at the man.

He nodded.

"You mean," I added, "that Yasmina would procure other girls for Ziggie or whomever?"

The man shrugged. "Procure? She got them from the road, from bus stations, and I figure she told them how to charge. Bet she got a commission, too."

I shot Vernon a glance. "Did she ever get girls for anyone else in the carnival?"

"Could be." The little man shrugged, crumpled his empty cigarette package and tossed it on the ground.

"You've all been questioned about Beaufont, right?" Vernon didn't wait for an answer. "You don't seem to have known him. Could Yasmina have been involved with him?"

The man shook his head. "Workers come and go. We don't memorize names, don't make friends much. Little people like us don't always get treated kindly by big people." He shot a nervous glance to his comrades. "Beaufont could have been around. We just don't remember him. If he had the hots for female, Yasmina would have found him."

The men edged away from us, moving among the trailers. The last one who passed us said under his breath, "Better her than us."

"Tried to join my act once," said a shrill voice from the trailer stoop. Julene held out her cup for Vernon to refill it.

"Yasmina wanted to be part of…?" I waved a hand in Jubile's direction.

"Only she wanted to take it a step farther. Make it look like, well, you know."

"On stage?"

"Yeah. Probably get us arrested." Julene wrapped her tiny fingers around the cup. The backs of her hands sported the liver spots of an old lady.

"Who told her no?" I asked.

"Who do you think?" She smiled over the cup. "Only one of us wields the whip."

I wondered about the day I saw Jubile slap her face. The woman had the harsh look of a carnival drifter, but she showed no signs of bruising or broken limbs.

"Don't mean she didn't come around after the act," chuckled Jubile who still had his eyes closed.

"Come round for what?" laughed Julene.

Jubile stopped laughing and opened his eyes. He grunted and reached for another doughnut.

"That's his sex!" said Julene in a high-pitched whisper, pointing to the doughnut box. "Don't go no further than that." She cackled between quick sips of hot coffee.

In the distance, Loman's patrol car pulled onto the grounds. Vernon and I nodded good-days to the fat man act and headed in his direction.

"Jubile is impotent?" I said.

"Could be." Vernon smiled. "Got lots of mental images about how he'd function if he weren't."

Loman's half-closed eyes looked as though they would shut any minute. The bags underneath showed signs of being up half the night.

"Just tried out every truck stop between here and Georgia," he said. "All got cheap gas. I'll give them that much credit."

"And coffee shops," said the uniform who joined him. "I've had enough eggs in six hours to grow feathers."

"Any data?" said Vernon.

Loman gave locations and scenarios much like the ones the dwarf had given us. Yasmina used truck stops as a sort of headquarters, but she worked the carnivals and any other traveling group that frequented cheap motels. And, she had occasionally appeared with another girl at her side.

"Anybody see Beaufont?" I asked.

"Nobody was sure," said Loman. "I showed the photo. Got lots of shrugs."

"The man was a serial killer," I said. "Late twenties, right? He didn't play cards with the other men much, and he doesn't seem to have made much of an impression when he worked the carnivals."

"Meaning?" Loman looked deflated.

"He blended in, didn't distract from the norm, and didn't become one of the boys. But, he looked for girls—quietly, and just maybe he used Yasmina to point him in the right direction."

Loman sighed. "You're probably right. Lots of people seem to remember the most recent victims as girls who came into the cafe with Yasmina."

The uniform, silent until now, asked the question at hand. "Who bumped off Yasmina? Some family member of one of the victims or a boyfriend?"

"A pimp?" asked Vernon.

"No evidence of one existing," said Loman. "Yasmina worked

on her own."

We stood in the cold morning, blowing fog and frowning. No one had the answer beyond the typical serial-killer pattern. But he had been found, and given the ultimate sentence, it seemed.

"Are we assuming that Beaufont was killed in retribution for his murders?" I asked.

The men glanced at each other. Loman replied, "Can't really assume that. It could have been robbery or a victim turning on her killer. The only thing we've got to go on is that the weapon and location of the wound are the same."

"Sounds like retribution," said Vernon.

We became silent as in the distance we watched Cannon emerge from his trailer and head for the coffee urn. He pulled a hooded sweatshirt over his head as he made the short trek. His mass of curly hair and beard looked the same as yesterday. It wasn't something he combed.

"He knows more than he's telling," I said.

Through the frigid air, a familiar voice sent out a "Whowhee!" We turned toward the parking lot where Pasquin and Edwin got out of Harlie's patrol car. He headed in our direction with Edwin trotting along in his uneven gait.

"Cold and frosty morning," said Pasquin who rubbed his hands together. He wore the heavy surplus coat and his battered straw hat. Edwin joined us with a silly grin, his hair sticking up in attention to the world. He had donned a lined army camouflage jacket and wore rubber wading boots.

"Why so early?" I asked.

Pasquin smiled and thumbed toward Edwin.

"I'm going to make one last search of the grounds for Sylvester," he said and pushed his hair up straighter. I figured a lifetime of this had permanently styled his hair that way. "Pasquin offered to help."

"We got sticks in the car," Pasquin said. "I don't yearn to bare hand a long snake that could swallow me whole."

Harlie followed, carrying two poles with curved metal endings. They belonged to Edwin who used them to capture swamp snakes for his own delight.

"I want to see either one of you tackle big old Sylvester," said Vernon.

Harlie juggled a set of keys. "Got to get going before people stir around too much. Fish and Game says no more searching here after today. They figure the snake has run off somewhere and froze to death."

"Do pythons freeze?" I asked.

"Why not?" said Pasquin. "Maybe they crack like lizards."

I watched Edwin and Pasquin follow Harlie to one of the Quonset huts. It had heaters, a place where a snake might find warmth. "Is that old tale really true?"

"If they find the thing, cracked or not, there's going to be a lot of whooping and hollering," laughed Vernon.

Loman and his deputy strolled toward the coffee urn. Before they arrived, I saw Cannon dart around a trailer and open a car door.

"Think we should follow him?" I nudged Vernon.

"Tony just pulled in," he said. He headed toward the parking lot.

I had no desire to listen to a grouchy chief detective, and Cannon's movements intrigued me. I headed for my own car. Backing out of a side entrance, I managed to pull up behind Cannon on the main street leading away from town. Tailing cars wasn't my talent, but I'd seen Vernon do it enough to avoid detection—I hoped.

Traffic was light for a cold morning in November. The few cars on the street were headed in the operation direction. Cannon drove his van at the speed limit. It was impossible to tell if he saw me in the rear view mirror, but the green van was battered and dirty, not easy to lose. He took the street until it turned into a highway that headed toward the springs and would finally end at the Gulf.

We passed tiny wood frame houses that had been turned into mechanic's shops, corner lots that had been turned into cement making quarries, and numerous trailer parks tucked back into trees. At a major crossroad, Cannon pulled into a gas station to fill up. I went past and found a shady dirt road that wouldn't be too visible from the main road. With any luck, he'd continue this way.

After waiting twenty minutes and thinking he may have taken the turnoff, I spied the green van moving slowly past. I waited until he was nearly a mile away and took off after him. We passed all the dirt lanes that ran into the thick forest. I slowed as we came to the Palmetto Springs turn-off, but Cannon kept on the main highway.

"Sure hope he's not going all the way to Panama City," I said.

When the terrain turned from high forest trees to low scrub and brackish water ponds, I knew we were near the coast. Cannon's van slowed. Without signaling, he turned onto a dirt lane. This would be my test. He could trick me here, wait for me and trap me in a situation where I could only back out to the main highway. I took a breath and turned after him.

Cannon's van kicked up enough dust to let me know he hadn't stopped. My little Honda bounced along the ruts. At one point, Cannon's van pulled over, pushing aside low sand-growing shrubs, and made way for a truck pulling a boat in the opposite direction. I pulled over, too, and the driver of the truck saluted as he edged his vehicle past me. By the time I continued the chase, Cannon's van was gone.

Easing down the rutted road, I kept my eyes peeled for anything that sat in the scrub brush on the sides. This didn't seem possible after awhile. The sides were puddles of tide water. In the distance,

I saw the top of sheds typical of boat ramps. The road forked and circled a clearing large enough to hold a dirt parking lot and two wooden structures. An inlet covered one entire side. A boat ramp had been built here, and someone was backing up to launch himself on a fishing trip.

Cannon's van rested near one of the wooden buildings. I parked at the other end of the lot and eased out, grabbing a hat from the back seat. Cramming the hat over my short gray-speckled brown locks, I hoped for the look of a fisherman.

The wooden structure turned out to be a bait and tackle shop that also sold a few grocery staples like sardines and chips, things that could sustain an all-day fishing trip. It had a useless screen door that stood open all the time. In the hot summers, the wooden door would have been open, but in the cold, it was shut tight. I moved away from it and pretended to be waiting for someone as two men entered. They nodded. Shoving open the warped door proved a bit difficult, and once they had done it, they left it open.

I moved to the edge of the doorway. Cannon stood a few feet away and spoke to someone.

"I'll be under the dock shed," he said. "Tell him to meet me there."

I took a chance and peeked inside. Cannon had purchased a soft drink and was speaking into his cell phone. I darted back to the side as he headed out and toward a tiny cement structure that read *Marlins* and *Mermaids* on opposite sides. Someone had decided all marlins were male, I guessed. He turned the soda bottle up and gulped the last of the liquid and tossed the bottle into a trash drum. He darted inside. When he came out, he was still adjusting his fly.

I looked at the docking shed. It would not be easy to hide there. For one thing, there was no other person around. Even if I sat at the opposite end, I'd be noticed. I finally decided that sitting in my car would give me a clear view even if I could hear nothing.

Cannon moved toward the boat shed and took a seat on a wooden bench. He stared out at the open water, doing nothing. I huddled down in my car, trying to stay warm. Finally a truck pulled into the lot and moved slowly as though the driver was unsure of his destination. He spied the space directly behind me and parked.

I pulled the hat closer to my head but watched from the side mirror. A familiar body emerged. The lanky, tubercular quality couldn't be missed.

"Ziggie!" I turned slightly away as he passed my car. The man pulled out a cigarette pack and lit up as he walked quickly toward the boat landing.

CHAPTER 19

Sitting in the cold Honda, I would have given anything to hear the conversation under the boat shed. Cannon gestured with one hand, scratching his mass of curls with the other. Ziggie stomped his feet to keep warm, smoked and paced as he listened. He finally nodded, tossed down a cigarette butt and hustled off to his truck. Cannon watched for a moment but made no move. I wanted to follow Ziggie, but I was afraid of being caught between him and Cannon on the narrow road.

Cannon turned suddenly and headed into the cement men's room. When he came out, he got into the van and drove away from the dock. Figuring he would return to the fairgrounds, I followed. But he turned a different way when he reached the main highway. He was taking the exact route I would use to get to my swamp house.

I sighed relief when Cannon didn't turn on my rutted road. Instead, he moved closer to Palmetto Springs Park and turned on a road that skirted the government boundaries. I couldn't follow him on the forest lane, too easily seen. I parked the Honda in a clump of trees near the paved road and walked down the dirt path. It was barely wide enough for Cannon's van; the sides would be scratched by overhanging scrub oak limbs.

Dodging the spear points of palmetto bushes and dipping under tree limbs, I walked the short distance to the edge of a pond. Cannon had driven halfway around and parked near a group of tall pines. He leaned against the side of the van and watched the water.

I stayed put in the trees at the end of the lane.

The wait didn't take long. Cannon stood up straight and looked to his right as though something were approaching. A man appeared and the two spoke in angry tones. I was too far away to understand their words, but the when the other man moved in front of Cannon and placed one hand on his shoulder, I recognized the face.

"Rinks!" I whispered. "He's hiding." I wanted to move closer and took the opportunity to move across the dirt lane into the trees behind Cannon's van. As I moved closer, the voices became louder and angrier.

By the time I was directly behind the van, the sound of flesh on flesh echoed throughout the forest. From a few trees back, I saw Cannon's curly head flat on the ground. Rinks stood over him.

"Get them off my back!" he yelled, then turned back into the forest.

My first instinct was to help Cannon off the ground. He had a nasty red spot near one eye but didn't seem to be bleeding. He groaned and sat on the ground, finally struggling to pull himself to the van. Opening the door, he reached inside and pulled out a pistol. He moved to the front and aimed the gun toward the path that Rinks took but he didn't shoot. The man was long gone, disappeared into a swamp terrain he would know well.

When I was sure Cannon's van was headed back to the fairgrounds, I turned off and drove to Fogarty Spring and Mama's Table. It was lunch time, and I decided to call Tony while sitting in front of one of her more famous Southern delights.

"You say Rinks is alive?" said Mama. She sat in a vacant chair near my window booth. "Got himself into some kind of trouble, I'll bet." She sipped on a hot tea spiced with a cinnamon stick. "Lots of talk about card games down in the woods."

I spoke into the cell phone and let Tony in on my tracking abilities.

He fumed silently, then said he'd meet me at Mama's—with Cannon along for the ride.

Mama took it easy this morning. She had one last cooking duty in the sheriff's booth and wasn't going to wear herself out in the morning.

"Cold weather has arrived," she said as a customer opened the door and let in a blast of arctic air. "Welcome to the Sunshine State."

"Mama," I said, stuffing a fried oyster into my mouth. The cook had made the plate special for me with extra hush puppies and a large bowl of cheese grits. Instead of the menu coleslaw, she had handed me a bowl of danzy peas fresh from someone's garden. They had been cooked with a piece of fat back for flavoring. "What's with you and Harlie?" I held my breath and hoped future treats were not in jeopardy.

Mama moved her broad hips to the other side of my booth. She stirred her tea. "Ought to add something strong to this if I'm going to have to talk about that man."

"You don't have to talk about him. I just wondered why all the bickering." I made a satisfied face when I bit off the end of a hush puppy.

"Guess I need to, " she said. "That pecan pie out of the oven yet?" She yelled into the kitchen. Without answering, the waitress brought her a piece on a saucer. "Can't very well talk about my past without some fuel, right?" She forked off a bite and put it in her mouth. "Um, that man just don't know what he's missed all these years."

"Harlie? Are you saying you could have married him?"

"Did."

"Did what?"

"Married him." Mama ate her pie steadily, stopping only for a sip of tea.

"You and Harlie were married?"

She shrugged, took a bite of pie, and glanced at me. "Still are."

"You're Harlie's wife?" I couldn't continue eating. In all the years I'd known Mama, she was a fabulous cook who ruled Fogarty Spring, who fed fishermen, flirted with them, and went off at night to live in her cabin in the woods. She hated being on water but loved living beside it. She and Pasquin had, as she called it, a "food thing going."

"On paper, yeah." She blushed. Her bottle-blond hair curled around her chubby face. When she smiled she seemed a female Bacchus. And she was smiling now. "We'd been sweethearts once upon a time. I think I told you that. He got the hots for somebody else, and I dumped him. Think that happened three or four times. Then one night we just run off to Georgia and got hitched." She laughed and yelled for more hot water and another tea bag.

"I used to hear about underage kids eloping across the Georgia border," I said.

"Bet you never heard about us," she smiled again. "Got hitched, had a wild and wooly wedding trip up to Savannah, then got back here and reality hit." She frowned and dunked her tea bag into the water like drowning a rat.

"He ran off with a floozy?" I tried to nibble on an oyster.

"The floozy was the military. Birdbrain never told me he'd enlisted. Just had to get married before he ran off to boot camp." She wound the tea bag and its string around her spoon and squeezed out the water.

"You got left here with no one," I said and sympathized.

"Honesty with me is pretty important," she said and squinted her eyes. "See this tea bag? I could have done that to him."

"And what happened when he came back?"

Mama leaned toward me, her face red now with anger.

"Nothing happened. I wouldn't let him in the door. I says to him, 'You lie to me, you ain't going to lie with me.'" She leaned back and smiled, satisfied that she'd told him. "You want some dessert?"

I tried eating the rest of the oysters and managed to down the peas. "Why didn't you divorce him?" I had seen Mama's temper a few times and never wanted to be the brunt of it. I could have been in dangerous waters with a question like that.

She cleared her dish and cup from the table. "Just didn't. Costs money, you know, and I figured he'd caused it, he could pay for it."

She moved into the kitchen to give orders for the evening. I finished eating and sipped on coffee until Tony's patrol car arrived. Vernon was with him.

"One of these days, Luanne, you're going to end up shot in a sinkhole and we'll never find you," said Tony.

"Vernon will dive for me," I said. "He'll find me." I couldn't resist a grin.

"We got Cannon out there in the car with a deputy." Tony gestured to his patrol car that sat at the river landing. "He ain't one bit happy about this."

"You're worried about happiness now, Tony?"

Mama brought coffee cups and poured for both the men. "Pie?"
Tony shook his head. Vernon smiled and nodded.

"He says he has no idea where Ziggic and Rinks are." Tony took the pie from Mama even though he hadn't ordered it. "You better be right about this."

"And if I'm not, you're going to ban me from the sheriff's department, not allow me to dive, and in general force me back to school marming and cooking where women belong." My resistance had broken down. Maybe it was Harlie's betrayal of Mama or Tony's persistent insinuation that I wasn't quite good enough, but I needed confrontation at the moment.

It didn't happen. Loman's car pulled up and he hurried into the dining area.

"Search of Ziggie's trailer didn't bring up much except he's been entertaining a woman there. Got an address of a motel in Gadsen County. Seems this Yasmina had a kind of permanent room in a dump over there. Got this." He passed a legal-size envelope to Tony. He didn't wait for him to open it. "Seems the woman got a few hundred dollars all of a sudden, just in this past week. Don't think any of her tricks would have paid her that much." He glanced at me and blushed.

"Maybe she did her belly dance, too, " I said.

"Still too much money for her, er, class." Loman shifted in the booth, his stomach pressing against the table.

"Well, Loman, hookers who travel truck stops can't be diamond studded." I pushed my coffee cup to the edge of the table for a refill.

"She got this money from somebody," he said and ordered pie.

"Blackmail?" Vernon asked.

"Check Ziggie's and Cannon's bank accounts," said Tony. He shoveled the last piece of pie into his mouth. "Let's go, Luanne. You need to show us exactly where you followed this man."

Tony let me ride with Loman. The thought of sitting in front and having Cannon stare at the back of my head didn't set well with me. Loman was another case. He hadn't been able to finish what he ordered, so he folded up several hush puppies in a napkin and laid them on the seat beside him. He drove with one hand, popped the cornmeal delights into his mouth with the other.

"You ever get grease on the radio?"

"All the time. On the steering wheel, too. Hand me a tissue." He pointed to the glove compartment.

"No guns in here, just candy bars and tissues." I passed the box to him. "I really feel safe now."

"Got confessions out of men who were offered chocolate," he grinned. His heavy lidded eyes looked as though he could sleep at any moment.

"What's this about card games?"

"Seems a group of men have these organized games and certain people belong. The stakes are high. 'Course it's illegal, and no law is going to uphold the debt somebody owes."

"I see, and if somebody loses big time and can't pay, the others go after him."

"Kind of a swamp mob action, I call it." He chewed on the last hush puppy. "Don't matter if it's uptown or in the creek, you're just as dead."

"Could Yasmina have been a gambler?"

"Doubt it. This is a man's club. Wouldn't have no women around except for...."

"Except for hooking," I finished his sentence for him. He nodded.

"May have hired some to cook or serve drinks, but haven't heard that yet."

We bumped onto the lane that took us to the boat dock. "You think Cannon knows about this?"

"Could be. Bet you Ziggie did, and most likely Rinks." He stood between me and the emerging Cannon.

I pointed out where Ziggie had met Cannon and gave Tony the license number on his truck. Cannon would say nothing.

"He's a friend, and I've promised," he said.

"Who's after him?" asked Tony.

Cannon shrugged. "He won't say. I'm just glad he's alive."

We headed back for the cars. Cannon avoided my eyes.

When we arrived at the narrow lane, Loman took the lead and followed my directions into the woods and toward the pond. "Da-yam!" he shouted every time the patrol car hit a bump or scraped against a tree limb. "Glad the boss is right behind us. I'd hate to have to explain the damage to this car."

The two cars came to a halt in front of the pond. I guided the men around to the spot where Rinks walloped Cannon in the face. Only a slight swelling under the curly beard was evidence that he'd been hit.

"Now, don't tell me Rinks is your friend," said Tony to Cannon. "He knocked you off your feet for some reason."

Cannon shuffled his feet on the sandy shore of the pond. He didn't want to say anything and grunted under his breath.

"Speak up," said Tony.

"Got himself in money trouble. That's about all I know."

"Why'd he hit you?" Loman moved in on one side, Vernon on the other. Tony stood between him and the forest. The only escape would be to jump in the pond.

"I wouldn't give him a loan," Cannon said. He closed his eyes and breathed relief. "He owes me, too, and I couldn't see giving him more."

The forest was silent, as though the snakes in their warm holes and the alligators sitting in cold sun rays wanted to hear more.

"Mr. Cannon," said Tony. "We're going to have to talk about all this gambling stuff."

Vernon and I didn't go to Tony's office. We had fair duty. Mama and Harlie had arrived at the booth and were setting up in silence. I felt queazy at first, knowing what I did about their lives. Their elopement had happened in the sixties. They had been married some forty years and no one knew—or at least I hadn't.

Pasquin joined us in the booth. He sat down hard on a straw chair and fanned himself with his hat. "That Edwin don't give up."

"No snake yet?" I pulled up a chair beside him.

He shook his head. "It's like he's lost a child. More concerned about it than Snake Boy is." Pasquin reached into a cooler and pulled out a can of soda. "Snake Boy wants the insurance," he chuckled. "Seems a little upset that Edwin is even trying to find him."

"I wonder how Snake Boy got Sylvester to disappear," I said. "Insurance fraud has been around a few years."

"Just what I told Edwin, but he won't have it. Says the snake got loose and is out there all alone somewhere."

Harlie headed off for the men's room, and Mama went to meet a deputy bringing in supplies. It was time to hit up the swamp genius.

"Pasquin, do you know that Mama is married to Harlie?" I turned my eyes, but not my head toward him.

"No!" But his protest didn't ring true.

"You do know, don't you?"

"Guess I helped them get to Georgia."

I looked at the old man. His face, lined and sagging, revealed eyes that shone with the mischief of a leprechaun.

"Harlie borrowed a truck from a friend to drive them up there, but Mama had to get away from her mama. I picked her up on the river and took her into Palmetto Springs to join him. Didn't want to get involved, but there was no stopping them." He chuckled. "Been a lot of changes over the years, but none in their marital status."

"Why didn't you tell me?" I pretended to slap at him.

"Just didn't think of it," he said. He leaned back in the chair. "It's been a consistency of the swamp, just like the gator buries her eggs in the mounds, like the anhinga spreads its wings to dry—just like them—Harlie and Mama have always had this attachment."

Mama returned to her spot in the booth, and we shut up about her.

"Okay, now tell me about gambling on the river," I said.

"Do better in a rocking chair on your porch," said Pasquin.

"Just pretend you're there," I said. "It's not sunset yet. I don't have any duties until the crowds get here. I've got all the time in the world to listen." I winked at Mama who had turned around to listen to us.

Pasquin placed his battered straw hat on his head and leaned back on two legs of the chair. He gazed off into the sky as though looking in the direction of his swamp would help him describe the scene.

"Been gambling on that river for a long time. Back in my day, they had some boats that run up and down, carrying customers who liked to play a little poker. For a while, somebody had a big boat anchored off the coast. Smaller boats would haul men out there for big gambling parties. Don't see that anymore. Drug runners got too dangerous for the more civilized card players." He accepted a coffee from Mama who had made it stronger than normal and filled it with sugar. "Lots of private games now, inside the vacation houses."

"What about big stakes games? You know, with men who play serious cards."

He nodded, sipped his coffee, and smiled approval at Mama. "I hear of a few places now and then."

"Rinks' place?"

He looked up in surprise. "Nope. But I hear some fellows use his landing to tie up and travel on land to a barn somewhere back in the woods." He grinned at me. "You planning on taking up poker,

Luanne?"

"Seems Rinks, Ziggie, and Cannon did." I nodded in the distance. The little men were standing around their trailer, gathering to get made up for the first evening performance.

"I heard Ziggie and Rinks are alive," said Pasquin.

"How in the world?" I had not said anything to him. Not one of us had the opportunity to let the information out to this old man of the swamp. It was like he had grown ears on the trees who listened for him.

"Edwin saw them both on one of his hunts for Sylvester."

CHAPTER 20

Edwin would have to answer to Tony. When I called to tell him Pasquin's information, he lost control. Between making nasty remarks about a meddlesome old man and a village idiot withholding information, he told me to make sure neither man left the grounds.

"I want to catch the clown act," I said. "Cannon isn't here to sub for Ziggie. Maybe one of the little guys will drive the cart."

"What are clowns doing at a fair?" asked Pasquin. "Don't they usually appear in a circus?"

"That's what I'd like to see." I didn't mention the adult nature of the Julene-Jubile act. Snake Boy was pretty obvious, but I planned to make a stink if I saw a bunch of little men in red noses, floppy ears, and nude below the waist. "Can you sell food for me during the first act?"

Pasquin glared at me, but he didn't say no. That meant yes from a man who had been my surrogate father and swamp guide for over forty years. "Wonder why one of them little men don't go after that little Julene?"

"She doesn't seem interested," I said. "Likes a full-sized man."

Pasquin chuckled. He eased off his seat and began setting out the napkin holders. Harlie had returned, his eyes darting from Pasquin to Mama.

The crowds came. Streams of teenagers and pockets of families with dads carrying their sons on their shoulders for one last jaunt into bizarre fun. Announcements came from the bull arena that the final riding contests would begin in thirty minutes. Men, full-sized, but dressed like Ziggie's clowns, rushed toward the fences. Their faces were painted and their clothes rag-tag, but they were cowboy in nature. These were the men who would distract the bull, prevent him from goring the thrown rider. Up close, they had the same carnival roughness as Ziggie's men. Their gnarled hands and wrinkled faces told stories of rope burns and beer nights.

I stood in front of the clown tent, its painted canvas sign laughing down at me in wide red clown mouths. A tall, thin clown had been painted driving a tiny car, his long legs poking straight out from the sides. Behind him, a half-dozen painted men looked happy and surprised.

A barker took his place next to the ticket booth. "See little men grow into big ones. Laugh until your belly pops. Take the kiddies. They love the tiny men." He droned into the microphone as people paid their money. I followed them.

Inside, there were a row of benches behind a rope. Between the rope and the back of the tent was empty space of dirt floor. One of the handlers hurried into the space and deposited a drum that had been painted blue and red. It resembled a wash tub turned upside down. He passed through the slit in the back opening. When the tent had filled, the barker came inside. I took a seat on the front row.

The barker told some jokes, the kind kids laughed at prior to Junior High. He was on his fourth, when a little man wobbled out and jerked on his coat. The dwarf, dressed in oversized shoes, a polka dot suit, and sporting flaring red sideburns, gestured for him to get out of the arena. A horn tooted, and out came the cart filled with little clowns and a big man driving. It began to chase the barker. The clown on the stage ran after it, trying to jump up with his buddies.

Children in the audience laughed and screeched as the antics of the little men approached the level of stooges. They conked each other with cloth clubs, rolled over and above each other in a leap frog movement. The tall clown didn't stay around. He parked the cart and left through the slit. After each tumble, the crowd applauded and the clowns began a new antic. The group began to jump hoops and cycle around on one wheelers. As they passed my seat, I could hear the huffing and puffing of aging lungs. Clown riders made a circle while those on foot stood between each one. They began to toss rings and juggle them high in the air. Pretending to compete, they tapped the cycles, causing the clowns to fall. Melee broke out as their juggling continued, now with the rings around their short legs and necks. When one man jumped high to catch a ring, he landed with an audible "oof" right in front of me. I leaned forward, my instinct to help him up. Something had happened. Money flew from his costume. It landed in the arena, and everyone howled. The other clowns paused for only a second, their crazy faces hiding a serious look behind the grease paint. They stared at the money, then at their fellow clown. He had frozen in one spot.

I leaned forward again to look at the bills that had fallen near the rope. They were real.

One of the clowns decided to make it part of the act and screeched. They all piled into the middle to grab the money, falling over each other until they made a mound. All except the one who dropped the money. He trotted around the back and ran through the slit in the canvas.

I didn't wait. I darted out the entrance and met the man as he scooted under the tent. He saw me and took off running toward the carnival rides. I followed him as far as the Merry-Go-Round and lost him. Searching the area, I spied him turning back toward the animal displays. He knew the set-up and could maneuver into small places. I ran towards him, shouting at Pasquin as I passed the sheriff's booth. "Get Tony!"

I pushed my body through throngs of children waiting for cotton candy and past teenagers who led their prize calves to the trucks that would take them to new farms or slaughter houses. The clown darted from one display to another, sometimes jumping beneath tables and traveling until he came to a wall. I felt silly, a full-grown woman chasing a tiny man and unable to catch him.

When the clown had reached the edge of the fairgrounds, the only place to turn was either the gate going out or the bull ring. Spying uniformed officers at the gates, he darted under the bull fence and joined the other clowns. The larger men, first puzzled by the addition, grew angry at his presence.

From a stall, a huge white brahma bull darted, tossing its behind high in the air, snorting ferocious protests at the ground as it tried to force off the rider. The young man on the bull gripped the rope in one hand, his other outstretched like an Ahab, beckoning others to join him in death. The rider had hold of two ropes. With a twist of his hand, the rope squeezed the bull's balls tighter. The animal jumped higher—which the rider hoped would make him more money if he could stay on. One squeeze too many and the bull hind quarters raised into the air and jerked sideways at the same time. The rider didn't have a chance. He flew some inches into the air and landed in the dirt. The animal, free of its tormentor, continued to buck, perhaps out of joy at seeing the downed rider within reach of its horns.

Clowns should have run into the arena, but the downed rider lay face down on the ground and covered his head with both arms. Other cowboy handlers rushed into the arena to distract the animal. From the side, a group of men dressed in silly costumes yelled and taunted the intruder clown. They danced and waved and jumped in front of him the same way they would have done in front of the bull. Ziggie's clown had run into forbidden territory. To escape the rodeo clowns, he headed into the arena and ran smack into a full-sized Chawbutt Nixon. The blow left the little man unconscious on the dirt. The other clowns, realizing their neglected duties, headed toward the bull to waylay the animal from tossing the little man to the crowds.

I yelled, "Hold that man," and climbed to the top of the fence.

"Yours, ma'am?" Chawbutt held the unconscious clown like a pig under one arm.

"Fortunately, these guys are used to tumbling around a lot. He's bruised, but he'll live." Cannon stood at the foot of the stretcher. Medics were about to load it and take the dwarf clown to the hospital.

"You know that?" asked Tony.

"These guys have had their share of falls, some a lot worse than this. Few broken bones over the years."

"He didn't do it as part of the show," I said. "He was running away from having to explain the money he dropped in the middle of his clown act."

"Money?" Cannon's eyes widened. "They don't carry money in the act."

"He did, and if I were the sheriff's detective, I'd find out why."

Tony glanced at me. "Did he gamble?"

"Could be," Cannon shrugged.

"Did he gamble?" Tony glared at Cannon, his face saying "don't play games with me."

"They all did sometimes, but not like Ziggie. Ziggie was the one with the habit."

"*Is*," I said. "Ziggie is alive. Remember?"

Cannon said nothing. He looked into the crowds. "This business is beginning to wear on me."

"Gambling business?" Tony asked.

"Carnival business."

"You've made a living at it. Got a nice little account in a Jacksonville bank." Tony said.

"You can't understand that, can you, sir?" Cannon's voice was bitter. "I saved up for a lot of years."

Tony said nothing more. He ordered Loman to follow the ambulance and ask the clown questions as soon as he could get clear of the emergency room. "And don't let him slip away from you." He looked my way as he said this.

I moved back to the sheriff's booth where Pasquin moved slowly between orders. People in the line were complaining about how long it was taking.

"What was that all about?" Pasquin said as he made change. He counted it deliberately into the outstretched hand.

"You've heard the expression, *follow the money*?" I took orders and yelled them back at Harlie or Mama.

Tony joined us in the booth. He didn't help and kept getting in the way of orders being passed from cook to counter. "I questioned Cannon about his involvement with Marie Beaufont," he said.

"Made passes at her?" I reached around him for an order of gator.

"Other way around, according to him. He says she wanted his check and tried to seduce him to get it. Even brought her mother a couple of times to help argue that the family needed it." Tony dodged a mustard bottle Harlie dropped.

"What was Rennie spending it on? Nobody can find any

drinking partners."

"Transportation maybe," said Tony. "He most likely picked up these girls at truck stops or on the road. Had to get there somehow, and we don't think he walked."

"You've got car rental slips to prove that?" I grabbed a package of napkins and stuffed them into the holder.

"None. He didn't rent a car. Could have taken the bus, but most likely he paid somebody to drive him."

"Somebody drove him to pick up girls to murder?" I paused. "There'd have to be two sickies out there to do that."

"Don't know if they were aware of what he was doing, but…" Tony shrugged. "You and Vernon need to be at the river tomorrow morning. You're going to ride the puller with White."

I stopped dead. "I have to do class schedules as soon as this booth job is over. Why me?"

"It's the only way to find evidence in the water. May be nothing there, but Marshall won't get on any boat, much less one where he has to stand. And we need a diver's eyes." He turned and went down the steps.

"Yes, sir! Indeed, sir!" I saluted to the wind.

It seemed the entirety of north Florida had turned out for the last night of the fair. No matter that the temperature was about to hit freezing, people just bundled up and ordered more hot chocolate. Harlie's forehead poured sweat in spite of the cold, and I dabbed it twice like a nurse helping out a surgeon. When I tried to do the same for Mama, she jerked away with a "get out of here!"

The last of the fried gator tail ran out early. She had chicken wings and was making them both Southern and Cajun style. No one cared. It was hot food and, eaten at the fair, tasted extra good.

Most of the animal displays had been removed along with the jam shows and arts and crafts exhibits. Only the rides, sideshows, and food booths remained. And these were the places the crowds gathered for one last uninhibited moment in the crazy house. Cannon, wrapped in a down jacket, stood in the carnival area like a troll guarding the bridge. He would collect the ticket sales and add to his Jacksonville account.

Pasquin finally gave out and took a seat behind the booth. He wrapped up tight in his army jacket and fell asleep in the cold. My body ached from the constant movement and long hours. Only a few hot dogs and chicken bits were left, but they kept coming. Close to midnight, Mama had had all she was going to take.

"Food is all gone!" She announced at the serving counter. "Try the cotton candy." She nodded toward the darkened booth. Cotton candy had already shut down. "Or not," she said, and began to lower the tarp. The crowd moaned disappointment but backed away. An all-night cafe just couldn't replace the excitement of a county fair.

"Call the clean-up crew, " said Mama as she sat in the chair Pasquin had vacated. "My feet and back have had it."

"Always did have hurting feet," said Harlie. "Don't know why you wanted to run your own place when standing on your feet hurt so much."

"Guess they didn't hurt quite so much back then." Mama closed her eyes.

"Here, raise them on this." Harlie brought over a crate that would serve as a stool. I stopped and stared. It was the first kind thing I'd seen either of them do.

Mama opened one eye, shoved off her shoes and raised them on the crate. She wiggled her toes, and Harlie dropped his jacket across them.

I wanted to wake up Pasquin to see this, but I didn't have the heart. I packed away the remaining napkins and unused plates, rubbed down the cooking surfaces and sat down on the steps to wait for the deputies who had cleaning detail. Behind me, Harlie scraped over another crate and sat on it. Only when I turned around did I realize he was sitting at the end of Mama's legs, massaging her feet. She kept her eyes closed, but her lips formed a smile.

"Wake up this old man and let's go," said Vernon. He whispered. Both Harlie and Mama had fallen asleep.

"What about them?" I asked. "They'll freeze to death."

"Deputies are on the way." Vernon nodded toward the car that had backed up to the supply trailer.

We drove away from the remnants of the carnival. Already, workers were disassembling the rides and packing them up for an early morning departure. Other workers raked out animal stalls and picked up trash from the grounds.

"Where will Cannon go next?" I asked.

"Says he has a gig in Jacksonville next week. Tony will keep a tail on him." Vernon squeezed my hand. "We got a cold ride on a boat tomorrow."

I moaned. "How early?"

"Man starts at eight. I can take the first shift if you're too sleepy. Only one of us can ride on that thing at a time." He tussled my hair. "And we have to stand."

I walked Pasquin into his house. For his eighty-plus years, he did well, but I didn't trust him out of a dead sleep. He plopped into one of his overstuffed chairs as soon as I opened the door. "Flip the heat on," he said.

When the blower was filling the room with heat, I asked if he needed help getting into bed.

"Haven't been asked that in years," he said. "But I can do it alone."

"I can have Vernon come in if you're embarrassed." I jerked off his straw hat and tossed it on a table.

"Take more than a silly swamp girl to embarrass me," he said. "Now let me tell you about Miss Mattie Belle…."

"Not tonight," I said and stretched.

I turned to go outside and join Vernon in the dry car heat. Opening the door meant a blast of frigid air.

"Cold tonight, Luanne, colder than a gator's tooth on ice. Stay clear of the cracking lizards."

CHAPTER 21

Overnight, the wind chill factor in Tallahassee was twenty-five, and that meant frigid for anyone living below Atlanta. But the metamorphic nature of the area changed everything by midmorning. A warming set in, causing a humid mist to rise off the river surface and fog up the view for miles. Vernon and I set out in heavy down coats, but stripped to sweatshirts by the time we each took a turn on the grass puller. White worked in shirt sleeves, his skin long since adjusted to the whimsical changes of river weather.

"It's not going to be easy to see anything in this fog," I said as I stood beside White at the top of the conveyor belt. He occupied the plastic seat attached to the boat and worked the gears. The two paddle wheels on either side turned at their highest speed and tossed water near my feet.

"Won't see anything," he said. "Grass is too thick." He slowed and turned the boat into the area where Yasmina's body had been found. On shore, deputies manned the crime scene area. A few moved slowly up and down the riverside, combing for evidence.

I leaned forward but the metal conveyor blocked the view of the river bottom. Concentrating on the side of the boat, I could see through the pristine water, clear to the top of the grass. "This stuff is pretty tall."

"And I just cleared it all out less than a month ago."

"You're right. I'm not going to see anything here."

"I got an idea," he said. "It may not be what your cop wants, but what if I pull up the grass and stop the belt in front. You can look into the grass there."

I smiled. Tony would shit a brick if I made my own decisions like this. "Do it," I said.

White revved up his gears, lowered the belt, and pulled up a load of green grass. It traveled towards me. Instead of conveying it into the back storage area, he stopped the movement and raised the belt. Long strands of hydrilla, aquarium grass, rested in front of me with tiny frogs and minnows jumping about, looking for water. White reached over with a gloved hand and swiped the animals into the water.

I borrowed one of his poles and poked around the grass. Nothing of any evidence appeared.

"Hydrilla cleans the water," he said. "Any blood or other stuff that didn't belong would be gone by now. You'd have to look for something man-made."

I nodded. "Like a knife or a wallet."

He turned on the belt and moved the load of grass to the back. Turning again to the area, he pulled up another load. On the third try, he had to travel to the shore truck to unload before coming back to the spot.

"We could do this all day," I said as I scanned the fourth load.

"I do this all day. You aren't slowing me down much."

We moved like this for nearly two hours, pulling, scanning, and traveling to the dump truck every third load. The area where Yasmina's body lay was clear as a bell now, the white sand visible from the surface.

"How close can you get to the shoreline?" I had an idea that anything not tied down may have drifted in the current, if it didn't catch on the grass, and something like a knife might burrow into the soft bank side dirt as it had on the side wall of the sinkhole.

"Close as you want," he said and pushed the gears back and forth until the side of the boat was nearly parallel with the bank. "You want me to pull the grass here?"

I nodded. He lowered the conveyor; grass along with mud from the side of the bank rode up on the belt.

"Stop!" The silvery metal shined like a beacon amongst the foliage, more alien to this natural setting than the grass itself. The curved blade had not a spot on it. Hydrilla had even cleaned the murder weapon.

"She's a natural," said White as we stood on shore. "Knew just where to look for that thing." He pointed to the knife that lay on top of an evidence bag.

Tony scowled at the man. "Don't talk about this, White. It's evidence and we'd just as soon not let anyone know what we found."

White smiled and thumbed my way. "She found," he said.

I had a sudden affection for the man. He knew how to get at Tony's core and grind it a little.

"Get it to Marshall and see if it's the murder weapon," Tony yelled at Loman.

Loman, standing close enough to hear a whisper, saluted and bagged the knife. He headed for a patrol car, chuckling all the way.

"Can I go home and work on a schedule now?" I tried not to grin, but Vernon stood behind Tony and showed teeth.

A gentle rain fell on the dry foliage outside the kitchen window, a welcome sound after the general warm-up began. I sat at the oak table used for breakfasts and any other jobs that had to be done away from the family china. Manny's partial schedule lay open before me. He had nothing but little darts and arrows, like doodling, all over the grid. It would be up to me to plug in the classes. I searched through the folder for enrollment data. Flipping through sheets on the faculty members, I tried to interest myself in their talents, as well as their desires, for certain classes. Some had requested areas they had never taught before and were not prepared academically.

"What could be their motive for wanting this class?" I let my mind wander. Most likely they needed a change, but I had to think of the students and what they needed. In the end, the whole thing would be academic, each person getting pretty much what he'd always had. "Tedium, but expertise," I mused.

I rested against the back of the chair and watched a cardinal that had flown down here from some cold northern state, poke around the dirt for worms. Another cardinal swooped down. The first one flared his red wings and jumped at the intruder. "Territory," I said. My mind focused on less natural things. "Motive?"

Beaufont had committed the ultimate in modern crime, the secretive slaughter of women, in the guise of the serial killer. Maybe he couldn't help himself, and maybe society had created him. Who had the motive to knock him off?

"His wife, surely," I thought. "If she knew, she'd be pretty pissed at the betrayal. And any number of family members of the victims, if they knew. Or something entirely different. Maybe Beaufont knew about the gambling or the hooking or something that got him killed. With a linoleum knife, the same thing he used?"

I called the crime scene lab and asked for Marshall.

"Luanne! You got Tony's tail in a twist again. Found the second murder weapon." He laughed into the receiver, his sound waves beating on my ear drum.

"So that was the weapon that killed Yasmina?"

"Most likely. Haven't had time to match it with her wounds, but my eye tells me it is. Funny thing is," he took a bite of something.

"Are you eating?"

"Sara brought fudge." Sara, the tech with the frown that eased up in the presence of the big man.

"You're kind of sweet on her?"

"Sweet on her fudge." He changed the subject. "Funny thing about the weapon, no, about this killing." He hiccuped.

"Yeah, Sara's got you all confused."

"Yasmina's neck was cut up, uneven. It was like she was fighting and somebody had to hold her still and slash at her." He grunted and took a sip of something.

"Why is that funny?"

"Beaufont must have surprised his victims, or somehow incapacitated them. He killed with a single slash across the throat. Any strong man should have been able to do that."

"Any strong man?"

"Yeah, anyone tall enough and strong enough to catch her from behind. Didn't happen that way."

"I think you said there were finger marks on her neck."

"Some, and on her arms, too. Fairly small, and I'd say not all from the same person."

"Marshall," a chill ran up my spine, "can you tell the difference between dwarf finger marks and other sizes."

Silence was followed by another sip. "I'll get back to you." He hung up.

I sat up straight. Could those little clowns have jumped Yasmina? Maybe she had money and they wanted it. I pictured a mad scene of clowns on a tall woman, yanking her hair and hauling her down on the ground. One, his puffy little hand gripping a linoleum knife, slashing at her. When she finally gurgled out her life, they rolled her off the shore and into the hydrilla grass.

"Doesn't make sense," I said. "Why would these guys use a linoleum knife? And her body wasn't rolled off the side. It was taken into the grass and weighted down. They used bricks."

What would the FBI people say about a serial killer in this situation? He had no regard for his victims. Chose to dump them in water without hiding their faces. No dignity for the most recent girls, and probably none for Gaylin. But Yasmina didn't fit the profile. She had been hidden in water, weighted so that she'd never come up with the body gases.

A sudden downpour of rain shook me from murder back to schedule. I pulled out the old one from last spring and filled in the blanks on the new one. I'd have to teach along with everyone else; the interim chair had no office or perks to go with the job.

I moved to the lap computer on the desk near the breakfast table and typed out letters for each of the linguistic faculty members. There would be no surprises from me. Same classes, same rooms, same times. If the dean wanted to change this, he could.

I was signing each letter when Pasquin yelled out his "Whoweeeeee" from the swamp path.

"Looks like the dry holes will fill up," said Pasquin. He shook the wet from his straw hat before brushing his feet on the mat. He had walked under a heavy canopy of trees that protected him from getting drenched.

"Take your wet shoes off and I'll give you some strong coffee," I said. " Better yet, you make the strong coffee."

He grinned and headed for the kitchen. One of his Cajun legacies was the coffee he made. "Must have been a Turk in that French quarter," he has often said. The brew will take off the back of your throat.

Pasquin was in no hurry. He moved like the forest—seasonal. Creature comfort came first, then any urgent message that might involve life or death. He placed his strong brew on the kitchen table, rested in a chair, and stretched his socked feet toward the heater vent.

"Edwin is about to worry me to death," he said between loud sips. "Up all night looking for that big snake. Says pythons are nocturnal and he figures he can find him at night. Heard this ruckus out by my shed last night—your Plato hound barking. Went to check and found Edwin poking around my rakes and things."

"He's been around here a few times, too, I think. How'd he get this way?" I licked the envelopes and stacked them on the desk.

"Follows in his daddy's tracks. Swamp people know snakes and some just like them better than others. Edwin took to the things in a big way. Too bad he ain't smart. He'd have made a good scientist. Probably found all kinds of uses for snake venom."

He chuckled at some private thought about his friend.

"Instead, he makes belts." I shuddered.

"Snake has got to be wrapped around him one way or the other."

"What will Edwin do with Sylvester if he finds him?"

"Oh, he'll make a big production out of finding him. He'll hand him over to Snake Boy and feel like a kid who has won a scout badge."

"I think Snake Boy would rather have the insurance money." I placed stamps on each envelope and breathed a sigh of relief that it was done. I planned to e-mail the schedule out to each faculty member tonight, but the official written letter notice would be posted before then.

"Speaking of insurance—you think that woman, the wife of that killer, got anything out of the carnival people?" He raised himself slowly, his knees cracking, and refilled his cup.

"Not much. I think Beaufont had a small life insurance policy. Vernon said it was so small it wouldn't even pay for his funeral."

"She ought to donate his body to science. Study the brain that killed like that."

"Well, she won't be burying him any time too soon. Crime lab is hanging on to his body."

I poured myself a cup of Pasquin's brew, added a heavy glop of milk, and sat with him at the table. The heat came on again, signaling the approach of a cool evening.

"Warming trend didn't last." He sipped and stared off somewhere, his aged brain clicking as fast as any younger man's.

"Pasquin," I began slowly.

"Uh-oh," he said and drew his thoughts back to the kitchen. "You want me to do something."

"You have any idea where the gambling took place, the stuff that went on with Rinks and Ziggie?"

"Don't know Ziggie, but I got a pretty good idea big gambling parties carried on in that big barn about a mile upstream from Rinks' place. He don't own it, but borrows it from the old farmer who lives near the bay. Wouldn't be surprised if that old farmer is one of the players."

"What does swamp gossip say about the goings-on over there?"

Pasquin pulled over another chair and eased his feet onto it. He sipped, touched his hat to see if it was dry, and sighed.

"Too high stakes," he said. "None of my swamp buddies go there anymore. Lots of fellows off the bay boats and from Tallahassee come in now. Big cash changes hands."

"Could Rinks have been in debt?"

"Most likely. So could his buddies and some who weren't his buddies."

"And if someone couldn't cover his losses?"

Pasquin shrugged. "Some fellows think you can beat money from a man."

"But what would be the use of shooting his alligators? Then the man wouldn't have any assets to ever pay his debt." I let my gaze wander toward the window. An oak branch had grown too near the house and was scraping the glass each time a breeze blew. "And there is Snake Boy who may have had some insurance." I stopped.

"What's on your mind, ma'am?" Pasquin removed his feet and sat upright.

"Just suppose Rinks needed money bad. If he had insurance and someone destroyed his crop—if alligators can be called crops— wouldn't he get a pay-off and be able to settle his debt?"

Pasquin shrugged. "Sounds good to me, but where is the man?"

"Hiding for some reason," I said. "And Ziggie, too." I looked at Pasquin and grinned. "Want to take a boat ride?"

The rain hadn't finished yet. It fell on us in Pasquin's boat as we turned from the main river into the lane that would lead us to Rinks' place and past. Pasquin had rigged a holder for a large umbrella to cover him and the controls of the motor. I sat at the other end with a plastic raincoat hood over my head.

"Won't be so bad once we get under the tree canopy," he said and slowed for a crop of hydrilla that threatened to recover its territory.

We passed Rinks' place. The yellow crime scene tape had fallen to the ground and rested in watery mud. The rain was only a mist now, and I removed the hood. Pasquin moved into a narrow lane that made a sharp angle. Tree limbs nearly clobbered us as we ducked and dodged.

"I can't see gamblers coming through this."

"They come by truck through the woods, from bay side," he said.

In the distance, I spotted the dark wood side of a large structure. It sat on an incline up from the river bank. There was a narrow landing with two boat ties, but no boats in sight.

"You planning on going up there?" Pasquin asked without expecting an answer. He knew. "Expect I'd better go with you."

He tied the boat, and we moved onto the shaky landing. Once up the bank, we had to go around the barn where the double doors stood slightly ajar. I listened, then squeezed inside the opening.

"You'll need this," said Pasquin and handed me a flashlight. "Most likely nobody in there 'cause the door was left open. I'll stay out here and watch for critters—the two-legged kind."

The barn had a floor that began a ways back from the doors. It had been swept clean and a series of round tables sat around, waiting for card players. The cops had been here. One table lay upturned as though detectives had searched the bottom for taped records. A spot on the floor marked a place where something square and heavy had set, possibly a safe. Either the players had removed it or the sheriff had it in the evidence room.

I moved to a cooler in back of the barn, a few yards away from the playing area. It was no longer plugged into the socket, but it was still filled. Warm beer cans floated in tepid water. Raising my sleeve, I sloshed around in the water and found nothing but more beer. Closing the lid, I stretched to peek behind the cooler. To one side, a cardboard box was filled with unopened bourbon bottles. Someone, possibly the search team, had cut open the lid and ripped it backwards. I knelt and removed each bottle. Behind one was the bill from a bay liquor store. When I withdrew another bottle, it had a different appearance. It's seal had been broken.

"Somebody has been around here," I said and backed away. "Took a sip of straight bourbon."

"Luanne!" Pasquin's voiced rasped a loud whisper. "Somebody's coming."

I darted out the door and joined Pasquin. A motor sounded from the other side of the barn as though a truck were pulling into the drive. We moved toward the landing where I motioned for Pasquin to untie and hide in the oak branches. He tried to protest, but I moved back up the hill and hid behind some scrub oaks.

A familiar young man slipped from the passenger side of the truck and took a look inside the barn. He motioned for the driver to follow him. Rinks slid out, carrying a pistol in one hand.

"Nobody's been here since the cops searched," said the young man, the very one who had sliced Ziggie's tire with an ax. "Won't nobody notice."

Rinks had to move the door back further to ease his large body into the opening. The young man followed. I tiptoed to the door and watched until they had gone all the way to the rear where the box of bourbon rested. Pressing myself against the wall, I stepped inside and stood silently in the shadows near the stairs to the loft. The men's voices were distinct from here.

"What you gonna do about getting that money?" said the young man.

"Zig says somebody stole it. Probably one of them girls he takes to his trailer. But he owes me big, and I ain't answering for his mistake." Rinks lifted the bourbon box. "Hope the store will take this back. Ain't been opened."

"You know where he is?" The young man looked frightened. He halfway helped Rinks with the box, but concentrated more on easing out the double doors.

"Cannon does. And if he don't produce, I'm going after that whole set-up he's traveling with." Rinks had to shove the door with his backside to get out with the box in his hands. He loaded it into the truck, and the two of them sped backwards into the forest until they came to the main road. I heard Rinks shift gears when he turned.

"Gambling debts," I said as I climbed into Pasquin's boat. "You were right. Sounds like Ziggie owes Rinks money, but the money—if he ever had it—got out of Ziggie's hands, and now Rinks is gunning for him."

"Swamp justice," Pasquin smiled. "Just you stay out of the firing line, you here?"

"I hear." I sat down and pulled the hood over my head as a drizzle started again. "And I bet I know where the money is."

Pasquin took off his hat and slapped it on his knee. "Okay, Ma'am, where?"

"A wee little man found it."

"Okay," said Tony. "The money belongs to Rinks, but was stolen from Ziggie's trailer by one of his own clowns." Tony shuffled his feet in the wet sawdust near the bull pen, abandoned now and threatening nothing but boards and straw. "Sounds plausible."

"And what does the little guy in the hospital say?"

Tony smiled. "Confessed to breaking into Ziggie's trailer and finding a wad of dough. He'd spent some of it already—on a woman over in Quincy." He lowered his head and opened into a big grin and what might have been a blush. "Guess that hooker got a *little* surprise." He shrugged. "But money is money."

Tony didn't joke much, not around me. I figured the sheriff's office must be sending out tall hooker/short john jokes like electrical currents.

"And he got caught when the bundle came loose during the show?" I could joke with the best of them, but I wasn't going to give in to Tony's mood.

Tony nodded. "Question is," he turned serious, "where did Ziggie get it in the first place. We got word that he lost in cards the last time he played."

"Cannon?" I smiled.

Tony looked toward the dwindling trailers. The last of the performers and organizers were heading out, long after Cannon had taken off with his crew—minus Ziggie.

"We know where he is." Tony turned toward Loman and began

to discuss the situation. He would send someone after Cannon or get one of his fellow officers in the next town to hold him.

"Can I be there when you question him?" I put both hands on my hips.

He hesitated. His male mind would weigh the options: let this female, who is not a deputy, add her two cents, or kick her butt out of the scene. "Get Vernon to bring you," he finally said.

Before he could turn his back on me, Tony's attention went to the far gate where a patrol car entered, siren off but lights flashing. All of us followed him to meet the uniformed deputy.

"Had to come this way and thought you'd like to know. The big fat man's vehicle broke down on the interstate. Highway patrol found him in the back seat with his legs stretched all the way to the front. There is no front seat, not on the passenger side. His little lady was driving in a special-made device for short people." He laughed. "Talk about the little engine that could."

"Was Cannon with him?"

"The whole shebang was traveling together. When they broke down, everybody stopped."

"Show us where." Tony shoved the man back into his car. Vernon and I piled in the back seat.

The group had traveled as far as Madison, near the Georgia border. They lined the interstate, slowing gawkers who had never seen a truck with a giant cobra painted on the side, or a group of clowns crowded on a cart. Julene stood on the grass shoulder along with all the clowns except the one in the hospital and Ziggie. They had hired a laborer to drive for them, both in and out of the act. The man couldn't stop giggling at the sight of Jubile attempting to get a good enough foot hold on the sloping shoulder to move his bulk from his magnified seat. Julene stared at the man as though she could have taken the whip to him right there on I-10.

Cannon bent over, speaking to the mechanic who had handed him a paper to sign. The big man's car would have to be towed, and Jubile would have to find a way to be transported in a regular car. The other trailers waited about a mile ahead.

When Cannon saw Tony, he stood up straight. "You're out of your territory, aren't you?"

Tony's body went stiff and the jaw began to agitate. "I'm going to ask you to come back and talk to us again. You can come on your own or I can get one of these highway patrolmen to set up something right here in this county."

Cannon eyed him, squinting in the midst of the curls. "Am I being arrested for something?"

"Not that I know of," said Tony.

Cannon turned to sign the paper the tow truck had given him. "Might as well. We're going to be awhile in this town."

I stood at the side of the road with the clowns and Julene, waiting for Tony to give the riding arrangements. He wasn't about to allow Cannon drive alone.

"What kind of gambling did Ziggie do back there?" I asked the question to the wind.

"Got in over his head," said one of his men. "Lost too much. Now we got to be slaves to Cannon for a long time just to keep ourselves fed." He scowled. "He's going to jail if we ever find him."

"And you think Cannon loaned him the money to pay off his debts?"

"Loaned! Hah!" Julene cackled, like sending out static electricity into the wind.

"Took it from the box receipts and told Ziggie it would have to be paid back from wages. Slave labor if you ask me."

"Can't you just quit and join another act, or make one of your own?" I turned to face the men. Their squashed faces with grotesque features stared at me.

"Contracted with Ziggie. If we go, we have to pay him off. Just as well stay and pay off his debts."

I sighed, "You guys need a business manager."

Laughter broke out on the side of I-10, high-pitched and nearly maniacal. "That's what he was in the beginning," said the shortest man in the group. "Our business manager. Some damn business!"

Jubile had finally managed to pull himself to the grass. His driver hurried to bring him a plastic chair from the trunk of the broken-down car. He planted his bulk and made the chair invisible. To those interstate travelers hurrying towards Disney World, he must have seemed one of the acts, a giant sitting on the side of the highway.

The tow truck hauled away Jubile's comfortable vehicle, leaving him to the devices of a man with a large pick-up. When they pushed the seat back, Jubile was able to fold his stomach enough to squeeze into the passenger side. The driver would have to push against thigh fat to shift gears, and Jubile's breathing would have to be shallow until they could catch up to his trailer in a rest park.

"A carnival behind the scenes is no fun," said Julene. "Can't fake the fun when reality hits." She frowned, near tears, and climbed into the clown car. The little men followed her.

Cannon couldn't sit still. He shifted from the edge of his chair to the back. He stretched his neck to take in the dull walls of the interview room, staring especially long at the two-way mirror.

Tony, Vernon, Loman, and I sat in the room with him. He didn't want a recorder, and he didn't want a lawyer.

"I didn't do anything illegal, just loaned out some money to one of my acts." He threw up both hands in protest.

"Where is Zigfield and where is Rinks?" Tony leaned toward him.

Cannon moved back slightly as though Tony's hot breath would scorch him. He shook his head.

"I've seen you with both, and we've been through this before," I said. "You know where they are and you know Rinks is gunning for Ziggie."

Cannon stared at me, his mouth slightly open. He shook his head again.

"You loaned money to Ziggie to pay off his debts, and the little clown stole the money. He can't pay Rinks, so Rinks goes after him."

Cannon let out a heavy sigh that sounded like he was going to heave. "That's not all Rinks did."

When Cannon offered no explanation, I asked, "He got rid of his own gators for the insurance, right?"

Cannon's eyes squinted. He tugged at the mass of curls in his beard. And nodded. "He was in debt, too. Ziggie's pay-off would have taken care of a lot of that, but he needed a lot more." Cannon looked up at each of us. "I wasn't there, but according to Ziggie, Rinks sent his help away and went out and blew the brains out of each gator. Made it look like sabotage or revenge." He began to laugh. "Only thing is, when he went to fill in the papers and collect the money, Ziggie's money got ripped off. Rinks couldn't afford the publicity with the robbery out in the open like that. He ups and disappears, just like Ziggie."

"And Ziggie contacted you?" asked Loman. He doodled on a note pad.

"Not exactly." Cannon squirmed, looking nervous and ready to jump. The uniform who stood at the door placed one hand closer to his gun belt.

"Ziggie thought it was that woman he had off and on in his trailer. He figured she had come across the money after a heated night of passion and took off with it." He began to shake his head. "And, no, I don't think he could have killed her. That had to be one of her other customers, and she had plenty."

"He had a motive," said Vernon.

"Ziggie might get angry, but I never saw him get brutal. You see how skinny he is. Yasmina was a big girl who could have broken his spine if she wanted to."

The men didn't pursue the Yasmina case. The fact that her throat had been cut was a secret, and since Cannon didn't seem to know that, they didn't tell him.

"Did Beaufont ever do any flooring work for you?" I asked.

Cannon frowned. "Flooring? Where would he do that?"

"Inside the trailers. Don't most of them have linoleum?"

He shook his head again. "Never had any refloored. No need to."

"Would anyone have any use for, say, the tools you'd use to lay flooring?" I wanted to avoid the kind of knife.

Cannon shook his head. "What's with you people?" Behind all the unruly curls, he appeared confused.

"We need to find Rinks and Ziggie," said Tony when I indicated I had nothing more to ask. "Can you tell us where they are?"

Cannon's eyes grew dark. He lowered his head and peered at us like a cave man eyeing prey. "Can, but why should I? Rinks killed his own stock of gators; Ziggie's money was stolen. Whatever beef they're in, it's with each other and not with the law."

Loman drew in a deep breath and leaned back in his chair. His face grew red, angry at someone telling him the law. Tony didn't move, but his face grew just as red.

"Because one has threatened to kill the other, that's why." Tony's position froze.

"Not to mention knocking me unconscious," I added, sending Tony daggers.

Cannon finally shrugged. "Zigs is in a motel with some of the carnival barkers. That's who he plays cards with, and a bunch of them took turns hiding him when he lost the money owed Rinks."

"Are you telling us Zigfield was in the caravan that sat out there on the interstate?" Tony's forehead began to sweat.

"Yeah," Cannon grinned. "Way up ahead, of course. Not even his little men knew he was there."

"And Rinks?" asked Vernon, cutting the tension of his fellow deputies.

"On a boat anchored somewhere off the Ochlockonee River. Belongs to his nephew's friend, he says. He got in touch with me. We met at the landing. That's about all I know."

"About?"

"All," he added.

Quiet hovered over the room, ready to explode into male frustration.

"Tell us about Rennie Beaufont," I said. It caught Cannon off guard.

"I've said all I can about Beaufont. He worked off and on for us. Didn't make a nuisance of himself."

"Did he gamble with Rinks and Ziggie or any of the other guys?"

"Not that I saw. Kept to himself most of the time. Or maybe he went home to his family. I know just about nothing about that man." Cannon grinned in relieved triumph.

"But you know his wife and you haven't told us about her," I pushed the point.

Cannon sifted through his beard. Tiny broken hairs drifted into the air, then onto his shirt. "She seems a pitiful thing. Always needing his check. Or maybe not needing it, but wanting it. She whined at me a lot, but I couldn't legally give it to her. Now, that mother of hers was something else." He made a half chuckle.

"How?" I asked.

"One time—we were in Ft. Walton Beach, I think—she showed up in need of money. I gave her the usual brush-off, so she shows up the same day with her mother. That woman threatened to call the cops. I told her to go ahead, that the money was his and I was under no obligation to give it to the wife." He leaned back and smiled. "She blew a fuse and said she had friends who could do a number on me and my carnival crew. I laughed at her and showed her the door and that's when the fuse popped. She took her chubby old lady's arm and swiped off my desk, went towards the door and did the same with the table there. Threw all my files into total confusion." He laughed.

"Violent nature, would you say?" I added.

Cannon grew quiet. "I got to thinking about her and decided to ask carnival security to come around more often. Even think I saw her one or two times in other cities, but I can't be sure." He sighed. "With a mother-in-law like that…" He looked up and didn't finish his thought.

"You know he's right," said Tony. "Nobody has broken a law here, unless you take the threat that Luanne overheard as serious." He glanced my way, the accusation clear in his black eyes.

Loman leaned forward. "Can't we insist on finding the two men on cause of knowing their general welfare?"

"As if the law cared whether either lived or died," I added.

Tony grunted. "Loman will check out the carnival group, and Vernon, you take Mother Theresa with you and find Rinks. Check in with Franklin County cops before you go charging down the river."

"There's an old shed around the curve in the bay," said Vernon. He stood in the patrol boat and guided it slowly through the manatee areas and into the open waters that would eventually become the Gulf of Mexico. "Cops have been getting some local calls about squatters."

"Who owns it?" I sat in the passenger chair and let the cool river breezes pass over my face. The weather had warmed to in-between, ideal.

"It's sitting on an otherwise vacant lot owned by somebody in Maine. Investment property most likely."

The boat bounced in the choppy bay waters. We met a few fishermen casting lines off boats. They nodded and saluted as we passed a shoreline of private landings and cement block vacation houses. Vernon slowed at a sandy spot that led up a path to a shed partially hidden in a clump of palmetto bushes. A rusted tin roof covered a car port and connected it to a shack that had new tin nailed over the old. The wood on the building had turned gray and one window was boarded up.

"He's here," I said. "At least that's the truck he was in the day I saw him at the gambling spot."

Vernon circled around the building; I waited by the landing until he signaled.

"Some young kid is inside. Can't see anybody else." He walked to the front door and knocked.

Something fell to the floor within, and feet scrambled over a wood floor. When they stopped, Vernon knocked again.

The door, its boards warped and gaping, scratched open a notch. A rusty chain was all that stood between Vernon and the frightened eyes of the young man inside.

"Yeah?" The voice had only recently changed as it croaked out a scared greeting.

"Here to see a Mr. Rinks." Vernon held up his sheriff's badge. He had no jurisdiction here, but this wasn't a criminal investigation.

"Oh, no!" the boy said and backed from the door. He flopped his hands up and down and made little hops on the floor like a kid who didn't know which way to turn.

"Let me make up your mind for you, son," said Vernon. "Open the door."

The movement stopped, and amid breathy "oh, nos," the boy unlatched the chain and held the door for us.

Vernon introduced himself and me and nodded for the kid to take a seat in the same chair he must have been in when we interrupted him. A piece of driftwood lay on the floor, a carving knife beside it.

"You do art work?" said Vernon as he leaned over and retrieved the knife. "Some people do nice things with driftwood." He pocketed the potential weapon.

"That's mine," said the boy, his hands trembling. He didn't know what to do with them except to fold and unfold them, first in front, then in back.

"Yes, it is," said Vernon. "Could we sit down?" He pulled up two wicker chairs that had seen too many days in Florida humidity. The areas where no one sat were nearly black with mildew. Vernon placed his between the kid and the front door; he put mine in a spot that could block any rush to a back exit.

"You—you want a beer?" The boy's adam's apple bobbed in a

rapid beat.

Vernon laughed, almost sneered, and didn't answer.

"We'd like to speak to Mr. Rinks," I said. "And you are?" I knew he was the young man I saw heave an ax into Ziggie's tire. The man with him that night wasn't Rinks.

"He's not here right now." Sweat broke out on the boy's forehead.

"When will he be here?" Vernon's back stiffened and he looked around the room.

"He…" The boy hesitated.

"You can tell us."

"He'll be back any minute. Just walked to a stand near the road to buy some stuff to eat." He gulped as though he'd caught himself in the cookie jar.

"We'll wait," I said and stood up to look at the hideout with a critical eye.

Seashells rested in various spots about the room. They had been collected years ago, it seemed. The once shiny pinks, speckles, and corals showed dingy yellow now. The ones in the window sills were covered in dust. Four wicker chairs sat randomly placed around the room. The only other furniture was the small kitchen table; two sleeping bags lay rolled up in a corner near a box.

"That looks familiar," I said and pointed to the bottles of Bourbon. Moving to the box, I found the same arrangement as they were in the gambling barn. "Find a buyer?"

The boy hiccuped and shook his head.

"Why not?"

"Liquor store said he needed them all back the same way."

I smiled. "Ah, the one open bottle."

"We didn't do that!" The boy's eyes watered.

"Who did?" asked Vernon, his voice demanding an answer.

The boy shook his head violently and backed against the wall.

A whistle sounded outside. The boy's head jerked toward the front door, his eyes wide with alarm. "Rinks is coming."

"Good," said Vernon and took a seat by the door. His right hand rested near his gun belt.

The kid looked ready to bolt, like a wild horse corralled inside a burning barn. "He's not going to like this."

When Rinks came through the door, he spied only the boy who had taken his whittling seat again. He held onto the chair with both hands. Rinks sat his bag on the table. Only then did he realize the room was too full. He made a rapid movement toward the door, but Vernon got there first, blocking his escape.

"Just some questions, sir. And before you start yelling attorney, I am assuring you we have nothing to charge you for right now—unless you have already submitted a phony insurance claim."

Rinks motioned for the boy to give him his chair. He heaved a sigh as he fell into it. "What do you want?"

"Does Zigfield owe you money?"

"Lots. Bastard had it and lost it."

"Try stolen. One of his performers stole it from his own trailer."

Rinks sneered with a half laugh. "He owes me big time."

"Gambling debts?"

"No, no. You aren't going to pin any illegal gambling charges on me." He started to stand, but Vernon raised one hand as if the magic of the gesture would seat him again.

"Did you threaten harm to Zigfield if the man didn't hand over the money?"

Rinks looked at Vernon with snake cold eyes. "Never."

"Then why do we have a witness that this young man axed a hole in his tire, and his companion hit Miss Fogarty in the face so hard she blacked out?"

The young man jumped as though an inner worm had bitten him. He looked ready to fly any minute. Rinks stared at me then back at Vernon.

"Do you know the Yasmina woman?" I asked. It through the man off guard.

Rinks stiffened again. "You mean the woman of the streets, a walking red light district?" He nodded. "Yeah. Saw her a few times. Heard tell she got killed."

Vernon nodded. "What about Beaufont?"

"He was always around somewhere. Didn't socialize much. It was his wife that came around looking for him. Scared little mouse. Some guy made a pass at her. Next time, she comes hauling Mommy with her."

"She showed up at the gambling barn, then?" I added.

"Yep, ah…" Rinks bit his lip. He had revealed the existence of such a place. "She showed up during some games. Interrupted the action."

Vernon stood up. "You need to come into Tallahassee and give a statement to the sheriff. Failure to do this could end up with someone taking blame for illegal gambling, whether he was in charge or not. And," Vernon turned and faced down the seated man, "…any threat to harm Zigfield will be taken most seriously."

Rinks, the big man who could handle alligators, even butcher one single-handed, shook and nodded his agreement to the statement.

"One more thing," said Vernon as we left the front door, "no false insurance claims. Get back to your farm and clean up the swamp. And tell that scum who hit Luanne I'd better never find him."

We left.

CHAPTER 23

We left, but we didn't go far. Rinks was on the move. He and the young man tossed the sleeping bags into the truck and threw dust as they fled their shabby hideaway.

"I'd follow him if I had a car," said Vernon. "He'd better be high-tailing it to the sheriff's office." Back in the boat, Vernon radioed the truck's license plate and description to his office. Word came back that Ziggie had been just where Cannon said he'd be and would return to make a statement.

"That's over, then," I said. "Those two are safe and, while somewhat shady, not big-time criminals."

I felt uneasy. The river breeze was turning cold again. We rode in silence except for the steady roar of the engine and the rhythmic lap of the water against the sides.

Once on the Palmetto River again, we waved to White who continued to sweep up the invading hydrilla in a losing battle to protect local nature.

When I finally dragged into the house near dusk, Plato greeted me with a yelp and a wet tongue. He jumped about, wanting to play. I tossed him a stick for a while then pleaded to sit on the porch. He seemed to understand, grabbed the stick and headed into the trees. He wouldn't return until he wanted more human companionship, something he took in small doses.

I sat in a rocker and watched the sun move into the river, turning the world around me black. Cold, unmoving air hovered like the ghost of swamp past. I had no will to move and wondered if this was what death might feel like in the beginning stages. Does death come in stages? It must have for those girls, for Gaylin. Did they know about the linoleum knife coming toward their throats, wielded by an expert who could cut a line to fit around a pedestal sink in a flash? Were they partially alive when he tossed their violated bodies into the water's edge and expected nature to hide his deed? Who knew?

The bitter cold enclosed my skin now, and I shivered. Who knew, indeed! I turned to the warmth of the living and picked up the phone in the darkness.

"Marshall?" I heard the big man's grunt on the other end. He often worked at night, preferring the solitude of a nearly empty building. "Tell me it was a linoleum knife in all the murder cases, including the last one."

"Tell you? I already told you it was. What's going on?"

"Does anyone see copycat in this second murder?" I shivered again. The thermostat was too low.

"Who would know except a few cops, me, you? And why copy a dead killer? Who's going to blame him?" Marshall's heavy breaths sounded like little crashing waves in my ear.

"Then why use such a weapon? It's not a common type of knife to have about unless you work in that field." I held my breath.

Marshall was silent. "You got a theory?"

"The act against Yasmina could have been revenge, getting back at her for setting a trap for the other girls. And it was a dirty kill, ragged cuts around the throat." I stopped.

"I think you're saying the second killer couldn't wield a knife with the expertise of Beaufont?"

"Right. Someone with lots of upper body strength and experience with that kind of blade."

Marshall's silence told me he was either agreeing or finding something to distract him in his office. "The cops are still looking at family members. No suspects so far. Maybe some truck driver fancied one and took it out on Yasmina. Hell! Maybe Cannon or Ziggie got tired of her hanging on and eliminated the problem."

"Do you believe any of that?"

"No. Unless they knew what Beaufont was doing, they wouldn't know about the knife. By the way, those finger marks weren't made by any dwarf. Small male fingers or a woman's maybe."

"I'll be in touch, Marshall." I hung up before he could lecture me on taking off by myself.

The burned-off dry lake looked like a black hole in space at night—you couldn't see it. The cold weather made it feel even closer to a vast nothingness. I parked the car where the diving trailer had been the day we went into the partially filled sinkhole. My boots made crunching sounds in the silence as I headed toward the edge of the lake. My flashlight darted among the low growing grass, jumping like a giant lightning bug in the darkness.

The high edge at the top of the bank ended somewhere near the sinkhole rim, the place where someone had tossed the body of a dead Rennie Beaufont. The ground here was bare; the grass already dead from drought had been trodden away by the constant movement of law enforcement.

I stood at the top and shined the light over the edge, down the side of the bank and aimed it at the sinkhole. The light traveled down, down, then up a slight rise before the hole. The heavy body of a dead male would roll down the bank easily, even continue to roll with good momentum until it fell into the hole—unless a slight rise in the terrain slowed it to a stop. "If Rennie had ended up in the hole, no one would have discovered him, wouldn't even have known he was missing." I stopped. People who worked the carnival talked about his coming and going, having nothing much to do with others. If he didn't come around, he wouldn't be missed if he was at the bottom of a sinkhole.

An animal squealed in the distance, another part of the food chain devoured. I pulled my down coat tighter around me. In the distance, tiny car lights flickered by on their way to warm houses after a day's toiling in the city. On the other side and behind the lake, heavy tree growth blotted out the few neighborhoods where one half of a couple waited for her quarreling partner to show up and agree to make it through another night. I turned around and walked through the bushes, into the trees, until I found the edge of Marie Beaufont's trailer park.

A bare bulb shined a harsh light over the unsteady steps of the tiny trailer. Marie's rusty pick-up, the thing that had pulled this trailer from town to town, carnival to carnival, sat detached on a patch of dead grass that served as a driveway. An older model sedan sat next to it.

A dim light shone in the window of the back bedrooms. I knocked on the door. It felt as if the entire structure shook.

The face that came to the door fit the terrain. Marie's eyes had sunk farther into her skinny face. The black circles that rimmed them bordered on clown grease. She must have been washing her hair, because it was turbaned in a worn blue towel.

"Oh, it's you," she said, her voice a monotone.

She moved aside and let me walk into the kitchen. It was dark except for a banker's lamp that threw a strong light across the tiny table. A woman sat shuffling a deck of cards into a game of solitaire. She looked up and stopped, one card in her hand, the rest of the deck in the other.

"Good evening, Mrs. Kelly," I said to Marie's mother. "Are you and the kids visiting?"

The older woman stared at me then at her daughter. She quietly shook her head.

"The kids are with neighbors in Live Oak," said Marie. "I'm having a bad time of it and Mother came to give me a little company." She picked up a dish cloth and wiped an already clean spot on the counter. "Are you here on business?"

"Business?" I was used to being the side-kick that got dragged along on jobs.

"About Rennie?" She folded the dish cloth and replaced it neatly across the tap.

"It's the linoleum knife," I said. "Did your husband have more than one?"

Eyes darted between mother and daughter. Marie bowed her head and shook it in despair.

"How would either of us know that?" said the mother, the anger in her voice daring me to bother her daughter.

"I mean, did he have a kit somewhere, something he used when he went on his jobs outside the carnival?" I suddenly felt afraid, like the cold air had seeped into the thin skin of the trailer and looked for someone to freeze.

"I gave all of Rennie's stuff to the sheriff. There's nothing—not one single thing—left of him in this trailer." Marie's cowed face turned defiant. She raised the sick eyes and stared at me like a queen who had pronounced sentence.

I drew in a deep breath. "Did you ever help your husband lay linoleum?"

Marie's face didn't move. Her haughtiness waned and she shot a look at her mother. The elder woman came to her defense.

"Never! My daughter took care of her children and worked as a waitress when necessary." She raised up from her chair and bent over the table towards me. "And she's having to do that now, because that sorry bastard rapist left her nothing. Not one damn dime!"

I let the silence surround us while I recalled the mention of a five-thousand dollar insurance policy. It wasn't much, but it was more than one damn dime. "I see," I said and backed toward the door. "If either of you remembers anything about a colleague of his or someone with a collection of knives, let us know." It was a feeble attempt to remove myself from the premises. Marie's eyes had filled with tears and she was losing her composure again. Her mother's eyes bore into me, and her stance at the table never faltered.

I left the trailer, backing down the rickety steps into the cold air. If any argument occurred at my leave, it was in whispered tones. I could hear nothing from outside. I shined the flashlight toward the park. A few trailers sat in tree coves, removed from each other's sight as though saving people the ugliness and too tight quarters for entire families. A baby cried in one, and I hoped it was the only child, not one of six or seven inside the cramped vehicle. I walked on old pavement, lanes that had been put down twenty years before, where grass had grown around it and eroded the edges. All the way through the park, past empty trailer spaces, to the office trailer. This one sat in plain view under a huge oak tree. A sign reading OFFICE rested in a window. There was no light on. I moved past and came to the garbage area. A large dumpster with plastic bags bulging under the lid sat beneath two bare bulbs on a wire. A few yards away, on a paved area, rested a wire drum. Inside were the ashes of burned material. The drum was there to burn things, raked leaves, mowed grass, and evidence that people once lived there.

I pulled a fallen limb from underneath the oak tree and broke off a branch. Using it for a probe, I poked around the ashes. The

wire drum hadn't been emptied for many burnings. Like the rest of
the park, it suffered from neglect. A good wind storm would blow
the top layer onto the broken pavement, but right now, it sat like
exposed dead for all to see.

Some things don't burn well: a metal bracelet, an earring, a belt
buckle, even some beads that didn't land quite in the fire. Melted
blobs still attached to a singed string fell to the side. I scooped what
I could find into my pocket and tossed the branch into the woods.
The windows of the trailers revealed no curious eyes, but I felt like
I was in a black spotlight. Still, cold air encircled me. I turned and
ran from the place.

"Serial killers often take trophies, right?" I dumped the items from
the ash drum onto Marshall Long's desk. Tony paced the narrow
foot space of the room, his head bowed, his hands in his pockets. I
had phoned them from the car after my visit to Marie's trailer park.

"There's no way to tell if these belonged to those girls," said
Tony.

Marshall picked up a metal bracelet with a ball point pen. "If a
name was engraved somewhere, we might be able to attach it to
someone, or if a relative could identify a piece of jewelry." He
raised the bracelet to the light and shook off some ash.

"And if not?"

"Then we have nothing," said Marshall. "If everyone uses that
drum to burn stuff, it could be anybody's."

"Look," I said and bent over the desk. I spoke to Marshall but I
was talking to Tony. "I think Marie and her mother found Rennie's
trophies and got rid of them, along with him. We didn't find anything in the trailer or in the sinkhole. What if we confront the
women, or better, just Marie, and tell her we found things belonging

to the girls in the ash pit. Don't accuse her, just let her know they were found. Maybe even make her think we suspect her husband burned them."

Marshall looked at Tony. "They had the bead box, Tony. Rennie kept that and his daughter discovered it. It must have been a trophy from the Gaylin Newberry killing."

Tony stood up, shook his head a few times, then said, "I'll have Loman find out from the park manager when the last time they fired up that drum. And we'll find out who, if any, of the tenants used it." He looked up at me and for a moment, I saw kindness in his eyes. It would be the only thanks coming for the evening.

Vernon had been called to a case in the north part of the county. I sat alone in my house in the swamp, huddling in a sweater next to a fire. Plato's jaunt into the woods got too cold. He lay down near the hearth, stretched and fell asleep. He whined once or twice, and his back leg trembled once. "Chasing a coon?" I whispered. He didn't open his eyes but his tail bounced once on the floor. The central heat kicked on and warmed up the room. Plato turned on his back, exposing his belly to the air. "You're not used to warm air, right?" He turned his face to me, his eyes wide open, a panting smile on his face. His tail swiped back and forth across the floor.

Somewhere in the distance a voice called out through the trees. Plato sat up in a bound, his ears perked forward. But the voice faded into the distance. It sounded a lot like Edwin on his quest to find Sylvester. Plato whined once and plopped back on the floor.

The morning brought frost. A white layer covered everything outside, especially the open grassy areas. Plato darted into the cold like a freed prisoner and sniffed the frozen dew. I sipped coffee and watched him head down Pasquin's path, most likely following

Edwin's scent from last night. The phone rang.

"It's cold, Tony. I don't want to dive today." This wasn't exactly true. I just wanted him to beg a little.

One of the deputies had gone fishing early in the morning, down river from where Yasmina's body was found. He had pulled up a woman's head scarf.

"The current could have washed it down there along with other stuff. I need the area searched." He sighed. "I'd ask Harry to do it alone, but he's, well…."

"Not all that reliable?" I knew it would be difficult for Tony to admit that.

"Get on your wet suit and meet us there."

Water's edge was colder than the forest floor. The wind chill from off the water made the air feel well below freezing. I suited up, ready to put on a tank, when Harry pulled up in a new van.

"You got rid of that vintage VW?" It had been his trademark, MacAllister, the archeologist who drives the '60s VW.

"Too hard on the leg," he said and tapped the one that had been shattered. "Needed more room."

"And Mitzi?"

"Mitzi doesn't do cold mornings," he said and grinned at me.

I slipped the tank straps around my shoulders, trying to ignore the fact that I'd ask such a petty question. My affair with Harry ended over two years ago, but he was a thorn that kept sticking me. "You are going down?"

"It's just a shore line search," he said and slipped the tank on his back. "Haven't done any caves lately."

We moved to the edge of the river. I pulled on my mask and walked into the water. My fins mashed down a new growth of hydrilla.

"Watch the grass and don't get tangled in it." I moved onto my belly then underwater.

Trying to stay beyond the line of grass, I pushed the growth aside and searched the shallow depths along the shore. Harry would start further down and we would meet halfway. I tucked beer bottles, tangled fishing line, and even a red wig into the waist bag.

I had been in the search a while, too long, it seemed, without meeting Harry. Surfacing, I saw him sitting on the bank. Tony and Loman stood over him.

"Sorry, Luanne," he called to me. "Got one hell of a cramp in this leg." Loman lifted Harry's tank off the ground and handed it to a uniformed deputy.

"Somebody get this bag and hand me another one." I lifted the full bag into the air. Harry shook his head, and Tony looked at Loman.

Loman's sleepy eyes opened wide for a second. He looked at his shoes, shrugged, and edged toward the muddy shoreline. I pushed the bag over the grass as far as I could. Loman couldn't reach it. He stepped into what he thought was a few inches of water. But the river is deceptive. At places it drops off suddenly into deep water. The man's foot darted downward, his body following it, straight into a thick growth of hydrilla. For a moment, his head disappeared beneath the surface.

Tony yelled. I dropped the bag and turned downward. Loman's lower body pulled against the strength of the hydrilla. Some of the shallow roots came up with his leg movement. His arms pushed against the cold water, bobbing his head atop then under the surface again.

Another pair of legs hit the water, squashing the hydrilla for a moment and lifting Loman by the arm pits. I swam to the bottom and tugged at the plants around Loman's legs. He finally pulled free.

I headed for clear water and the surface to see what had happened on shore. Tony, wet from the waist down, had lugged Loman to the bank edge. The big man lay on his back, laughing to the sky. His belly, soaked shirt and jacket, shook with each loud guffaw. Uniformed deputies stood around the two men and laughed with him. Tony chuckled and tried to wipe away the bits of grass and mud. Only Harry sat stone-faced, his embarrassment at doing nothing written in his eyes.

When the search was finished, I had come up with two bags of river garbage. Maybe Marshall could tell if any of it belonged to Yasmina or her killer. Even the scarf the fisherman had found could have belonged to a weekend boater.

The big find of the day had been Harry. My once diving hero who studied underwater structures, who defied cave systems that had killed the best of divers, and had investigated more than one bloody crime for Tony Amado, had become useless. He wasn't even able to navigate shallow waters to pull out an overweight deputy trapped in hydrilla grass.

CHAPTER 24

"This stuff belonged to women, but nobody can tell if they are trophies." Tony pushed the ash drum items around on his desk. "But maybe we can bluff them, make them think it came from Beaufont's stash."

I rolled my eyes. Tony wouldn't admit where the idea came from, but most everyone in the room knew.

"We've got a suspicious-looking bank withdrawal and deposit." He glanced my way, averting his eyes as quickly as possible. "Yasmina receives two grand the same day Marie collects a check for that much. Nothing to go on, but just maybe Yasmina knew something."

I nodded and shot a smile in Vernon's direction.

In Tony's office after the river search, Loman laughed at himself and shook his head over his fall into deep hydrilla. It would be a tale told in the sheriff's department for years to come.

"Loman will hit the park manager with a search warrant to confiscate the contents of the ash drum. You and Luanne will go inside with me. Just follow my lead." Tony spoke to Vernon, but nodded my way at his last command. He gathered up the items and stuffed them in the paper evidence bag.

Two patrol cars pulled into the park entrance. We didn't stop to see if Loman found the manager at home, but pulled around the narrow lanes to the Beaufont residence. In daylight, it might be called quaint, a neat little trailer tucked among large oak trees. It could be the artist's retreat where he went to paint or write the novel based on an old Southern family. Instead, it was the moving home of a serial killer who had fooled his family into thinking he liked the drifter's life, going from carnival to carnival, from one flooring company to another. When all the time, he was stalking one female after another.

The truck and sedan were still in their parking places. Vernon parked the patrol car directly behind them, blocking any kind of rush to run.

"We have to talk to you about your husband," said Tony as we stood at the bottom of the steps. Marie's mother peeked over her daughter's shoulder.

"I was just cleaning up," said Marie. She lifted the dust cloth as though the men needed proof. She stood aside and we entered the tiny living space.

"I'd like you to see these," said Tony. He stood at one end of the table. Vernon was at the other, placing the two women across from each other. I pulled up a chair behind Marie.

Tony lifted the brown bag and dumped the contents onto the green table top. A film of ash rose briefly in the air. He leaned over with his pen and pushed them apart, showing girl things—bracelet, earring, an old lipstick case.

Marie's eyes opened wide in their dark sockets. Her face paled. Her mother moved backward slightly as though something from the items might touch her. Both women sat in silence.

"We think they are trophies your husband took off his victims," said Tony. "That's one characteristic of the type of kill… person he was." He waited and still no word came from the women. "We'd like to know if you found anything here that could have belonged to one of the victims." He waited again.

"Where did you get these things?" Marie's voice was barely a whisper. Her eyes were closed now.

"The ash can up by the manager's office. Got a man up there now gathering the whole business."

Marie's eyes opened and glanced toward her mother. The elder woman rose quietly and went to the door. She leaned out far enough to see the patrol car and men standing around the ash drum. Nodding at her daughter, she resumed her seat at the table.

"You don't think he actually burned those things, do you?" Marie's eyes blazed now. Tears and anger shot into her skinny face.

"Marie!" Her mother leaned over and took her daughter's hand. "Leave her alone! She doesn't need to hear about things taken from dead women."

"Her daughter had a bead box that belonged to one victim," I said from behind. Marie jumped and turned slightly toward me.

"Not anymore!" she said, her voice a hiss by now.

"Have you found other items?" Tony repeated his question.

"Of course not!" The mother gripped her daughter's hand.

"You clean a lot," I said. "Surely you must have come across some items that didn't belong to either you or your daughter."

"Oh, I clean! You bet I clean." Marie tugged her hand away from her mother and waved the dust cloth in the air. "But he's still here. He's still here!" She nearly yelled at her mother.

"You want to wipe him out of your life?" She didn't answer me. "I can't blame you for that."

Except for Marie's choking sobs, no one made a sound. Vernon waited for the most uncomfortable moment in the silence.

"When did you first find out your husband was killing women?"

The older woman gasped and grabbed at her daughter's hand, but Marie dodged her and pulled back her entire body, scratching the chair legs on the floor.

"Enough!" She rocked and pounded the table with a fist. "Enough!"

"You'll have to leave," her mother cried. "She's not well."

"No!" Marie bolted for the sofa that doubled as a bed. She stared at all of us from across the tiny room. "Do you have any idea what it's like to wake up one morning and realize your own husband has been knifing women—not one—but many over the years he has been married to you?"

"Don't, Marie!" Her mother stood and moved toward her.

"Stay back, or so help me, Mother!" Marie balled up a pale fist and shook it at her.

"I couldn't deal with the idea that this man had done all those things. I never suspected way back when a girl from the carnival went missing. But it kept happening. He stayed away from me too often. Came home late from 'drinking with his buddies.'" Marie's voice mimicked her husband. "He never went to bars with his buddies." She stopped and gasped into her dust cloth. "Lies! He told lies and killed."

Tony moved toward Marie. "Ma'am, I have to read you your rights. Just in case what you're about to say is a confession."

Marie stopped, seeming to hold her breath. "Read away."

Tony went through the Miranda rights and asked if she wanted to continue talking.

"Did I find souvenirs from his massacres? That's what you asked, isn't it, Detective Amado? Well, you bet your jolly little life I did. The coincidence of time and murders grated on my brain. I pulled his suitcase down, the one he stashed in the back of trailer. He said never to touch that, that he kept tools in there and didn't want them disturbed. Kept it locked."

She swiped a sleeve across her nose. "But getting mad gives you strength. Did you know that? I broke the damn lock. And there they were. All those things girls wore. Trophies as you call them. Trophies and a linoleum knife. And pictures." She sobbed and nodded. "Yes, he took pictures of the bodies after he'd slashed the throats and done the other things.

"I had to get rid of them, but I didn't know how. If he found out." She closed her eyes. "So I did what I've always done. I called my mother."

We turned to look at the woman still sitting at the table. Her face had turned ashen white, but her eyes still flashed anger. "You want to read me my rights, too?"

Tony turned and blurted out the Miranda warnings.

"She came up here and took the trophies. She said I couldn't live here any longer, that my kids wouldn't be safe."

A silence fell across the room. Marie sat up, seeming to gain composure. Her eyes stared somewhere far off. "Rennie often came home by getting a ride. The ride would let him off up on the highway, and he'd walk around the dry lake to the trailer. He'd been to a floor job that day; didn't knock off until after dark. We waited for him out there."

She stopped and stared into nothingness. "I tripped him in the darkness. Mother had the knife." She turned slowly toward her mother. "Yes, Mr. Amado, we found things that belonged to those girls. My mother said she'd burn them."

The elder woman stood up. "But I never burned them here. Not in this ash drum."

Marie lifted her eyes toward her mother, then slowly focused on the dining table. "Then what are these?"

"Things I sifted from the ash drum the other night," I said. "No one ever said who they belonged to."

Marie's eye sockets burned. She had been tricked, but the fury she shot about the room wasn't directed at me. She turned on her mother.

"She's the one!" Marie stood now, her finger pointing as lethally as a sharp knife. "I tripped him, but she sliced his neck. Used the linoleum knife, the same one he used on those girls."

"Marie, sit down!" The mother stood but Marie was having none of it. She thrust her body toward her mother like an animal defending territory.

"And that's not all! When that other slut came here and said she had guessed what we'd done and asked for money, she," Marie's finger pointed like a bullet, "is the one who decided what we'd do."

Marie's mother paled and she sat down again. "I never thought you'd tell," she whispered to herself. "Think of your children."

"Children! Just think of them! Not only do they have one sick father who killed girls for pleasure, they've got a mother and a grand-mother who…" She stopped and gasped, a hand flew over her mouth. She sank to the sofa and rocked like an autistic child.

"Yasmina was on a blackmail kick, willing to soak Marie and her mother for the pitiful bit of money they had each month. Marie never enjoyed a penny of that insurance. Never had a chance." Tony paced his office.

Vernon and I stood leaning against the wall. There was no place to sit. The chairs acted as storage spots for all the files and evidence bags. We had waited around for Marie and her mother to be charged with two counts of murder. When the lawyer appeared, the mother decided to confess it all and throw herself on the mercy of the court as a mother trying to protect her child. Tony even invited me into the room to hear her confess.

"We agreed to pay Yasmina. Did pay her once. But when she came around again, Marie was having to work more hours serving tables just to feed herself." Mrs. Kelly's eyes looked up and the passion of a cornered animal shot at all of us. "My duty is to protect my daughter, and I would not sit by and see her collect dirty plates from overfed truck drivers at all hours of the night. Not when she'd have to turn around and dole it all out to some hooker who slept with the same truck drivers! I would not stand for it!" She rose part way off the chair and slammed her fist on the interview table. Her lawyer and Tony rose with her. "Oh, yes," she said as she sat down again. "I got that bitch. We told her to meet us at the water's edge. It's a place I went fishing once with my son-in-law." She laughed and squeezed her eyes shut. "Would you believe Rennie took me fishing out on the very river where he was dumping bodies?" She pushed her graying hair back from her forehead and asked for some water.

"We got her to meet us there. Marie didn't want to go, but I wasn't sure I could handle it alone. We went early, before the time we gave Yasmina, and waited in the bushes. I told her to meet us at the boat. She walked right by us, down the path that leads to the shore. I just jumped from the bushes and shoved her with my body against a pine tree."

She took more gulps of water and placed the empty glass on the table.

"She had that long stringy hair, you see. Easy to grab hold of and hold her head back. I yelled for Marie to grab her arms, but Yasmina was stronger. I had to dodge her hands and go at her throat at the same time I held her hair. Marie struggled to hold her but they both ended up on the ground." She hesitated, closed her eyes, and whispered, "That's when I made the final cut." She lifted her hand and made the gesture of slicing across a neck. "Did to her what Rennie had done to lord knows how many women."

Mrs. Kelly opened her eyes wide and exhaled.

"And the body?"

She nodded. "We didn't want it found. I'd collected some bricks somebody had piled near a construction site in Live Oak. We tied them with a rope. It took both of us to drag Yasmina to the water's edge and shove her into the boat. We tied the rope around her waist." She chuckled a bit. "There wasn't room in the little row boat for the body and the two of us. Marie stayed on shore. I rowed out to a spot where the grass was thick and the water seemed deep. Nearly fell out of the boat myself, trying to roll her over." She placed both palms on the table and smiled. "But I did it."

The silence that followed was broken when Tony spoke to the tape that the confession was over. Mrs. Kelly's lawyer released her to a deputy. We waited for him to leave then sat in silence again.

"Guess the woman didn't know about White and his hydrilla pulling machine," said Tony.

"Swamp justice," I sighed.

We all jumped when my cell phone rang.

"Luanne," said the dean, "I've got some good news for you. Seems Manny had been making a concoction of exotic herb tea that affected his brain. Soon as it wore off in the hospital, he was okay. He can do the schedules. You don't have to worry about it now."

I looked at the phone, speechless.

"Luanne?"

"Thanks a lot, sir. Perhaps you can send letters to the department faculty to explain why their winter assignments are no longer valid?"

The north Florida cold spell wasn't going away. The mercury kept dropping, even during the rest of the day. It would be another night when locals would have to cover delicate plants and let faucets drip to prevent pipes from freezing.

"Vernon, you ever hear about lizards freezing and popping open during a bitter cold?" I stroked his hand that rested on the gear shift.

"Old tale, if you ask me." He grinned. "Lots of people believe it happens, but I never saw a split lizard lying around the swamp floor."

I lay my head back on the car seat. The sun shined brightly through the cold. It would take a cloud cover to warm up the place. "It's almost dinner time. Let's see what Mama is offering tonight."

Vernon slowed, and in the middle of a deserted paved road, made a U-turn. He passed the Palmetto Springs turn-off and took a narrow paved lane to Fogarty Spring.

"Looks like everybody was ready to get away from fairground treats," he said as he parked next to two patrol cars. "Even Harlie." He jabbed a finger at the heavy man who descended the steps carrying a large bag of take-out eats.

"Not eating in?" I asked as we passed him on the steps.

"Got desk duty tonight." He placed the bag in the trunk of one of the cars, waved, and drove toward the lane.

"For all that fussing they did in the booth, he seems rather happy," said Vernon.

"You ever hear about his wife?" I smiled.

"Never knew he was married."

"Then come along, big boy. I've got a tale to tell you."

CHAPTER 25

Mama's busboy shoved two tables together. Law enforcement in the form of Loman, Tony, two uniformed patrols, and Vernon sat with me and shared a huge place of fried mullet. It sat in the middle, skirted by a bowl of cheese grits and another of cole slaw. Baskets of hush puppies rested at each end, next to the pitchers of iced tea.

Loman ordered a side dish of oysters on the half shell and sat lifting and sliding them down his throat, all the while eyeing the diminishing platter of fish filets.

"Don't worry, I'll refill," said Mama. She patted him on his back.

During the feast, served family style, Mama joked about some of the people she had to feed during her time in the cafe. No one said anything about carnivals, or killers, or bad marriages. When the door opened and a herd of cowboy types entered, she laughed, "And look what we have here."

Rodeo bull riders invaded the place. You couldn't see much, just hats, big leather belts, and boots. They crowded into booths and around tables where extra chairs had to be provided. The talk was loud and boasting about conquering the big name bulls such as Bodacious, Pearl Jam, and Maneater.

"Had to use a ball rope but good on that old bull last night. They ought to retire that sucker," said one. "Got any raw oysters?" he asked the waitress.

"Caught a rider over in Crestview using liquid rosin on his rope. Got him expelled right out," said a familiar voice.

I peeked around Mama. Chawbutt Nixon hadn't removed his hat yet, but the caterpillar mustache gave him away. "Oh, dear," I said and scrunched into the seat.

"You heading out to Valdosta?" asked another.

"Yeah," said Chawbutt. "Got some new bulls up there this time." He ordered and looked around the room.

"Well, I'll be!" He grinned, and I realized my scrunching hadn't worked. He stood, hiked his belt and walked bowlegged toward our table.

"Ya'll don't get too far away, do you?" He grinned. No tobacco plug, but his teeth had the yellow stains of a lifetime user. "How you, ma'am?" He tipped the wide hat and gazed at me.

"Doing fine," I said.

Loman looked up from his half shells and grinned at me. I bumped his leg under the table.

"You gonna be around later?"

I looked from Loman to Mama and tried to say with my eyes, "Help, this man is asking me out."

I shook my head. "I'm really a professor, and I have lots of work to do tonight."

Chawbutt stood like a man who had been goosed by one of the bull horns. His hand was still on the hat brim. "A professor?" he asked and might as well have said "a Martian?"

"Of linguistics," I added.

"Of what?"

"It's all about how people talk," said Loman. "She studies everybody, you know. Writes down their peculiar ways of saying things. I bet she's even got the lingo of bull riders down somewhere."

"That true?" Chawbutt grinned.

I shrugged and bumped Loman again.

"Then you know all about us?"

"Not exactly," I said. "But enough." I sighed and went for it. "You are a member of a group of intersociallary speakers who has created its own jargon not only for the purpose of communicating with the trade but also to exclude others to the point that you give the impression of being exclusive and beyond the ability of the ordinary standard speaker to comprehend." I popped a hush puppy into my mouth.

Chawbutt stood in silence, his eyes peering from beneath the hat brim. His grin had disappeared. He was about to say something else, when we heard the familiar, "Whoweeeeee" from outside.

"Now what's that old man doing out on the river in this cold?" Mama said and rose to go and hold the door for Pasquin who rushed up the stairs.

"Thought I might have to use your phone, but looks like what I need is here." Pasquin reached over and grabbed a fish filet. "Edwin is in a state. Won't quit weeping and wailing about that big snake. You got to get down there and see what you can do." He took a bite out of the fish.

"He needs a doctor," said Loman. "That snake ain't never going to be found."

"Nope, you got it wrong. He found him, only not in exactly the physical condition he wanted to find him." Pasquin grabbed another piece of fish, wrapped it in a napkin, and stuffed it in his coat pocket. "You guys coming?"

Chawbutt hadn't moved. He turned and watched us move around him to the cars. Tony called Fish and Game to send someone to meet us at the slough down from the fairgrounds. Three patrol cars formed the caravan to see what had happened to Snake Boy's big loss.

"Thanks for getting me out of that mess, Sylvester," I said out loud in the car.

The slough between the two gum swamp ponds was so nasty no one had ever named it. The ponds, havens for alligators and frogs, rested at the bottom of the hill, below the fairgrounds. The slough was mostly mud, tree debris, and shallow water run-off where homeless drifters discarded cheap wine bottles and empty cigarette packs.

We parked the cars next to the street on the incline and walked into the trees. Edwin, sitting on the high bank, stared into the muddy water. His eyes rimmed red, he started bellowing as soon as he saw Pasquin.

"Look what he done to Sylvester," he blubbered.

At the bottom of the bank, a line stretched for nearly six feet in the shallow water. We had to look close, because the line was only slightly lighter in color than the mud. Sylvester lay still, his head facing south, his tail north, and the twain not meeting in the middle. Something had chomped out that part.

Vernon moved down the bank and leaned over. We all followed, bowing like religious folks to the snake god. "Alligator for sure," said Vernon. He stifled a laugh.

"Damn gators!" Edwin cried from above us. "Like they ain't got enough to eat."

We said nothing, just kept bending over. The Fish and Game warden joined us. Edwin watched our backsides from his perch on the bank.

"Wonder why the gator didn't finish eating him," I said.

Pasquin raised himself, glanced back at Edwin, and said, "Don't think he liked foreign food."

Marshall Long had joined the late diners at Mama's Table when we returned after Sylvester had been removed by the game warden. Edwin was still a mess, but he agreed to some fried shrimp. The

bull riders had left, according to Mama, after consuming seafood
and shooting bull you-know-what about their adventures.

"Sara just put away your Gaylin, Luanne. Locked her up in storage." Marshall popped a hush puppy in his mouth.

"Why don't you bring Sara here once in a while?" I tossed him a
cold shrimp.

"Don't know. She doesn't much like to eat." He shrugged.

"But she likes you," I said.

He shivered.

Beepers began to sound in pockets. Smiles and jokes ended.
Something was happening at a gas station near the main highway.

"You'll get a ride from Pasquin?" said Vernon as he squeezed
my shoulder.

It was a typical scenario. Happiness lasted a short time. Then
some crazy decided to blast it all away.

I sat with Pasquin and sipped strong coffee. We watched Edwin
eat and become a bit more settled with the full stomach. When his
contentment turned to grogginess, we decided it was time to hit the
cold river and take the man home.

Night engulfed us along with the cold. Only the headlight on
Pasquin's boat gave a semblance of reality on the black water. He
knew where the thick cypress knees grew and how to dodge their
encroaching knobs. The putter of the motor was joined by an occasional jump of some creature into the water. And once a screech
owl pierced the darkness from a distant tree.

We edged closer to shore. Pasquin slowed the boat to nearly a
stop and plowed through hydrilla that even now in the cold had
locked onto the bottom and grew like green snakes in bundles. We
made it to shore without having to clear the propeller.

Pasquin unloaded his friend. We watched Edwin walk through
the dark woods toward his little house with the snakes, dead and

alive, in the back yard. He didn't use a flashlight. Like Pasquin, he knew the way and the ways of the swamp. His head hung a little low tonight, the loss of Sylvester weighing heavy on his brain.

At my landing, I climbed out of the boat and invited the old man in for a warm pot of tea. "Not tonight, ma'am. This old man's got to get home and climb under an electric blanket."

I stood for a moment and listened to the slight lapping of water against the shore. Pasquin listened, too. Two loud cracks popped somewhere on the forest floor.

"Lizards cracking," he whispered.

OH, WELL. THANK YOU FOR INDULGING ME. IF WE BAG ANYTHING GOOD, I'LL BRING SOME BACK FOR YOU.

IT'S A DEAL. GOOD LUCK!

CLOP CLOP

MUCH BETTER NOW. FOLLOW T[HE] ROAD UNTIL YO[U] HIT SHANDONG AND KEEP YOUR EYES PEALED.

I WILL. THANK YOU AGAIN, MY FRIEND. I OWE YOU FOR THIS.

THIS IS AS FAR AS I GO, CHONG LIN. TIME TO CHANGE YOUR CLOTHES.

GOOD LUCK.

So once more, Chong Lin found himself all alone and crossing the snowy landscape.

UNTIL WE MEET AGAIN, JIN CHAI!

HWOOOSH

99

103

SKREE

YOU KNOW, JUST THIS MORNING A FORTUNETELLER TOLD ME THAT DESPITE THIS HARSH WINTER, THE SPRING BOUNTY WOULD SURPASS EXPECTATIONS.

AND HE WAS RIGHT! IF I'M NOT MISTAKEN, YOU'RE CHONG LIN, AND THERE'S A 3,000-GOLD-COIN PRICE ON YOUR HEAD!

WHO ARE YOU? WHAT ARE YOU TALKING ABOUT?

I'M NOT CHONG LIN. MY NAME IS JIANG.

YOU'VE GOT THE WRONG MAN.

YOU CAN CHANGE YOUR NAME. BUT YOU CAN'T CHANGE YOUR FACE!

107

109

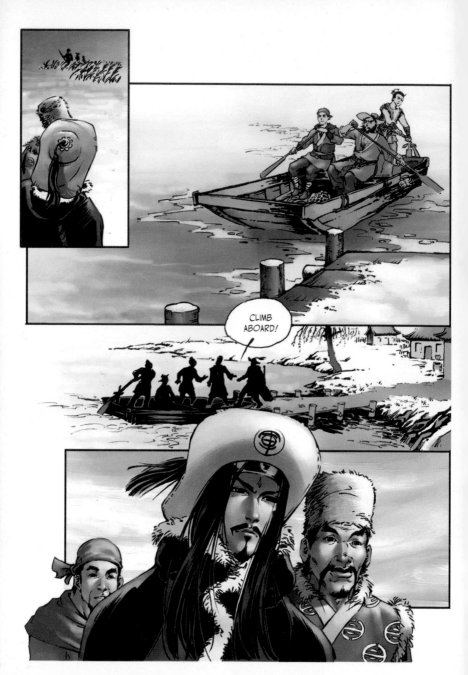

CLIMB ABOARD!

113

WELL, PICK YOUR JAW
UP OFF THE GROUND.
WAIT UNTIL YOU SEE
WHAT'S AT THE TOP
OF THESE STEPS.

117

BY THE HEAVENS. THIS IS A PLACE FIT FOR AN EMPEROR.

119

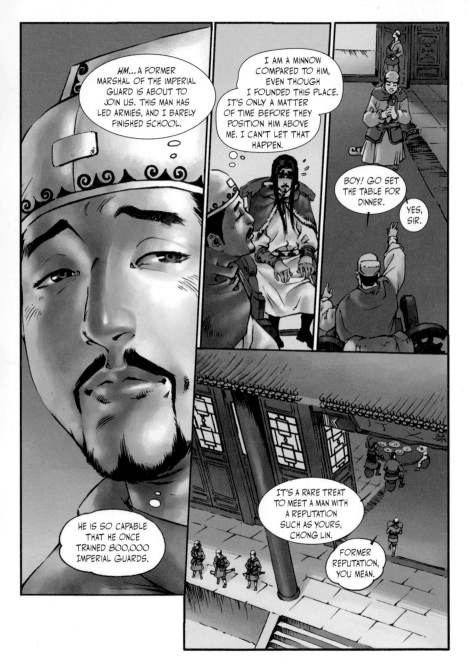

123

WELL, THAT'S JUST IT. THE THINGS THAT DISCREDIT YOU OUT THERE ONLY ENHANCE YOUR REPUTATION IN LIANGSHAN.

HERE HERE!

The five men ate and drank long into the evening, until finally Lun Wang decided to speak his mind.

WELL, THEN?

BRING THE TRAY!

125

127

129

Chong Lin hid among the mountain trails all day, but nobody passed through, so he returned empty handed.

WELL, CHONG LIN? DID YOU SUCCEED?

NO, I DID NOT. THERE IS NOTHING TO SAY.

HM...

OH, WELL. BETTER LUCK TOMORROW. TWO DAYS LEFT.

YES. TWO DAYS LEFT...

But even though Chong Lin headed in a different direction, no one appeared. Then, after noon...

LOOK! A WHOLE GROUP OF PEOPLE HEADING THIS WAY!

LET'S GO! WE'VE GOT NO TIME TO LOSE.

WHAT IF WE HEADED SOUTH TODAY INSTEAD?

GOOD IDEA.

QUIET! HEAD DOWN. THERE ARE TOO MANY. WE'RE OUTNUMBERED.

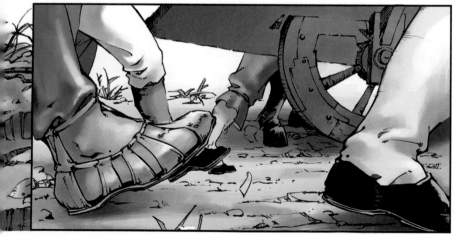

135

DAMN IT ALL! AS AN INNOCENT MAN, I WAS AS GOOD AS DEAD. NOW I HAVE A CHANCE AT LIFE, BUT I MUST KILL SOMEONE TO DO IT. THERE IS NO END TO THE ABSURDITY OF THIS WORLD!

DON'T WORRY. I'M SURE YOU'LL SUCCEED.

BAM

The next day, Chong Lin headed east and waited for the first sign of an approach.

137

139

IT'S NOT A MATTER OF WANT. I *NEED* YOUR HEAD.

SIGH... TAKE THESE GOODS BACK TO THE FORTRESS. I'LL WAIT HERE TO SEE IF ANYONE ELSE COMES BY.

GOOD IDEA! THEY MIGHT GIVE YOU AN EXTENSION FOR THIS.

I'LL BE BACK SOON. GOOD LUCK!

149

"Invaluable...beautiful artwork...commendable efforts to bring the characters to life." – *Publishers Weekly*

Legends from China
THREE KINGDOMS

Our heroes' journey is far from over. Join Bei Liu, Yu Guan, and Fei Zhang as they battle enemies and allies alike, determined to end the war for China's future and restore peace to the land.

Three Kingdoms volumes 1–20, available in **bookstores** and on **Amazon.com**

Vol. 01

Vol. 02

Vol. 03

Vol. 04

Vol. 05

Vol. 06

Vol. 07

Vol. 08

Vol. 09

Vol. 10

Vol. 11

Vol. 12

Vol. 13

Vol. 14

Vol. 15

Vol. 16

Vol. 17

Vol. 18

Vol. 19

Vol. 20